BRAZEN

She tilted her head back. "I am not accustomed to you."

"We have only just met." Did her imagination fool her, or did he draw breath more quickly?

"I would not be accustomed to you had we known each other these last twenty years. Every moment with you is new, different, exciting." She stood on tiptoe, and, trembling, brazenly dusted his lips with hers as she imagined someone of her reputation would do. He inhaled sharply, then his arms encircled her, drawing her deeper and deeper into a haze of passion. She had never had her lips alone give her so much pleasure. She had never before felt so protected and so vulnerable all at once.

He tugged gently at one of her curls, dangling against her bare back, with his hand. "I have wanted to do that all night."

BOOK YOUR PLACE ON OUR WEBSITE AND MAKE THE READING CONNECTION!

We've created a customized website just for our very special readers, where you can get the inside scoop on everything that's going on with Zebra, Pinnacle and Kensington books.

When you come online, you'll have the exciting opportunity to:

- View covers of upcoming books
- Read sample chapters
- Learn about our future publishing schedule (listed by publication month *and author*)
- Find out when your favorite authors will be visiting a city near you
- Search for and order backlist books from our online catalog
- Check out author bios and background information
- Send e-mail to your favorite authors
- Meet the Kensington staff online
- Join us in weekly chats with authors, readers and other guests
- Get writing guidelines
- AND MUCH MORE!

**Visit our website at
http://www.kensingtonbooks.com**

A Delightful Folly

Glenda Garland

ZEBRA BOOKS
Kensington Publishing Corp.
www.kensingtonbooks.com

ZEBRA BOOKS are published by

Kensington Publishing Corp.
850 Third Avenue
New York, NY 10022

All Kensington titles, imprints and distributed lines are available at special quantity discounts for bulk purchases for sales promotion, premiums, fund-raising, educational or institutional use.

Special book excerpts or customized printings can also be created to fit specific needs. For details, write or phone the office of the Kensington Special Sales Manager: Kensington Publishing Corp., 850 Third Avenue, New York, NY 10022. Attn. Special Sales Department. Phone: 1-800-221-2647.

First Printing: March 2005
10 9 8 7 6 5 4 3 2 1

Printed in the United States of America

For my parents-in-law, Bob and Barbara Garland,
who have shared their good name
with love, encouragement,
and a cheerful accommodation of raisin avoidance.

Chapter One

As Benedict Hadley, Viscount Fitzhugh, moved through the chattering, perfumed crush at Lady Guildham's ball, searching, he grumbled at his father's appeal that he come to London and renew his childhood friendship with Alexander Letellier.

"He seems to be at one of life's little crossroads," his father, the earl of Hadley, had written.

In Benedict's opinion, Letellier always appeared to be at one of life's little crossroads. But the appeal's novelty had impressed Benedict enough to disrupt his life and come.

Was it still raining in Bath? Surely it had stopped by now, since he had left three days ago. What investing opportunities would he miss by coming here for such a length of time?

Benedict excused himself to many as he avoided broad backs only to bump into elbows, but saw no one he knew among the other gentlemen who also wore the black-and-white evening wear Brummell had made fashionable.

Would that Weston's tailoring could provide sufficient armor against the noise.

As he passed, feminine mouths disappeared behind fans, leaving pairs of bright eyes poised between curls and feathers of all hues. What attribute or disadvantage provided meat for the gossip behind those fans?

Upon Benedict's arrival in London, his father had reported that their neighbor Mrs. Bourre had said that women would want to crack Benedict like a nut. Benedict and his father had shared a wince over that.

Then his father had said, "Don't understand modern sensibilities. Not at all. Cracking indeed. Just don't flirt with any little birds who can't feather their own nests. Remember what I asked you here for. Find out what is on Letellier's mind."

One little bird's mother, a not unattractive woman in her early forties, cut directly across Benedict's path, a rather plain, blond chick in tow. "Lord Fitzhugh, how lovely to see you back in London. How long has it been?"

Long enough for Benedict to have forgotten her name. However, he remembered where they had met: a dinner party hosted by a friend's family. He could still see the room's oblong shape and floral molding behind her. But her name? "I have been frequently in London, ma'am, but have not partaken of the Season's delights. You are well?"

"Indeed, yes. How very kind of you to inquire. This is my daughter, Eliza. She is making her come-out this year. Give Lord Fitzhugh a curtsy, child."

Benedict bowed, cursing inside. "My great pleasure." He did not want to display himself for half an hour dancing with someone whose surname he could not recall.

"Lady Archer, you will never guess who has shown up at my ball!" It was Lady Guildham, an unlikely rescuer, but one took what one could get. Benedict bowed, murmured an excuse while Lady Archer—that was her name—bent heads together with their hostess, and headed back toward the ballroom entrance.

Letellier had not progressed this far.

Really, Benedict had barely met Lady Archer when he was but a lad of twenty-one. What qualities did she imagine he had, to be pushing her daughter at him in such fashion?

Would natural philosophy progress to such a point that it could determine whether society's interest in one stemmed from personal merit, or a calculation of one's monetary assets? What sort of contraption could measure, weigh, and answer that most delicate of questions? What would it look like? The detailed drawings of Newton, Galileo, Huygens, and Fontana rose in Benedict's mind, but while he could readily imagine them able to pull him this way and that, he could not feel so sanguine about what they would need to wrap metallic pincers about first.

Would there not need to be some sort of metaphysical component, as yet undiscovered? One that did not resemble old Maria, the Gypsy fortune-teller, with her twisted nose and wrinkles upon wrinkles?

Benedict smothered the smile such an image brought. Who knew how it might be interpreted?

Would an instrument with such a component hurt to use? Would it strip away all one's illusions of oneself? Or would future generations not care whether it hurt, so long as it was accurate, and precise?

Benedict doubted any such contraption would look like the dazzlingly lovely woman standing next to Letellier, near the ballroom entrance. She wore a cream dress of the first style, finely embroidered in cream, and trimmed in emerald green. A magnificent emerald pendant decorated her throat. The piled arrangement of her coppery hair brought out the regal oval of her face and displayed the delicate line of her throat and shoulders. She coolly surveyed the ballroom with a tilt to her bow-shaped lips.

Such a woman would hurt to use, Benedict thought absurdly. Such a woman hurt to look at, for wanting what a mere mortal should not be entitled to. Besides, her gaze measured entirely according to her own agenda.

What did she see in Alexander Letellier that made her stand next to him and his three friends? Converse with him, no less, in tones not heard over the crowd and the musicians beginning the next dance?

It certainly could not be his sartorial taste.

Although by deed a Corinthian, Letellier defied expectation by dressing more like a dandy. Tonight he wore a gold coat that teetered on the brink of yellow, with white breeches. It did not so much clash with the lady's dress as attempt to throw it in the shade.

Not very gallant. More like ludicrous.

Still, Benedict thought, trying to be fair to his childhood friend, had fashion permitted him to powder his dark hair, the effect might have been striking. Letellier was not an unhandsome man, either, except for his heavy eyebrows, which could make his snapping dark Gallic eyes appear small.

Letellier saw him coming, and a sly, roguish smile spread like ink over his features. "And look. Here we have Fitzhugh, emerging from some far corner of Lady Guildham's delightful ballroom to pay us a visit." He tipped his head toward his fair companion. "Why do you think he exerts himself so? I know, he has come to meet you, dear lady. Your beauty has entranced him, as it did me." His French accent, never lost from his childhood, softened what could have been a provocative speech.

"He looks a respectable man," the lady said in a low, musical voice. She was older than Benedict had thought, perhaps close to his own twenty-eight. A woman who had seen something of the world and kept her own counsel. Demimonde?

Was he becoming broad-minded, or merely cynical?

Or was he trying to come up with some flaw in her so she did not overmaster him?

"Eminently respectable," Letellier said, drawing chuckles from his companions. "Yes, you are right. Much more respectable than I. Although"—and he tapped his lips with a knuckle—"perhaps what draws him here is not your delectable self, but a desire to assess my state of sobriety, and its likely implications for my head at first light tomorrow. Not very sporting, Fitzhugh. I have not mentioned it, dear lady, but I am to duel Fitzhugh here in the morning."

Benedict had the lady's full attention. Her eyes were a brilliant greenish hazel, the color of new leaves waving against copper beech bark. Thick dark lashes framed them under arched brows. An elemental force lurked in those eyes, the undeniable call of woman to man, as potent as the lever that could move the world.

Her bow-shaped mouth parted, and she dipped one proud cheekbone toward him as though getting a half inch closer to him would reveal all his inner secrets. The sensation intrigued and perturbed him.

"It is best, then," she said to Benedict, "that I got to know you tonight, sir."

She was a lady, then. Even a woman as socially skilled as the highest of the demimonde would have asked who had challenged whom, and why.

The cool response did not, however, fit with those eyes. They betrayed the intense interest of someone who placed such an event on a grander painting than a twenty-by-twenty square of turf and two ritually crossed swords.

"Is she not everything everyone has ever said?" Letellier asked in an admiring tone.

The lady's lashes flickered down, and Benedict wracked his memory for a list of beautiful women known to be in

London this Season. Benedict acknowledged his current lack of social savoir faire, and regretted it.

"What do you think, Fitzhugh?"

"Let us say I do not know the lady's name," Benedict replied, summoning up every calm face he had ever turned toward his father when that gentleman ranted about Benedict's inexplicable desire to do things his own way. As there had been many such events as he had grown up, Benedict had the confidence that comes from much practice.

Or so he thought until the lady's lashes flicked up, disconcerting him.

But Benedict managed to say, "It is, however, unkind of you to lead her to believe we duel anywhere outside Monsieur Marguillier's *salle,* and not at first light, if you please, but at the eminently respectable hour of eleven o'clock. Your head will be quite recovered tomorrow from any excesses it might lead you into tonight."

Letellier laughed, and put an arm across Benedict's shoulders. Since Benedict topped Letellier by some five inches, the motion perforce dragged at him. "You are the most amusing fellow, Cousin."

"Cousin?" the lady said.

"Oh, nothing official," Letellier said, withdrawing his arm. "His father, Lord Hadley, assisted my mother and me in escaping France. Fitzhugh and I played together as boys. And now he has come to London. The angels cried his presence from London Bridge, and wept tears of joy. What else could a poor relation such as myself do but invite him to cross swords with me?"

The lady did not rise to the bait, but said, "All my fears are allayed, then."

"Do not think me from the woods yet, dear lady. When last we crossed swords, Fitzhugh knocked me senseless."

"They were sticks, not swords," Benedict said, "and I

could not anticipate the rabbit's hole you fell into. It was the rock you landed on that knocked you senseless."

One of Letellier's friends laughed. Letellier glared at him, and he choked back his laughter in a nervous hiccup.

The keen lady observed this with apparent placidity. "Are there rabbit holes at the fencing *salle*? Rocks? No? Then you will, belike, enjoy yourselves in your gentlemanly fashion."

"You are not convinced that gentlemen truly enjoy fencing," Letellier said.

"I am not oblivious to the allures of exercise."

Letellier gave her a smile that hovered at the precipice of being a leer, and then backed away from the edge. Benedict found himself bristling, although bristling at Letellier was the last thing he should do. On odd moments Benedict allowed himself to believe his father finally regarded him as having some small competencies. On even moments, he reminded himself that his father did not consider investing in various ventures as anything more than rolling dice.

Maybe this beautiful woman was Letellier's most recent little crossroads. Blast his father, Benedict thought. Why must he be so concerned about Letellier?

Was he supposed to encourage the lady to continue by Letellier's side, or was he supposed to cool the lady's ardor for Letellier? She appeared, now that he had observed her up close and in conversation, not to be completely in thrall to Letellier's charm. She remained, however, and that had to indicate, well, something.

Or maybe the lady had met Letellier only that evening, and Benedict, all unknowing, just had to be spontaneous. Benedict did not appreciate needing to be spontaneous. Not all problems solved themselves by having someone plow ahead willy-nilly. Had he not proved that, at least as far as his new business ventures went, despite his father's telling him all his life that deliberation never accomplished anything?

Benedict took a deep breath and stopped ranting in his head. He *would* prove his worth.

The lady's sidelong hazel glance also helped him recall himself. She had not been looking at him the way so many other young women and their mothers had been looking at him. Regret washed over him, followed by a profound sense of relief. Were he never measured by such a woman, he would never be found wanting.

"There can be more allure to fencing than mere exercise, my lady," Letellier said, kissing her hand. "Say you will bet on me to best Fitzhugh here. The first three unanswered touches."

A debate raged in her eyes, hidden from Letellier, but plain and freshly intriguing to Benedict. He did not know whether this woman had caused his father's worry about Letellier. He began to believe, however, that she would soon. She affected him strongly enough that she would have the same effect on others. Thus Benedict considered his duty clear.

"Do you not believe, Letellier, that the lady should be given a relative assessment of our skills?"

Letellier's friend laughed again, but this time with a hand before his mouth.

"There are no rabbit holes," the lady said. "That is enough for me to know. One hundred pounds on you, Mr. Letellier. Who shall take it up?"

Letellier's friends were silent. Letellier flushed.

"You are known to be a swordsman, then, sir," the lady said to Benedict.

"He is known to be many things," Letellier said, "all of them dull. I have had occasion to fence often over the past year, whereas you have been far too preoccupied poring over your dull figures. I may surprise you."

"Will you not take up my bet?" the lady asked Benedict, playing with her fan.

Benedict bowed. "Much as I regret turning down any desire of a lady, a fine opponent is its own reward to me. Have Letellier announce your bet tomorrow at Monsieur Marguillier's salon. There will be someone present who will be happy to take it up. There always is. Better for you, too."

"How is that, sir?"

"Likely he will have a better measure of my boyhood friend's skills, freshly honed this past year."

"There, my dear, did I not tell you? He *is* dull." This time Letellier did not correct his friends' laughter.

"What will they know of yours?" she asked Benedict.

"I am an open book, ma'am."

Speculation rippled through every line of her face. Benedict concentrated on being as closed a book as he could. A smooth, unblemished leather binding of dark brown, perhaps, concealing whether he was a natural history, a book of sermons, or the newest, wickedest poetry. She intrigued him, but it would do no one any good to reveal it.

She smiled, quietly, and he wondered if she thought she had cut open a leaf.

"Do you know, Fitzhugh, I am reminded that I do not yet have a good reason why you came over here."

"Merely for your company," Benedict said.

Letellier scrunched up a corner of his mouth. "Hadley and Aunt Bourre have dispatched you."

"Not expressly."

"Indeed?"

"My father could not attend this evening. As to Aunt

Bourre, she has Dorrie to attend to. I thought you would like company."

Letellier still looked skeptical.

"*Aunt* Bourre?" the lady asked.

"Another honorary relative," Letellier said. "Apart from my mother, who is ill in Kent, all my relatives in England are honorary." He made it sound very extravagant. "But I cannot believe you, Fitzhugh."

Benedict raised a brow. "Very well. Since you refuse to be convinced I could seek out your company for your company, I shall withdraw. Gentlemen, ma'am." He bowed, pretended not to feel so distressed by how the lady's eyes widened. Could a woman who had attached herself to Letellier's company not want Benedict to leave? Or did she merely marvel at the rapidity of his exit?

He felt the churl, but neither did he wish to remain as Letellier's whipping boy. Letellier would not respect him for it.

He had walked four steps away when Letellier said, as if on cue, "Balls bring out the worst in me, Fitzhugh. If you wish to join us later, we are for the Red Falcon."

"Thank you," Benedict said over his shoulder. He stalked back the way he had come, not noticing either the gentlemen who removed themselves and their lady companions from his path, or the ladies' thoughtful looks. He thought only that it was a fine thing so many couples danced so that he could better manage the crowd.

Damn Letellier for not having the courtesy to name his companion. Benedict wanted desperately to place her, so he might know what to do about her. He well imagined his father's scorn should he report that some unknown but dangerously beautiful woman had attached herself to Letellier. Blast the whole messy situation.

"There you are, Fitzhugh," said Miss Dorrie Bourre,

who had to do a little hop-step to catch his arm. Tipping her head, she said, "I have been looking for you."

"My dear," he said with much more enthusiasm than was proper for such a public forum. "You have found me." He cursed himself as her eyes widened.

Dorrie was not some mystery beauty who perplexed and befuddled. Her dear face, its sweet circle broken only by her pointy chin, deep dimples, and firm mouth, all topped by wheat-colored curls, had called out to him all his life. From the chilly atmosphere of his own home, he had often traveled the mile to her warm one, and watched her grow into a splendid young woman. She had enough lively curiosity to prevent boredom, and a common sense Benedict found soothing.

Dorrie did not deserve to have him embarrass her in public. He had done that twice already. The first time, last summer, almost a long year ago, he had given in to an impulse more like his father's than his own and proposed marriage. She had refused, saying he was like a brother to her, and he had left for Bath.

Benedict's arrival in London three days ago had occasioned her second embarrassment, for how could they meet again without awkwardness? Had his father not appealed to him, Benedict would have stayed away a little longer.

Embarrassing her again would not persuade her to give him another chance.

"The next dance, it is supposed to be ours," she said, and looked like she regretted it.

Gently Benedict took her hand and set it upon his arm. She allowed him the privilege, and they strolled toward the marble colonnade where Benedict had last seen Dorrie's mother, whom Benedict and Letellier both called Aunt Bourre.

"I have been speaking," Benedict said, "to Letellier. It was an odd experience."

"All *my* experiences with him are odd," Dorrie said. "He has never been an easy person to know. Not like you, Fitzhugh."

Perhaps, Benedict thought, warmed, she was close to forgiving him for his proposal of last year, and accepting him as her adopted brother again. It would be enough. For now.

"I do not remember Mama's mentioning he would be here," Dorrie said. "She has, however, been quite worried about him."

If Aunt Bourre was worried about Letellier, it would explain his father's worry. Any friend of Aunt Bourre's loyal heart automatically earned Hadley's regard and concern. Benedict tried to remember this fact to his father's credit whenever they were angry and disappointed with each other.

Benedict had to remember that frequently.

He wished, though, that his father had decided to apply himself, and not Benedict, to the problem. "Really?"

"Really," replied Dorrie. "Before you ask, though, she would not tell me why, but she has been most interested in any letters that come from Madame Letellier. Yesterday, after reading one before we were to go out, she forgot her favorite cherry-blossom bonnet and then the name of our hostess, Lady Willoughby, who is a kindly lady for all she has the dreadful sense to mix the most awful combinations of colors in her dress. Yesterday it was blue and brown. Ugh.

"But Mama had to introduce my other cousins, Emma and Edmund Tunbridge—you will remember them—and Emma is coming out this Season, and Mama just stood there blinking. I patted Mama on the back as if she had a cough and introduced my cousins myself. Fortunately

Mama did cough and excuse herself, so I knew she was not lost to all awareness of her situation. But really, she and Lady Willoughby have been friends these past fourteen years, ever since they met when my cousin Barnabas married Lady Willoughby's niece. Can you ever remember a time when my mother was not deeply sensitive to a social situation?"

Benedict tried and could not. He had long thought Aunt Bourre one of the most socially graceful women he had ever met. She could find a kind word to say to anyone she wished to find one for. She could turn aside rudeness with a smile. And she had the happy ability not to take everything that happened as being personally directed at her.

Benedict had long tried to emulate her, at least in his thoughts.

"So of course I am happy you are come to London," Dorrie continued.

Benedict's heart soared with hope . . .

"If anyone can puzzle out what worries Mama about Letellier, it is you."

. . . and dropped to the silver buckles of his black shoes.

"Oh, the music is beginning for the dance. We shall not have time to go to Mama if we are to join the line."

"I think I may say with perfect equanimity that your mother will regard your dancing with me with—"

"Equanimity," Dorrie said, and laughed.

Benedict elected to be happy with that. It felt wonderful to dance with Dorrie, to watch her round face flush with pleasure and exertion. Benedict forgot to think about the beautiful, exotic lady every second.

Until, that is, he saw her coming down the line. She and Letellier were only five couples up. She looked down the line, and focused on him.

What did she mean by it?

"Letellier *has* been making up to Lady Jane Compton," Dorrie was saying, "but I do not think that—"

"He is coming down the line," Benedict said, wondering whether Lady Jane Compton wore cream and green.

Dorrie looked and would have missed a step but for Benedict's already holding her hand. "My God. He is dancing with Lady Notorious. *That* will set the fox among the pigeons."

Chapter Two

Nothing about Alexander Letellier impressed Esme except his complete embrace of profligacy. He spread his smiles about until one had to smile or feel the harpy. Esme felt the latter. She could not answer for the feather-headed gentlemen who toadied and paid court to him. His smiles themselves tried so hard they bordered on their own leering parody. His accent she had at first found melodious; then all melody fell into dissonance as he dropped it and picked it up, dusted it off, and set it back upon his lips as it pleased him.

Too little could not be said about his canary-bright coat, for it cawed as none of the black-coated gentlemen's did. He knew it, of course, and played their strings, not by gliding a bow over them, but by plucking them in harsh staccato.

Less than an evening with him, and Esme loathed him.

She could easily comprehend, however, how dear Jane might be captivated. A rambunctious eighteen, Jane thought she knew the world and all its flavors. A man who seemed to dare and dare again, until he had pressed any experience of all its sweet oil, must compel. Esme had reports that Letellier had jumped the wall of the Iddesford House garden, climbed a tree, and serenaded Jane at her bedroom window.

Nor had that incident marked the end of his attentions. Whenever Jane attended a ball, Letellier persuaded her to dance at least once with him. He took his bows during her at-home hours, a large bouquet of exotic flowers always to hand.

Hearing of Letellier's interest in Jane, and knowing who some of his friends were, Esme had come to London to intervene. Intervention, however, required creativity, for on no account could Esme work directly with Jane's mother, Augusta, Countess of Iddesford.

In Augusta's view, Esme had the bad *ton* to be the *dowager* Countess of Iddesford, and twenty-three years younger than Augusta. No matter that the marriage had been forced upon Esme by her domineering father and her infatuated late husband, Charles. No matter that the succession had passed without ruffle or perturbation to Augusta's husband, John. Augusta and John hated Esme for what she was and never bothered to find out who she was.

Nor had Charles discouraged their lack of curiosity. He had not wanted to appear the fool for falling in love with someone fifty years his junior, and so had been happy to use Esme as an excuse not to socialize with his son and daughter-in-law. Esme regretted that she had been too young, and, initially, too resentful of her own situation to go against his wishes.

But Esme had learned to care for Charles, if not to love him, and Charles had had hopes for his grand-daughter Jane.

Esme's creativity ran in simple, but, she hoped, elegant lines. If she could not work with Augusta, she would use that very fact to deceive Letellier. Letellier easily believed her desire to frustrate Jane's parents and promote the match.

Letellier's friend Fitzhugh surprised Esme, though. As

he had strolled up to them, all ease and grace, with his well-proportioned, rectangular face and hair the color of ash, she had considered him a fine specimen of English manhood. No more, no less.

He had noticed her, of course, the way nine men of ten noticed her. Esme had given up the struggle with her face and figure. They would be considered lovely, even if she dressed in rags and let her hair hang in tangles. Since rags made her itch and tangles pained her head, she dressed to please herself.

Let the men of Britain cope.

Lord Fitzhugh had not, however, come across the room to notice her more closely. He had been looking for Letellier, and despite noticing her, he had replied without either stuttering or pulling back his shoulders and puffing out his chest, as so many other men did.

He had professed himself ignorant of her identity.

Esme knew what people called her. After her mourning for Charles, she had set on reentering society on her own. She would not look to her father for assistance, nor would the other Iddesfords have assisted her. But gentlemen had paid attention, and she had accepted their attention. In public. Privately, only one gentleman had been allowed in. His name was Gillespie. Equally privately, he had been tossed back out.

When the whispers started, however, she did not doubt for a second that Gillespie had very publicly painted their last meeting differently than it had happened.

Nor did she have to work her imagination hard to understand how the rumors developed a life of their own and followed her across Europe. She could count on any gentleman with whom she conversed to either make something up or remain silent. Who would want to admit failure where it was reputed so many others had already succeeded?

Either choice led to one conclusion, and furthered her wretched reputation. Esme took no pleasure in it, but as the years went on and she could do nothing about it, she had learned to accept it.

Still, she had been warmed to discover someone who did not know her and her reputation. Better yet, he had resisted Letellier's baits and snares, and her own attempts to draw him in. A man who knew his own mind must refresh.

And yet . . . he had seemed eager to continue in Letellier's company. That was a pretty little conundrum. How could any man who knew his own mind desire to be in Letellier's presence? Letellier had as good as sent him away with his teasing, too. What did it mean that Letellier regarded this Fitzhugh as someone not worthy to pay him court?

Fitzhugh danced with the kind of restrained grace a fencer might employ. Having such a man make love to her the way he danced would be quite an experience.

No one believed she would not do just as she pleased. No one would accuse her of an overabundance of virtue. Maybe, after she had detached Letellier from Jane, she could finally indulge herself.

With Fitzhugh.

What was she thinking?

But who was the mousy creature he was partnering with such easy amicability?

The girl was not prattling. No, Fitzhugh and the mouse shared the ease of long acquaintance. But neither did she look on him as one would a lover, nor a potential suitor.

Yes, Fitzhugh puzzled Esme excessively, and intrigued her. So as the number of couples between herself and Letellier, and Fitzhugh and his mystery girl, decreased, Esme indulged in a seldom-used, but not-forgotten game of darting glances at him. The trick involved letting Fitzhugh, and possibly his little partner, know she was aware of him without having Letellier cotton to it.

It turned out to be far easier than she had anticipated. Letellier, not so lost in his admiration of her that he neglected to make sure others admired him for having her, noticed her speaking glances toward Fitzhugh not at all. Fitzhugh himself momentarily acquired that wonderful expression one gets when one thinks one is being waved to and then realizes the waver intended to wave at someone behind one.

So, Esme thought, much struck, *he is modest.*

The girl, however, understood the situation exactly, and narrowed her eyes at Esme as the two passed each other.

Esme merely smiled, which served to cover any number of sins. Despite his bemused expression, Fitzhugh took her hand in a firm but gentle grip. Did he handle his rapier in such a way? Could he maintain that sort of pressure, and control?

What a shivery, delicious, intoxicating thought.

Esme had to remember what step came next, for all she had done the sequence twenty times. It was a good thing she did, too, for Letellier's next comments took her aback.

"My dearest Dorrie, don't you look too sweet. Has Fitzhugh told you he is joining us at the Red Falcon after this tedious party? He wants to get to know my lady better. What chance do you think he has?"

That pricked Fitzhugh's calm, although he quickly reined in the anger that flared across his face. Unfortunately he was also required to let go her hand, and Esme to take up Letellier's. Esme repressed a chill.

The girl said, "La, Letellier, where did you find such

a coat? I do believe even my cousin Miss Tunbridge has not found a shop selling such exotics."

"Charming, dear Dorrie. Charming."

"I look forward to it, Letellier," Fitzhugh said. The two gentlemen grimaced smiles at each other, and they were sailing past, on to the next couple, down the line.

Esme could not help but follow Fitzhugh's progress. His dancing remained even, an amiable smile on his face, although the girl Dorrie was hissing something.

"I wondered whether Fitzhugh would find a woman who could stir his blood enough to make him forget his little squirrel. Apparently you can do it with your eyes alone. It is well he did not look back at you just now. I should hate such an automaton to lose his step."

"You do not have a high opinion of him."

"On the contrary. I have the highest opinion of him. He has always been the perfect son. He never disagrees, but always does what he is told."

"Does that not understate the matter?"

"You are a wicked, wicked woman," he said with pleasure.

"So everyone says," Esme said.

"Is this your way of amusing yourself of an evening?"

"Sir?"

"Seeing how many men you may charm with just your eyes?"

"Tonight it is merely sauce."

"That does remind me of a question I had."

"What am I doing with you?" Esme asked.

Letellier threw his head back and laughed. "You are a treasure among women, my dear. I believe I shall enjoy fencing with you as much as I do Fitzhugh."

"You must be more explicit in your meaning of fencing, sir," Esme said with an easy but practiced tip of her head that exposed her neck in invitation.

Letellier licked his lips. "Is there more to fencing?"

That she must congratulate herself on this response . . . "Maybe, but first I shall help you sharpen your sword." And she looked expressively about her.

Letellier took the hint. He was not unintelligent, just repellent. For the rest of the dance, he spoke of fashion. He laughed over any extreme not his own. The Mushrooms who tugged at cravats and laces as if they had never worn evening clothes before, the Tulips with their collar points excessively high, the women with feathers in their turbans rivaling the collar points for height—all came under Letellier's scrutiny.

Esme laughed in genuine pleasure when he pointed out Lady Boxborough, whose yard-long ostrich plume was steadily leaking down her back. "She will put out someone's eye," Esme said.

"Willing, or not?" he said, and studied her carefully.

"Ten pounds, regardless of intent," Esme flashed back, and curtsied to end the dance.

Yes, she had his character. He smiled his acceptance and drew her arm through his. Esme hated the presumption of it, but did not demur. Someone of her reputation would not, and she had to play on her reputation now.

They strolled toward the punch bowl, which Esme saw for a mere second before black-coated gentlemen surrounded it, anxious to relieve their ladies' thirst. The crowding there left the middle of the ballroom curiously depopulated.

She turned to Letellier. "I sought you out because I have a proposition for you."

"I did not think, me, that it was for my good looks."

"You want to marry my step-granddaughter, Lady Jane Compton."

"Do I?"

"You have made no secret of your attentions."

He shrugged. "True."

"The family does not encourage your suit."

"Also true."

"The family does not encourage my presence in society."

"Ahh," he said. Then, just when she thought she had him lured, he asked, "Is it that you are more than twenty years younger than my lady the current countess?"

"My daughter-in-law does know how to count, yes. But that is not all."

"Oh?" he asked.

"I believe she thought I would poison her husband with chocolate-covered cherries. That is, after all, the way she would do it, were she ever roused sufficiently."

Letellier laughed, and Esme could not contain her own smile. She did not have to lie about disliking Augusta.

"Then she believed I would present my late husband with a son." *Would that not have been a miracle? Poor Charles.*

"As you were burying his half-brother, no doubt."

"I cannot speak for her lurid imaginings, but *you* have imagination, sir."

"Do I?" he asked disingenuously.

"You got into the Iddesford garden. That is no mean feat."

"Your daughter-in-law," he said, enjoying calling a woman of fifty Esme's daughter-in-law, "did not appreciate my gesture."

"Did Jane?"

"But certainly."

"I thought so. I know her well."

Finally, finally, he took the lure. "How well?"

"Enough to help you get her."

"And what, dear lady," he asked, running a finger from her lips to her chin, "would you get in return?"

Esme held herself still. It had been all well and fine to plan, but here, in the crux of it, she could not deny her rush of feeling. *I* will *fulfill my promise to you, poor lonely Charles.*

She could, however, put a cool face on it. She said, "You would be a good match for Jane. She has high spirits, as I can see you do. You would be grateful to me, I am sure, since her dowry is ample enough to fit all Cheshire within it. And then there is the satisfaction of Lord and Lady Iddesford's knowing I have bested them. That would be sweet. And perhaps, as we get to know each other better, we may . . ."

Again he ran a finger along her mouth, catching her lip before descending to her chin. Wearing his edgy smile, he bent to kiss her, no conflict in his mind between his pursuit of Jane and his belief that he would bed Esme. And, likely, that Esme would enjoy it.

The snake.

As she smelled his musky cologne, she turned her head so his lips landed on her cheek, a brand sealing their bargain.

Fitzhugh and the girl emerged from the punch-going crowd. The girl held a glass and her chin high. Fitzhugh had his arms crossed, and what likely passed for a scowl on his face. Amazing that his bland expression hinted so eloquently at his feelings. Amazing that Esme could feel them as a brand upon her other cheek.

Esme sighed, recognizing that look as easily as breathing. The girl had told him who Esme was. Well, she thought with a courage she did not feel, what was life without challenge?

"You are a magnificent creature," Letellier said.

I am a lying fool, Esme thought, and smiled mechanically. She should be rejoicing. She should be conserving her strength and her wits to deal with this slippery snake of a man. And yet she bemoaned being an object to him before a man whom she had met only briefly. She put her hand over her right cheek, where she felt Fitzhugh's invisible brand burn.

"What is wrong?"

"Nothing. Some punch, sir?"

Chapter Three

The Red Falcon took its name from some forgotten lore. In the dim light—each table had one and only one candle set in the center—no red falcons could be found painted on the walls, or under the rough-hewn plank tables, or in the rooms for stores in the back. Nor did a single carving sit perched above a ceiling beam. Benedict imagined one in the shadows, winking, but that was all the place could supply.

Likely its current inhabitants cared very little. Although the establishment gave the illusion of a club for the definitely not aristocratic, the only patrons not aristocratic were the serving girls. One lissome creature led Benedict to a corner table, where Letellier, his lady friend, and his cronies sat. Tall walls of rough-hewn planks loosely chinked together separated them from adjoining tables. A bench wrapped along the walls, and, since Letellier's cronies had taken the room on the left side, Benedict perforce sat to the right, by the lady.

The serving girl bent to take Benedict's order for brandy, her curls tickling his ear, and said, "If the gentleman desires anything, I would be happy to see if it's something we serve." She was clean and fresh, for all her accent told its tale.

Benedict thanked her gravely, deciding that the Falcon was not going to be an Exotic Experience, at least not yet.

"What did our little Dorrie say when you told her you were coming out here?" Letellier said by way of greeting.

"Miss Bourre is none of your concern." Benedict did not want to look at the lady. He had identified the feeling she stirred within him. It was lust. Not the casual lust one felt when a pretty woman passed and one had a half hour to occupy. No, this resembled the kind of lust that lasted for weeks or months, that could not satisfy itself in one chance encounter.

Benedict did not want such feelings. He loved Dorrie. He knew he did. He had all his life. He had let his desire get the better of his common sense last summer. Now he knew better.

Or he hoped so. It must be so.

The lady had eschewed a mask as other ladies often wore when coming to such places. She had, however, added a loosely tied, hooded green cloak. The cloak and the green trim of her dress framed a triangle of creamy skin that moved enticingly with her breathing. The hood sloped at an angle, with more piled in a heap across the left shoulder than the right, as though she had whisked it off with abandon.

Her gaze trapped Benedict's, her eyes catlike. Interesting shadows accrued beyond a thin halo reflected by her coppery curls. She did not smile a greeting, nor did she appear in the least triumphant, as Letellier did, at his arrival.

And Benedict cursed himself for thinking that she would. Dorrie had told him who she was. Her connection to Letellier puzzled Dorrie and baffled Benedict. Letellier did not belong to that fascinating class of men the dowager Countess of Iddesford attached to herself.

If he was what such a beauty now wanted, how the mighty had fallen.

And whatever Benedict's feelings for her, she would never be interested in a man like himself, Benedict thought with a burn of self-disgusted disappointment. Not even if she *were* in her declining years.

Hard to imagine this woman ever declining. Youth could always recommend itself, but true beauty demanded its own reckoning. She would be beautiful when she was eighty.

"Gallant as always," Letellier said, but dropped the subject of Dorrie. "You will have a brandy with us?"

"I have ordered one," Benedict said.

"Tell me, Cousin, did you never learn your rhetoric, or do you make a study of answering in the most concise way possible?"

One of Letellier's cronies snickered. Benedict decided he was tired of Letellier's cronies' snickering. "No," he replied, knowing it would bring a laugh.

It did, but not by either Letellier or Lady Iddesford. Then, as his cronies subsided, Letellier barked a laugh. "But this really is too, too much, Fitzhugh. First the invitation to fence. Then crossing a ballroom—a highly strenuous activity. And now, now you commit yourself to be seen in my company when no one could conclude anything else but that you sought it out. I must have the story. *Did* your father and Aunt Bourre put you up to this? Really, I must know."

For all his extravagance of phrasing, Letellier truly wanted to know. The cronies picked up on his tone, too, for they wriggled straighter in their seats. The lady, too, moved her shoulders, freeing her single emerald on its gold chain from its prison within the cloak's ties. It invaded the green-framed triangle of creamy flesh and winked like a third eye.

Benedict glanced at the cronies. They protested, but Letellier had them in such control that one piercing look silenced them. They slumped off.

"And the lady?" Benedict asked, not looking at her.

"She may stay. I have discovered in my lady a tricky mind that rivals my own."

That comment led to any number of awful and fantastic implications. "Do you know," Benedict said, keeping his voice light, "that the lady and I have not been introduced?"

"You are not likely to be so here, either," Letellier said.

"Point taken."

"Well?"

Letellier's mocking did not impress Benedict, but Letellier with a sense of urgency did. "My father invited me to Town," Benedict said. "You know he has ever pushed me toward the Corinthian set. I believe he thought that if I began fencing with you, my old friend, I should do it more often."

Although she steadily regarded the candle, Benedict could tell the lady had caught his slight emphasis on "my old friend," for her bow-shaped mouth twitched.

Letellier laughed. "Does he not pay any attention to the matters of people younger than ancient?"

"When he was our age, I am certain of it."

"So you did not correct him."

There would have been no point to it. The thought must have shown in Benedict's face, for Letellier said, "No, you did not. Oh well, so he set up our appointment tomorrow. Point one has *an* explanation."

"I believe Aunt Bourre had expressed a desire to see me."

Letellier snorted.

"I begin to wonder if your suspicions are correct, Letellier. Perhaps my father and Aunt Bourre invited me to Town with the sole and express purpose of looking you up. You are acting very much as you did last time."

"And what of it?" Letellier asked.

"Did I not help you then?"

"I was not the father of that trull's child."

No thanks for paying off the girl, though. Benedict wished he could be rid of the odd feeling that Letellier thought the less of him, as though Benedict had been tried and found wanting—for kindness.

"But that is history," Letellier said. "I do not need your help this time."

"Very well. I will not offer any. But spare me the overly amusing snide comments. Even you do not utter such entertainments from the goodness of your heart."

Lady Iddesford smiled, and as she did, the gathers of her hood slid farther off her shoulder, toward Letellier. She reached with her ungloved right hand to flip them back, but Letellier caught her hand on her shoulder. Caressing it with his index finger, he said, "It is you who would be amusingly snide, Cousin. But very well. You shall know all. I have finally decided it is time for me to poke my, er, nose into parson's mousetrap."

Distaste over Letellier's caressing Lady Iddesford gave way to a dismay and disgust so profound, Benedict had to swallow before he could say, "And when do I wish you both happy?"

Lady Iddesford froze, her eyes widening. Then as quickly as she had reacted, she looked away from Letellier. To hide her startled horror? The situation puzzled more and more.

"You *are* a wit, dear Fitzhugh. Is he not droll, my dear?"

"Exceedingly," the lady said.

Her voice, forming those four syllables, was the only well-tuned note in the Red Falcon's raucous carillon.

"I wish to marry this lady's granddaughter."

"Step-granddaughter, sir, please."

"My deepest apologies. I would not have thought it necessary to remind a woman as beautiful and gracious as yourself that you could not possibly be old enough to be someone's grandmother."

"This gentleman," the lady said, now looking back over her captured hand to Letellier, and then, boldly, at Benedict, "will like his matters put precisely."

Good God, Benedict thought, shaken as much by her look as her accuracy.

Then another thought struck him. *You were right, Dorrie. He* is *setting the fox among the pigeons.* In heated, half-whispered words, Dorrie had told him something of the woman sitting next to him. How she had caught the elderly earl of Iddesford's fancy and forced a marriage. How she had treated him and the rest of the family with contempt after the marriage. How she had likely wasted away whatever funds the earl had left her in a whirlwind spree across England and Europe, taking only the most interesting, courted, and high-placed gentlemen as her lovers.

Benedict had heard some of it himself. Within the Corinthian circles, some gentleman would remark that could he but do so-and-so better, he would be worthy to attract the attention of a Lady Iddesford. Then that same person would wonder whom she had taken hold of lately, which invariably led to heated discussion of where the lady might be residing, and half-mocking, half-deadly earnest competition among them to be the one who could raise her fortunes.

Benedict had wondered, idly, how much of what he had heard was true. Confronted now by this beautiful woman, who could seduce with a flicker of her brilliant eyes but who could also regard Letellier, her apparent partner in conspiracy, with horror, the question gained an intense, painful urgency.

"You have read my dear friend aright, I do believe, ma'am," Letellier said. "What do you think, Fitzhugh?"

"That you would yet prevaricate."

"Definitely aright. I am ecstatic with pleasure," said Letellier, giving a little staged shiver. When that produced no response, he went on. "I wish to marry this lady's step-granddaughter, and she has agreed to help me do it."

"I had heard there was parental opposition," Benedict said.

"Who could believe it?" Letellier said.

"Is it true?"

"They want a duke for the girl," Letellier said, waving his hand dismissively.

"Which one?"

"Breshirewood," the lady said.

"He's a popular fellow, that one," Benedict said before he could help it. Only that evening, he had overheard Aunt Bourre tell her sister Lady Tunbridge that Dorrie might fancy the duke.

Lady Iddesford had distracted Benedict from madly comparing any and all of his assets against those of the duke of Breshirewood. Now all the inequalities in situation and fortune flooded him.

"The wind blows that way, does it?" Letellier said, and a note of sympathy entered his expression, hovered there like an uninvited guest at a wedding, flushed with shame, and departed.

The lady followed this interchange avidly. Benedict burned to know what she was thinking. Benedict burned to be the one who could capture her hand, and hold it, unprotested.

Instead he said, "So, you want to marry the girl."

Letellier released Lady Iddesford's hand to clasp his breast just beneath his foamy cravat. "I am smitten. Desperately, uncontrollably, hopelessly smitten." He grinned, and drank some wine.

Then the lady, straightening her hood at last, moved a few inches closer to Benedict. It was the most natural and casual of movements, the kind one makes when one has sat in one position too long. Then she set her hands down on the bench, and although Benedict did not know whether her right hand touched Letellier's thigh, her left certainly touched Benedict's leg.

A shudder tickled Benedict's spine, and he straightened, trying to disguise it, as she had. She recognized her effect on him, however. A trace of female superiority gleamed beneath the lowered lashes. Then, madness beyond all madness, she ran her forefinger along his leg under the table, then went back, criss-crossing, rousing him as no other gesture had ever roused him. It was such a little thing, but so potent.

What was she playing at? She should not be doing this. She should not be making him feel like this.

Then Benedict realized she was spelling the letter *E* on his leg. Since Letellier's wine glass yet screened his face, Benedict raised his brows slightly at the lady. She responded by spelling out rapidly *A-S-Y*. Easy.

What did she mean by *easy*?

He would get no more clues, though, for she folded her hands neatly on the table. The emerald at her neck winked with her breathing. Had its frequency increased, or did Benedict merely tease himself?

Letellier thumped his wine glass down on the table, and made the candle flame jump. "I fancy the girl. It's time I was married. And she has a fine dowry."

"All excellent reasons for marriage," Benedict said.

"So you may tell your father and Aunt Bourre that

they may shortly wish me happy. For this wonderful woman"—Letellier recaptured the dowager's hand—"has offered to help me do it."

"How lucky," Benedict said. Again, those greenish hazel eyes, so wide and limpid, snared him. Her lips parted slightly.

"Letellier." It was blond, large-boned Merton, the crony who laughed the least of the three of them.

"What?" Letellier asked in irritation.

"He's come in."

Letellier went carefully blank, then he kissed the lady's hand and released it. "Do excuse me a moment, my dear, friend Fitzhugh. I have something I must attend to."

Alone with Benedict, Lady Iddesford looked down at her hands, and hunched her shoulders a little forward, so that her necklace dangled in the air two inches above the green border of her dress. Benedict did not know what to think. Every time he thought he had her assigned to a nice mental column, she became something completely irreconcilable.

Finally she collected herself. "Thank you," she said.

"I beg your pardon. For what?"

She lifted her chin. "For heeding me, of course."

"I did not heed you, ma'am."

"You stopped poking at him, did you not?"

"I took my own counsel, ma'am. I have known him a long time. And unlike Letellier, I never poke."

Her brows rose. "You make a fine piece of parchment."

The hot flush of desire her words caused made him harsher than he might have been. "Suppose you tell me why you are helping Letellier when you clearly despise him?"

Chapter Four

His legs lived up to all the promise she had seen in them dancing. If Esme had not been so intent on sending him a message, and sending it quickly, she might have tried to see what else he let her get away with. Truly, she had never developed a desire this strong before, nor acted upon it.

"Do you think he knows?" she asked.

That made him blink. "I beg your pardon."

"You beg my pardon too much, sir," she said, wryly.

"You are the most incomprehensible woman I have ever met."

"Indeed? Why?"

"Are you going to answer my question?" He tipped his head in the direction Letellier and the broad-beamed Merton had gone. "He'll be back soon."

"You think this business of his will not keep him long."

"I think he would be a fool to leave a woman he is so obviously *smitten* with alone with anyone he does not trust implicitly."

Congratulations, Esme told herself. Letellier might not trust her entirely, but lust had a way of blinkering men. The question was, how little would Letellier see? And how much would Fitzhugh?

"It is a shame," she said, dropping her chin so she

could regard him from lidded eyes, "that he does not trust you more."

"Do you want him to?"

Now he had *her* blinking. She fingered her wine glass, set it away from her. "I want him to trust me."

"We return, again, to our previous question."

"Why should I trust you when he does not?"

"Woman," he said, "you could give soap a lesson on being slippery."

She had to chuckle. Her gaze snarled with his, and suddenly the Red Falcon lost all its air. She licked her lips, and tried again to draw breath despite his avid following of her gesture.

"My lady—" he began.

Then, from a booth nearby, she heard the braying voice she remembered all too well and stopped breathing for another reason altogether. "—and then it all fell apart. But say, have you seen her? He told me she was here—"

Esme fumbled for her hood, could not make her hands work properly. Fitzhugh untangled the folds, and brought it forward. He tucked a copper curl inside the hood, his warm fingers creating a tiny waltz of sensation along her collarbone. Suddenly he was breathing like he had run a race. He lifted both hands from her shoulders, and they hovered there before he clasped them together. "No one can see you," he said.

"It's Gillespie," she said, gratitude making her name the hated name. "I cannot let Gillespie see me."

"He shall not."

And then Gillespie stood there, at their booth, his handsome, slightly effeminate face with its fine bones and upturned nose. His blond hair and gray eyes were not unlike Fitzhugh's. "I say. Fitzhugh. Never seen you here before."

He was looking, not at Fitzhugh, but at her, trying to see within the shadows of her hood. Fitzhugh touched her leg, much as she had done to him, indicating that she should move closer to him. She would be no closer to Gillespie, and at a greater angle, partially blocked by Fitzhugh's body, so she moved, making it the wiggle of someone who finds her companion desirable. Had Gillespie not been there, she would have felt no mockery in the pretense, either.

"Never been here before," Benedict said.

"Say, I hear you fence Letellier tomorrow."

"True."

Gillespie did not enjoy running up against Fitzhugh's terrifying ability to form a minimal response to any conversational sally. "I heard Lady Iddesford was with Letellier."

"Oh?"

A flush trickled into Gillespie's face, and Esme recognized that he was half drunk. "You haven't seen her, have you?"

"Is Letellier here?"

"That was a joke, wasn't it?"

A profound stillness settled over Fitzhugh as his whole body tightened next to hers. "You may describe it that way."

"Right. No offense, Fitzhugh," Gillespie said, backing off, but resenting it, for he said, "Who's the little sweet you have with you, then, eh?"

"None of your business." Fitzhugh took Esme's hand and stood up from the bench, guiding her with him.

"Always the gentleman, eh?"

"Privacy," Fitzhugh said. "This place advertised privacy."

Esme stood, shadowing Fitzhugh's right shoulder.

"Do not let it be said I scared you away," Gillespie said.

Esme could not see the expression on Fitzhugh's face, but Gillespie held up his hands. "Peace, my lord. Peace."

"Excuse us." Fitzhugh led Esme toward the door.

Esme did not see what Gillespie next tried to do, but she felt a tug at her hood. Fitzhugh released her hand, and she pulled her hood forward again and turned.

Fitzhugh had Gillespie's arm twisted up behind his back. In the sudden hush that fell over the Red Falcon, Fitzhugh's words resonated. "Try that again, and I shall call you out."

"Right. Right you are. A thousand apologies. Really. Never meant to offend. Just a little fun."

"Be more inventive," Fitzhugh said, and cast Gillespie from him so that he stumbled deeper into the pub and crashed into an unoccupied table. Gillespie shook his head, dazed, as Fitzhugh ushered her out into the cool, soft spring air.

"Thank you," she said, as he led her up the dark street. Muffled talking and laughter from other taverns and pubs sounded their way.

"You are welcome," he replied. Somehow he anticipated to the second when her knees buckled, for he drew an arm about her waist under her cloak and drew her firmly to him, still walking. "We must get you home. Which way?"

She should resent the liberty. She should, as she had resented Letellier's taking her hand so often. But she did not. She appreciated his support, and with every step, feeling his body solid and warm next to hers, she appreciated it for more than support. "I am staying at Lady Howard's town house."

"That old harridan?"

"She likes me," Esme said with dignity. "Upper Brook Street, near Park Lane."

"Yes. Is she in residence?"

"No. She has not been well. We wintered together in Yorkshire, where not even one crocus has yet dared pop its head above the snow. Do you know I began to resent the fire that kept me warm because it had to keep me warm? Then when I had a letter about Jane and Letellier, I—"

"You what?"

"Came down," she said repressively. "He will be annoyed we left."

"Letellier?"

"Yes."

"He must have left himself. I did not see him."

"Oh," Esme said, dismayed. She had not noticed, so focused had she been on escaping Gillespie. Why had Letellier left?

A door opened to their right, spilling light and two young gentlemen onto the street. Wine-soaked and spluttering, they picked themselves up and tried to get back inside, but the door closed before they could.

"Damn me," said one.

"Damn you, too," said the other.

They fell with uproarious laughter. Then one tried to tip his hat at Esme, only to find it gone. "Sorry, sorry."

Fitzhugh smiled faintly. "Best call for it in the morning."

"Excellent advice, my lord. Excellent. Thank you," the young gentleman said, then ruined the effect by hiccupping and swaying so violently his friend had to catch him before he fell.

Fitzhugh shook his head, but his mood had lightened.

"You may let me go now, *my lord*."

"My identity was unknown to you?"

"Your surname was not," Esme said. "But your identity is."

"Benedict Hadley, Viscount Fitzhugh, only son and heir to the earl of Hadley. At your service, ma'am."

"Esmeralda, Dowager Countess of Iddesford. But you knew that."

"Yes."

"I am pleased to meet you. Formally, as it were."

"As it were. The pleasure is all mine."

She could not decide whether he regarded her with disdain. "You really could let go of me now."

"No," he replied. "I really could not." They walked steadily up the street, and crossed the intersecting street. The young gentlemen could barely be heard, and for the space of a block, she felt her world reduced to those points of contact between them, hip to hip, his arm about her waist.

"It suits you, your name. Not many names do," he said.

"I must ascribe it to luck. I mean, what odds are that one's mother or father may recognize those qualities in you as a wee baby? I was lucky. My mother looked at my eyes and insisted I be called Esmerelda. With an 'e' where the first 'a' should be. It is the Spanish spelling, and her mother was a hidalga. She was a shrewd woman, I think. The 'e' gave my father something to disagree with her about. From all accounts, she gave in on the 'a' but got to keep the name. Not that—never mind."

Esme realized she was babbling again. She had been about to say that her mother had not been able to bear her father much longer, but had run away to her relatives in Spain.

The rhythmic motion of walking against him affected her strongly. However she had denied her body its wants over the last years, she had never denied that she wanted. She wanted Lord Fitzhugh more than she had wanted anyone. Could she indulge herself, if only in a kiss? Would he keep it their secret?

Could she dare ask?

They stopped at the next intersection, bright with lanterns, to let a carriage pass them by.

"You have very striking eyes," he said.

"So do you. I have never seen someone speak so much saying so little. It is all in here." She touched him lightly along the brow. She had to touch him, or expire from restraint.

Whether he willed it or not, his face stretched toward her hand. Then he said, softly, "You would hurt to use. And not be accurate at all."

"What?" she asked, bemused.

"Nothing," he replied. "A conceit of mine."

"You have fancies, and whims?"

"Constantly."

"And yet—" She would have told him how surprising his pursuit of his country mouse was. Miss Bourre looked as if she had never had a fancy or whim in her life. But saying such a thing would have been unfair of her, and presumptuous. What did she know of this Miss Bourre except what she looked like and Letellier's opinion?

"And yet?"

"And yet you never seem to stray from your path," she said, hoping he accepted the answer.

"I am on no path I expected to be tonight."

"I am sorry. I—"

"Do not regard it."

"But I do regard it, my lord. I regard it highly. He was the very last person I wanted to see." She both wanted him to ask why and dreaded forming an answer. But she had learned enough of him to know she need not have worried.

"There is a hackney carriage up the street," he said. "If you would like?"

"No," she said. "No. They always stink of tobacco. May we please continue walking?"

"Your slippers are very slight."

"I have danced far longer in them."

"Then I am yours to command."

They let the hackney pass them before crossing the street, hopping a little over some raised bricks, and plunging down the next street. For several blocks it stood quiet, with more residences than businesses, and those the kind open during the day. No one else walked upon it, and it was too early for the carriages of the rich and powerful to start rolling back to their homes. Even as they worked their way north and west and the streets became more well-to-do and better lighted, it was quiet, and peaceful, with only the sound of her light slippers and his shoes upon the cobbles and bricks.

Fitzhugh continued to hold his arm about her waist, although she was past needing the support. She did not protest, though. She would have protested its removal. The rhythm of his body beat in sync with the excitement in her heart.

On the South Audley corner of Grosvenor Square, they passed a tall statue of an angel in flowing marble robes, which stood glowing in reflected lantern light among a little alcove of shrubs and flowering trees. "Could we pause a moment?"

He obliged. "Are your slippers wearing thin?"

"No." She pushed a little at a gate in the tall, black, iron fence surrounding the middle of the square. It opened inward. She pulled a dark green mask from her reticule. "Give me a hand?" she asked.

"What do you mean to do?"

"I have wanted to gag her since I entered London. Oh, I cannot get it. This dress does not give me the same freedom of movement as—"

"As what?" he asked, expression intent.

"As what I wore before I put up my hair," she replied.

"I should be willing to bet you were a proper hoyden."

"Is much explained?" she asked, then chewed her lip.

"I was never a hoyden," he replied after a pause. "What would be the male equivalent?"

"Hellion?"

"Close enough. I was never a hellion. Did your father never beat you?"

"Not as much as he could have had cause to," Esme said. "But the times he did, it was worth it." She tried again to tie the mask around the angel's mouth, but even standing on tiptoe, she could not get both arms high enough.

"Allow me." He stepped up onto the statue's pedestal, balancing lightly on two corners, then tied the mask around the statue's mouth. "How is it?"

"Much better."

"Does it not need to be a little to the left?"

He was teasing her. "No, but now that you mention it, perhaps a little down. No, not quite. No, that is too far. Back up again, if you please. Yes, perfect."

"You are quite certain it is placed correctly now?"

"Well . . ." She laughed.

He jumped down. "You have a lovely laugh."

"Thank you, sir," she said.

"Why did we perform this exercise?" he asked.

"Her smile is far too smug. She thinks she knows something, and I do not want her talking."

"What could she possibly know?"

"Who knows how people come up with half the things they believe they know?"

"Reasoning?"

"You give our fellow creatures too much credit, my lord."

He stepped back, glanced from the mask to Esme. "Someone will remove the mask tomorrow."

"Yes, but she will be quiet tonight. And it will drive people crazy not to know who did it."

"You are a very unusual woman."

She chuckled.

"What is so funny?"

"That is not the adjective most use to describe me. I like it. Shall we?"

This time, she took his arm. They walked half a block, then Fitzhugh said, "It has been a very interesting night."

"Yes."

"I did not expect to go to the Red Falcon tonight."

"Why did you, then?"

He hesitated. "To rescue a beautiful woman."

"But you could know nothing of Gillespie and—" She blushed. "You thought to rescue me from Letellier?"

"I wondered."

"I have been taking care of myself very adequately for the last eight years of my life, my lord. It is a rare day when I need rescuing from a man."

"Rarer still to need rescuing from two."

"Sarcasm does not become you."

"I was not being sarcastic," he replied.

She did not appreciate his being correct, and withdrawing her hand, walked on, arms folded. "I needed no rescuing from Letellier. And Gillespie, he was not supposed to be in London. He was supposed to be in—"

"Russia. Yes, I know." Effortlessly he had caught up to her. "But you trouble to know where he is."

"Did you not notice my saying I know how to look after myself? Here, we make a left here. Upper Brook Street."

"All precautions cannot work all the time."

"I have thanked you for Gillespie. Him I should not have wanted to meet. But Letellier, him I can handle."

"Because you will help him with your step-granddaughter?"

"Do say that a little louder, sir. They could not hear you in Yorkshire." He did not even dignify her rant with a scowl, which made her feel like a cat. "We are almost to Lady Howard's house. Can your curiosity wait?"

Again he said nothing, just gave her the steady look that let her know she had behaved badly. They completed their last long, half block in silence.

With Esme in residence, Lady Howard's staff kept the lanterns well lit. But it was Williams, Esme's own major-domo, his salt-and-pepper hair a match for his formal black jacket, who let them into the gracious foyer with its checkerboard floor, warm oak paneling and stair, and medieval tapestries. Lady Howard liked tapestries, particularly ones of ladies and unicorns, and hunts.

"My lady," he said with the polite neutrality on his blunt face that he adopted when he had worried over her. Then he raised his brows in reference to Fitzhugh, who had his arms crossed and was surveying the gold-and-crystal chandelier.

Had he regarded their walk home as a mere interlude before business? Had he indulged himself by stoking her feelings?

"Good evening, Mr. Williams. This is Lord Fitzhugh."

Williams grimaced at her even as Fitzhugh picked up on the address. "*Mr.* Williams?" he asked. "You are not Lady Iddesford's butler?"

"Her majordomo, my lord."

"An interesting title to have," said Fitzhugh with his deceptive blandness.

"Mr. Williams is one of the reasons I can take very

good care of myself. He has been with me for five years now."

"And he's a big, tall fellow, with what, fifteen years' experience and two stone on me, and no one knows I am here. Do I consider myself in danger?"

"Don't be ridiculous," Esme said.

But Fitzhugh and Williams kept regarding each other. Really, men were odd. Then she relented. Williams had not had occasion to escort men into her household. She had given up all that concurrent with his joining her staff. And Fitzhugh, he had already had to stare down Letellier and Gillespie that night.

"Mr. Williams, Lord Fitzhugh helped me avoid Gillespie not an hour ago."

That brought warmth into Williams' face. "My lord, you have my thanks. I learned after you left for the evening, my lady, that he had come back to England. I did not expect he would be out and about and at the same place as you. I am sorry."

"Do not trouble yourself over it any more," Esme said, detaching her cloak. "Lord Fitzhugh and I have something to discuss in the library. Will you excuse us?"

Williams took her cloak and opened the door to the library for them. Then he closed the door behind them.

A large fire crackled cheerfully in a heavily carved fireplace, and the ormolu clock set firmly in the middle of the mantel proclaimed that it was only shortly after two o'clock. The rest of the room was too dark for Esme's taste. She lit a brace of candles on the large desk before the fire with a taper, and the room's green furniture picked up dim color.

"Do you want something to drink?"

"No. You did not need to tell him to wait up for you, did you?" Fitzhugh asked, bracing a shoulder against the closer edge of the mantel, his arms still folded.

Esme leaned against the desk edge. Although her shoes had begun pinching, she preferred to be on her feet. Lord Fitzhugh was not a man to be treated like a tame, milk-fed tomcat. He had handled Gillespie, and teased her over gagging the statue. He moved wonderful fluidly, and he made her feel tingly all over.

"There is not much I *need* to tell him," Esme said. "Mr. Williams used to be a don. He taught history."

"That relieves my mind. He may numb an assailant's brain by excessive quoting of dates and arcane facts. His looking like a stevedore does not hurt, either."

"Now you are truly sarcastic."

He tipped his head, considering. "Yes."

"Why?"

"I remembered that you are conspiring with Letellier."

"But you are his friend. Surely you support his marrying the lady he chooses."

"I may be his friend." He paused. "But I am not sure I would let Letellier near anything young or innocent, to say nothing of young, innocent, and female."

"And that lets me out. I see."

"You have spent the last quarter hour proclaiming your ability to protect yourself."

He was right, but the fact that he did not disagree with her set her blood to steaming and crackling like the fire.

"Besides," he continued, "it is no innocent thing to use a daughter to harm a mother and father."

"It made perfect sense to Letellier," she said, and could not help but grimace at what had come out of her mouth.

He noticed. "So you can be honest with yourself. I regard that as promising."

"Promising for what?"

"I would like you to stop. I think you could stop. So, please, stop."

They stared at each other a long, tense moment. Esme's nerves danced a solitary reel, crying out for a partner. But despite their interlude, there was no longer anything of the partner about Fitzhugh. He had become all disdain.

"Why should I? Especially now that I know you would like someone as pretty and vivacious as Jane available to distract His Grace the Duke of Breshirewood. That would solve some of your problems nicely, would it not?"

"It might," he said. "Then again, it might not matter. What matter a hundred dukes if she cannot see me as a man?"

"She is a fool," Esme said, and straightened. She took the two steps that separated them.

Although she did not see him move, she could not deny that he seemed to have straightened, grown taller. "She is accustomed to me," he said. "There is a difference."

She tilted her head back. "I am not accustomed to you."

"We have only just met." Did her imagination fool her, or did he draw breath more quickly?

"I would not be accustomed to you had we known each other these last twenty years. Every moment with you is new, different, exciting." She stood on tiptoe, and, trembling, brazenly dusted his lips with hers as she imagined someone of her reputation would do. He inhaled sharply, then his arms encircled her, drawing her deeper and deeper into a haze of passion whose expression of delight fired and pervaded every fiber of her being. She had never had her lips alone give her so much pleasure. She had never before felt so protected and so vulnerable all at once.

He tugged gently at one of her curls, dangling against

her bare back, with his hand. "I have wanted to do that all night."

"I, too. Could we, maybe . . . ?" she asked, stretching toward him again.

But he untwined her hands from his back and hair, and held them within his, in between them. "It is the last thing I should have done."

Esme's heart froze. "Why do you say that?"

"Because I wish to marry someone else."

"It did not stop you a moment ago."

"It should have." His tone, so flat and spare, made her long to hear it charged with emotion again.

"But it did not."

"No."

"Then—" she began, softly.

"I have heard much of your reputation this evening, madam. Your unprecedented arrival in London—"

"You believe all you have heard about me." Now her voice fell oddly flat, discordant even to her own ears.

"You have shown me the rumors are true. I *do* go on reason, madam."

The unfairness of it all swelled within Esme. She spluttered, wrenched her hands from his, and turned her back to him. "Leave."

"We will need to continue our discussion, my lady."

"You may continue it as long as you have breath. I am going to bed. Alone."

"Thank you for that clarification."

She took a deep breath and recalled her own dignity. "Thank you again for your assistance with Gillespie. I was in your debt." She walked around the desk edge farthest from him and opened the library door. Williams was on his feet in a trice.

"Lord Fitzhugh is leaving, Mr. Williams."

Fitzhugh yet stood by the mantel, some twenty feet inside the room, his back to the door.

"May I escort you out, my lord," Williams said in the kind of voice that would have woken up any sleepy student sitting in the far benches.

Then Esme noticed the other two footmen of Lady Howard's household skulking in the shadows of the staircase.

Fitzhugh came out slowly, one fisted hand propped over his mouth by the other, folded arm. His gray eyes managed to look thoughtful and alert. With deliberation he took her hand.

Esme cursed inside, as her body begged for him to kiss her hand and her mind implored her Maker he would not.

He bowed over her hand. "It was my pleasure to be of service." His gaze flicked sideways, and Esme knew he had seen the other footmen. "Good night," he said simply.

"My lord," Williams said, and showed him the door.

The door closed behind him, and Williams told the footmen to get on to bed. Then he turned back to Esme.

"Why is it, Mr. Williams," said Esme, surprising herself with the detachment of her own voice, "that one can draw so many wrong conclusions from the same set of facts?"

"Interpretation says as much about the interpreter as the facts themselves, my lady. Have I not told you that before?"

"Time and again, Mr. Williams. But I never want to believe it." She squeezed his wrist, summoned her stiff-upper-lip smile. She could not possibly bear sympathy now. "Do not mind me. It has been a long and eventful evening. Good night."

Chapter Five

On the street, Benedict watched the lights from the foyer go out, then the lights along the stair. After that, he saw no other movement. Presumably she kept her bedroom to the back.

The cool, damp spring air thickening around him, he could not help but marvel at how unanticipated and extraordinary this evening of befriending Letellier had been.

God, he must fence Letellier in less than nine hours. When was eleven o'clock a civilized hour? Had he said it was a civilized hour?

But meeting Lady Iddesford had changed the shape of the evening, taken it and pulled it radically. Why *did* she aid Letellier when she did not like him? Did she dislike her son- and daughter-in-law so very much?

Everyone spoke of her as a dilettante of men. She certainly knew how to use her body, from the way she carried herself, all graceful poise, to the sleek way she proffered him her forbidden fruit. Within five minutes of their beginning their walk along the dark London streets, she could have asked for his arm only.

But she had continued walking hip to hip with him, a sensual rhythm that wore away his resistance. Having stoked him this way, she had thought a little lightheartedness and flattery would have him entirely under her spell.

God help him, she had nearly succeeded. As he had imagined, kissing Lady Iddesford approached heaven. Whatever Benedict's head told him about what happened to mere mortals who flew too close to heaven, his heart had agreed to soar.

At least for a little while. Then he had had his head to answer to again, and his head had told him he was a pitiful worm who did not deserve the love of a good woman like Dorrie Bourre when he could be so taken in by a lady notorious.

Nor had Lady Iddesford reacted well to coming back to earth.

But . . . but was it not curious the way she had thanked him, even after they had argued, for helping her avoid Gillespie? There had been pride there, certainly, as one might expect, given her position. And dignified nobility.

"Is it really three o'clock, Mama?"

Benedict looked over his shoulder. A carriage had come down the street, stamping and jingling, and he had not noticed it. Good Lord, was that Miss Archer alighting from it, followed by her mother?

"Yes, it really is. You must get used to these hours, my dear. The Season is only beginning."

"But who is that gentleman standing in front of Lady Howard's house? Is Lady Howard at home?"

"Hush, daughter. It's time for bed."

Did she pitch that just a trifle louder? Regardless of whether she or his own imagination had given him the prod, Benedict bowed to it. Hadley House was not far at the brisk walk he could do without Lady Iddesford attached to his hip.

Still, it felt farther than it should have.

Donaldson, his father's butler, took his hat at the door

and said, "I hope you had an enjoyable evening, my lord. The earl is waiting for you in the library."

"Of course," Benedict said. Libraries were just going to be bad luck for him this evening. All the weight of learning meant as nothing beside the pressure two people could apply to one's spirit. He smiled, ruefully. "If you have no other duties tonight, Donaldson, hie thee hither."

"Very good, my lord," Donaldson said. "Thank you."

His father glowered from a broad, studded maroon leather chair with his stout legs up on a studded leather ottoman. A matching chair stood calling Benedict's name. Two brandy glasses decorated the side table between the two chairs, the one near his father considerably lower in volume. His father glanced pointedly at the grandfather clock's ornate face, his graying ginger sideburns roused. "Where in Satan's blazes you been, sir?"

As a reprimand, Benedict had to regard this as easy.

He sat down, took a sip of the smooth brandy, and forced a level tone. "After the ball, I joined Letellier at the Red Falcon. It is—"

"Yes, yes, I know where it is. What did you speak about?"

"Sir, I do not—"

"Give me none of your hesitations or impulses of caution. I sent for you to befriend him, not to listen to you hedge."

Benedict took a couple of deep, slow breaths, masking them behind sipping some brandy, before he replied. "Sir, what I was about to say was that I do not think Letellier was entirely honest with me this evening."

"I never thought he would be. He never was a forthright child, and he's grown into a veritable gut-twisting man. So?"

Fine, Benedict thought. "He wants to wed Lady Jane Compton. He professes himself in love. Lady Iddesford is helping him."

"Lady Iddesford? Oh, the young, exceptionally delectable, *Dowager* Lady Iddesford."

"That's her," Benedict said neutrally, disliking his father's overeager tone.

"I do not know a man alive who would not want to find her on his arm. How did Letellier manage it?"

"Lady Jane is her step-granddaughter. Compton is—"

"The family name. That's right. That's right. So, she wants to put one right in Iddesford's eye, does she? Never heard there was any love lost there."

"Apparently not." And apparently, assuming that Lady Iddesford would enjoy revenging herself in such a way required no intuitive leap. Sometimes what looked like a duck was indeed a duck, but Benedict applauded himself for staying long enough to put the notion—her—to the test.

Liar, liar, liar. She acted differently than any other woman. I wanted to kiss her and see what she would do.

"—do you think?"

"I am sorry, sir. I was not attending," Benedict said.

His father scowled, then spoke slowly, putting distance between his words. "If Lady Iddesford is aiding Letellier, what sort of plan do they have, do you think?"

"Letellier left to meet someone before he could be specific, sir."

His father kept scowling.

"If that is all, sir?"

"Sit down, sir. Sit down."

Wary, Benedict settled back into his chair.

His father played with the heavy, dull chain of his pocket watch. Benedict could not count the times he had watched, in pretty much the same state of emotion, while his father had let the links go chink, chink, chink between his fingers.

"Mrs. Bourre," his father finally said, "had another letter from Madame Letellier after returning from the ball."

So Benedict surmised he was no longer supposed to be ignorant of any letters or concerns on either Aunt Bourre's or Letellier's mother's part. He nodded.

"Madame reports that Letellier has applied to the lawyers for all available funds. All. Down to the last sou. Your head works like a balance sheet. What does that say to you?"

Benedict had already started some mental positing. Then he realized his father did not deride him for it, and felt the warm glow of approval. Perhaps even need. "There are no reports of gambling debts?"

"No. He has many vices, but gambling to excess is not one of them."

"Then likely he is investing in something."

"Or someone," his father growled. "Iddesford's will split his fortune between his family and his widow, and we all know what happened to that."

Dorrie had voiced similar concerns when she had filled him in on the mystery lady's identity. "How would you feel if you saw your money wasted, spent abroad on entertainment of the most extreme sort?" Dorrie had asked. "For that is what they say she did. Why else would she live in Lady Howard's house, instead of taking her own lodgings?"

Benedict replied to his father the same way he had replied to Dorrie. "Iddesford, I understand, capitalized on a fair income and increased it tenfold. Half of a whole lot is still a whole lot."

"Question of pride, sir, isn't it?" his father said.

"It is indeed. All around." Put starkly like that, it was

easy to believe that Letellier had invested in Lady Iddesford to help him reap the hand of Lady Jane Compton.

Benedict could yet feel her lips warm and insistent on
his, her hands twining in his hair, her soft breasts pressed
against him. Her desire for him had pulsed along every
fiber of her. And every fiber of his being had answered
the call.

There would be no more of that.

How much would Letellier pay her?

"I shall endeavor to find out where the money is going,
Father," Benedict said. "I have contacts in the City."

"Thought you might," the earl said in the tone one
uses when one must admit being thankful for a thing
one has long and publicly regarded as of dubious merit.

"I will inquire about appointments."

"Appointments?" his father asked. "You are a viscount."

"Appointments. In the meantime, maybe I will learn
more from Letellier himself tomorrow at Monsieur
Marguillier's."

His father frowned, then nodded. "Man to man, no
beautiful woman in between. You be careful there,
Fitzhugh, and keep your hands well and at your sides."

Benedict resisted the impulse to tell his father he was
not an idiot. He *had* been an idiot to kiss Lady Iddesford.
He hoped he could depend on her not wanting it known
that a man had resisted her charms.

Terrible thoughts, those.

"Woman's not respectable, anyway," his father said.
"You have Dorrie to be thinking of."

"Do you think Dorrie will ever regard me as a suitor?"

"Who can tell with women? But it would be a good
match for her. You will be earl someday."

Kind of you to consider it from Dorrie's perspective, sir. "She
may be interested in Breshirewood."

"Ah? Really? He's a fine lad. Go get some sleep. You

look blue-deviled. And remember, a strong arm and a bit of daring will do you best tomorrow, not your dancing about."

"Yes, sir," Benedict said, and bit his tongue.

Esme screamed and hit out against the arms trying to hold her down. They held her, forced her arms onto the pillow, but she kept struggling, kicking against the blankets that imprisoned her legs. She would not let him. She would not permit him. But he was so much stronger.

"No, my lady, it's but a dream," said a woman's voice. But Esme heard the fear in it, and would not be fooled. She struggled all the harder.

"My lady," said a deep male voice. "You're having a nightmare."

"No!" Esme cried. Then of a sudden she opened her eyes and beheld both Gillespie's and Williams' faces inches from hers. Slowly the image of Gillespie faded, and Esme realized it was Williams' hands holding her. Esme went limp with relief. "You are not Gillespie."

"No, ma'am. No, that I am not," Williams said, and released her. He stood, and Esme thought she could see a darkening spot on his brow. "It was a nightmare."

Esme propped herself up on an elbow, ran her other hand through damp, tousled curls she must have loosened from her nightly braid. Her maid, Sally Percival, sat worriedly at the edge of her bed, her white cap surpassing even Esme's gold bed hangings for brilliance in the dim light.

"A nightmare."

"Yes, my lady," Williams said. "Percival heard you screaming and summoned me."

"I hit you, Mr. Williams?"

He touched his forehead. "There will be no mark in

the morning, my lady. Never worry about me. It was seeing him again this evening, was it not? I had wondered."

Tears cascaded without warning down her cheeks. They felt shockingly hot and left behind an odd, intense cold.

"The brandy, Percival," Williams said.

"Yes, sir."

A second or two later Williams pressed the glass against Esme's lips. "Drink, my lady. Drink for both of us."

Esme managed a gulp and a smile for his jest. The brandy burned, but Esme welcomed it. Every second the dream of Gillespie holding her down, intending to rape her, receded. It was ridiculous to still have this fear. He had not even seen her that evening.

"I am so sorry, my lady."

"It is not your fault. My wrap, please, Percival. And do light some candles."

"My lady," Percival said, and held up the deep green robe Esme kept at the foot of her bed. She helped Esme into it, and began lighting candles from a taper while Esme invited Williams to come sit with her in the gold chairs near the fire.

"I do not know if I can do this, Mr. Williams," she said.

He pressed the brandy glass back into her cold fingers. "I remember someone telling you that once."

Esme smiled at him. "What would I do without you, sir?"

"You will manage. It may not be pleasant, but you will manage."

Esme gazed into the fire. "Lord Fitzhugh hates me."

"Do I deny him the house?"

"No," Esme said quickly. Too quickly. "No. He believes as I do, that Mr. Letellier would not suit Jane. His opposition to me may increase Mr. Letellier's confidence."

"A funny friendship."

"To say the least."

"It is too bad Letellier moved into those small quarters and took only his manservant to valet for him," Williams said. "A larger household has so many more possibilities for sneaking and the finding out of things."

"One of his friends mentioned he yet keeps a horse," Esme said. "Possibilities there?"

"I will set someone on it. And I will let our maid in Iddesford's household know that she should try to listen in on conversations between Lady Jane and Letellier. Then I will get someone—today!—into Gillespie's ménage, and another following him on the streets. We will have no more surprises."

"I should be very grateful," Esme said. "Now that I know he is about, I shall know what to do."

"And the earl of Hadley's household?" Williams asked, glancing up at her from a too-casual perusal of his fingertips. "Do you want someone there?"

"I do not think that necessary. What Lord Fitzhugh will do, he will do from an excess of good intentions."

"Sometimes good intentions are the worst devil there is."

"I shall maintain my guard, then," Esme said lightly. What matter that she had delighted at his helping her gag the statue? What matter how wickedly wonderful Fitzhugh's kiss had made her feel? She had a promise to keep. She would not bend to the allure of him. That she promised herself.

Chapter Six

Benedict stood loosely *en garde*, surveying Letellier five yards away through the dark netting of his fencing mask. Letellier had arrived at their match a quarter hour late, dressed in a scream of lime green coat and blue unmentionables, and apologized profusely and at volume before changing into Monsieur Marguillier's preferred white fencing clothes. Benedict had never seen Monsieur himself out of them. They suited his lithe, whiplike body, but it did make one wonder if one would recognize him on the street.

Monsieur's long, narrowish space occupied the top floor of the highest house on that row, so it had the advantage of big windows along the walls for light, and narrow stairs that tested one's mettle merely getting there. Opposite the longest stretch of windows, a smaller rectangular space separated by stone columns served as spectator lounge.

Fully thirty gentlemen had turned out for this match, and fully half of them had been there when Benedict came in. Observing their rowdy conversation, Monsieur had said to Benedict, "There is great interest in this. Who has seen you fence this last year?"

"Squirrels, Monsieur."

And Monsieur had laughed.

Letellier fetched off his mask, and, before Monsieur

could protest, said to the crowd, "Your attention, gentlemen. We cannot begin yet. There is the matter of a wager."

Benedict had forgotten Lady Iddesford's wager. Now he found he hated the notion of her name coming into this room of gentlemen, or being connected with his.

"The dowager countess of Iddesford has wagered one hundred pounds that I will beat Fitzhugh quite soundly. Will anyone take up the bet?"

"I will, rather. At two to one."

Good God, Benedict thought, *Gillespie.* Benedict forced a bow at the sign of confidence.

This interchange set the crowd of gentlemen buzzing and elbowing each other with knowing smiles. New bets went around until Monsieur, frowning, called a halt.

"Your mask, sir," he said to Letellier.

Letellier slipped his mask back on and assumed *en garde.* With an amused wariness, Benedict noted that Letellier's wrist looked firmer, and remembered what his first teacher had said about fencing.

"The true art of the sword," the wiry old Gypsy had said in heavily accented English, "is that once some skill has been achieved, it reveals the mind of the man. A daring man will attack with daring. A sloppy man will attack in the high ward when he himself is. A subtle man will find out what his opponent is. And a master will be subtle, *and* able to adjust."

Benedict let Letellier test his blade, with beat attacks, feints, parries, lunges and withdrawals, reverses and counterreverses, and calmly gave up steps, watching.

This went on for some minutes, and the murmur among the spectators steadily rose in volume. Monsieur, however, put no stop to it. He stood against one of the stone columns, fist pressed against his mouth, watching intently, his arms occasionally twitching as he fenced vicariously with them.

Benedict enjoyed himself. Letellier was breathing deeply and attempting to conceal the faint tremors of his sword arm by trying to vary the direction and speed of his attacks. Benedict was not fooled. He knew what kind of man Letellier was, and his fencing merely confirmed it.

Letellier tapped Benedict's sword tip, and with a twist of his wrist, Benedict tapped him back, safely guarded. "You think you play with me," Letellier said in a hissing undertone.

"All fencing here is play," Benedict answered, but he knew he was not being entirely honest. Competition's gleeful song rang in his blood like a Sunday carillon. Its sweet harmony triumphed in the likely possibility that he could prove, before Letellier and all these assembled gentlemen, that if anyone deserved a woman as beautiful as Lady Iddesford, it was he.

The picture of her rising in his mind, its accompanying lust, conspired to throw him off his step, and consequently, his guard. Letellier had not tired so much that he did not take advantage. His sword hit Benedict squarely in the shoulder.

"First hit to Mr. Letellier," Monsieur said, and raised his brows.

Benedict ignored the sudden buzz from the crowd and gathered his wandering wits. He had planned to let Letellier win, but he no longer found it palatable. He found it, in fact, positively repugnant. *He* would win, but he would do it in a way that preserved Letellier's honor. After all, he needed to stay close to the man. And what better challenge to his skill than to allow Letellier to get that close?

Benedict let Letellier come forward, as he was wont to

do. When Letellier's too-quick advance set him off guard, Benedict took the opening, thrust upward, and accepted Monsieur's judgment of his first hit.

Benedict let Letellier come on again. But this time he held his ground as Letellier tapped and lunged and thrust his way in search of a hole in Benedict's guard. Finding none after several minutes, Letellier's attack went wild, and Benedict did not hesitate to touch him directly over his heart.

"Lord Fitzhugh's second hit," Monsieur announced.

They stepped back, saluted each other, and resumed. Now Benedict found the going much more difficult. Although his arm had not tired, and he did not breathe as heavily as Letellier, the very undisciplined nature of Letellier's defense made it difficult to give Letellier an opening to take his second hit. At last Benedict managed it by pretending to disengage too soon.

Letellier thrust at his stomach, with unnecessary force. "Ha!" he said, intending to provoke.

This time, as they began, Benedict again let Letellier into his guard, and Letellier, thinking he had the easy victory, lunged for the thrust that would hurt as well as score. To do so, however, he had to decide the proper distance. Too far and he would have to bring his arm back and then overextend it. Too close and he would also be unguarded. He chose too far.

With his greater reach and steady wrist, Benedict merely flicked his sword back to the straight line and made his own thrust. Another hit to Letellier's heart.

Letellier reared his head back in surprise, then his gloved hand clenched around his sword hilt.

"Third hit and match to Lord Fitzhugh," Monsieur said.

Benedict saluted Letellier and Monsieur. Letellier, reminded of his manners, did likewise. Then Benedict barely had time to remove his mask before there was a press of gentlemen, congratulating him.

Benedict accepted the congratulations with aplomb, aware of Letellier's anger, Gillespie's gloating, and Monsieur's scrutiny. He escaped into one of the back rooms to change, but was shortly followed by Monsieur.

"They are making arrangements to cover their bets?" Benedict asked.

Monsieur nodded. "An interesting match, my lord. You are cool. He is hot. More reckless than is good for him. He overreached himself. But you know that."

Benedict nodded. Now that the battle lust had left him, it worried him that Letellier, shown Benedict's skill at the beginning of the match, could believe he had come so close to winning of his own merit. How easily could Letellier be tricked thus in other matters?

Was Letellier using Lady Iddesford, or was Lady Iddesford using Letellier?

"Would you, my lord, do me the honor of fencing with me within the week? No charge for a lesson, I assure you. I should merely like the practice of an equal—nay, dare I say, likely a superior."

They shook hands and made plans to meet. Then Benedict remembered that Lady Iddesford owed Gillespie one hundred pounds.

Letellier had changed quickly. He stood talking to Gillespie about that very matter. As Benedict came up to them, Gillespie was protesting with a self-deprecating smile, "Yes, it would seem most presumptuous, indeed, pressing, even, but the lady and I share an acquaintance of some years. Now that I have learned she is in Town, I am most eager to renew it."

"An awkward way to renew an acquaintance, to be sure, sir," Benedict said. "Dunning the lady for a hundred pounds."

A chuckle ran through the remaining gentlemen.

Gillespie gave him a chilly smile.

Benedict did not know what had prompted him to say that, but Gillespie's smile served as reward enough.

Letellier laughed, but his eyes were hot and calculating. "Yes, Gillespie. You can't have that. Let me serve as your go-between, and I will renew your acquaintance tonight. The lady has promised to accompany me to Lady Tunbridge's."

"Kind of you, Letellier, I must say. She is a fine piece of woman. Very fine." Then Gillespie decided to go on the attack. "Wish I could have seen how fine the woman you were hiding last night was."

Letellier turned sardonic. "My dear Fitzhugh, did you pick up someone else? Or was that indeed my lady?"

"You had left, sir," Benedict said, wishing Letellier would halt this conversation, made dreadful before all these avid gentlemen. "Of course I escorted the lady home."

"Of course," Letellier said. "Gillespie, you met Lady Iddesford last night, it appears. What a good joke, no?"

Gillespie's expression said, decidedly, *no*, even as smiles around them said definitely *yes*. Then Gillespie said, "Mayhap I should ask our champion here to serve as go-between for Lady Iddesford and myself, Letellier. She seemed fairly attached to him. Will you be at Lady Tunbridge's tonight, sir?"

Letellier smiled thinly. "He will be."

It was the truth, and Benedict resented them all: Gillespie for being a cad; Letellier for being at one of life's little crossroads and prickly about his amour propre to boot; and Lady Iddesford for increasing the wedge between them.

He looked forward to avoiding Lady Iddesford that

night, and dancing as many dances with Dorrie as she would allow.

"I do not understand the woman," Dorrie said as she and Benedict danced the *boulanger* in Lady Tunbridge's wide, white-and-gilt ballroom, with mirrors running down one long side.

"Which woman?" Benedict asked, pretending ignorance.

Dorrie's expression said he should not be daft. "Lady Iddesford, of course."

"Which one?" Benedict inquired. "They are both here."

"Oh? Oh!" She looked about her, and saw what Benedict had noted with some consternation a few minutes before. The dowager Lady Iddesford stood on the next to lowest stair of the broad stone staircase by which one entered the room. A crowd of gentlemen had not yet permitted her to descend the entire way.

Not surprising, Benedict thought, since the dress she wore, which matched her coppery hair, had announced her presence more eloquently than any call. She had arranged her hair deceptively simply, in a high chignon surrounded by a very whisper of a pearl turban, and loose, dangling curls brushed her shoulders like the most sublime, silky ribbons. It was the kind of style only a woman as beautiful as she could wear without appearing ridiculously overreaching.

Having attracted her audience, she was keeping them, and telling them something they found quite hilarious. Benedict told himself he did not think any the less of them for hanging upon her every word. He had been tempted to himself.

Gillespie was not among them.

"I did not see her," Dorrie said. "Where is the other Lady Iddesford? Have they met each other yet?"

"I do not believe so. She is over there, third mirror from the short wall, watching Lady Jane dance with young Tatling." She also wore a frown on her full face that Hades would have been pleased to call his own. It would not be fair to compare her face or figure to someone about twenty-five years her junior, but Benedict could not deny that she lacked the sense of style to make herself look more than a fine dress worn by a portly woman. Red, too, was not her best color.

"Young Tatling, as you would have him, is a mere two years younger than you."

Benedict shrugged as he danced.

"Were you ever young, Fitzhugh?"

"I seem to recall it, dimly." It was not a new observation of hers, and this his standard response. Tonight, though, he found himself wanting to be younger, to be the kind of man he had been last night. That man did not worry about what harmless pranks he performed. That man would willingly include himself in the group surrounding Lady Iddesford and not care whether he would be laughed at.

That man was weak in the head.

The dance ended, and many watched Lady Jane Compton walk in the opposite direction of her mama, and toward her step-grandmother. The two ladies, one the pretty blond debutante in white, one the notorious, fiery young widow, embraced with all signs of friendship. The gentlemen around them were charmed.

Benedict, however, glanced back over his shoulder and said, sotto voce, to Dorrie, "Here comes the other Lady Iddesford."

"Oh, my aunt Tunbridge will be so distressed if there is a scene during Emma's come-out ball. However did

Lady Notorious come to be here? Come. Help me."
Dorrie tugged at Benedict to intercept Lady Iddesford
the elder.

Benedict allowed himself to be moved, although he
watched the other. With appreciation for good strat-
egy, Benedict saw Letellier descend the stairs to meet
Lady Jane as if the whole event had been choreo-
graphed for the stage. She received him with every
evidence of pleasure.

Dorrie fetched Benedict so shortly before the countess that she brought herself up like a ship that had had
its anchor dropped during full sail. Benedict bowed, and
Dorrie curtsied as they excused themselves. Then Dorrie said, "My lady, is the ball not delightful? And I know
my aunt Tunbridge so appreciated your coming with
dear Lady Jane. Did you know we met last summer when
she came to stay with her cousins?"

"She did not mention it," the countess said, her chin
high, as much from pride, Benedict decided, as from
trying to look past his shoulder and see her step-
mother-in-law and daughter. A sense of the ludicrous
began tickling Benedict.

"We had the nicest picnic together," Dorrie was saying,
and described it. Benedict stood stolidly, letting her talk
and preventing the countess from escaping.

When the countess made a move to leave, Dorrie said,
"Did you hear about the prank someone pulled last
night in Grosvenor Square?"

"No," the countess said, diverted.

"Why, someone fixed a mask over an angel statue's
mouth."

"The one in the middle of the square? By South Audley Street?"

Dorrie nodded.

"Of all things I dislike, it is young men who think

drink gives them license to deface public property." The countess continued on for a full minute. Then she said, "You must excuse me, Miss Bourre. Jane is not currently partnered for this dance, and I wish to—" She broke off as the lovely dowager appeared at Benedict's elbow, bringing with her the intriguing and exotic scent of frangipani.

"My dear Augusta, how are you? And dear Iddesford? All well? So happy. Now, you must not worry about dear Jane. She and Mr. Letellier have entered the line. There, do you see? Does she not look like perfection itself? How I love seeing a petite blond next to a strapping, dark man. The splendid contrast! I do declare, it overwhelms me." She opened her fan with the merest flick of her wrist and fanned herself. No sign of heat had entered her face. She looked beautiful and perfect.

"But Augusta," she continued, "you look overheated. You must take care not to. Flushed cheeks can clash so horribly with a red dress. Red is an exceptionally difficult color to wear."

Watching the ladies Iddesford was like seeing a cup slip from someone's hands and being too far away to catch it before it crashed into thousands of sharp splinters upon the floor.

The older Lady Iddesford swelled visibly, like a dark red tulip coming up from the ground, about to say something scathing.

Dorrie squeezed Benedict's arm painfully. He did not hesitate; he had recognized the inevitability of what he would be asked to do.

"Lady Iddesford," he said to the woman who had kissed him passionately the night before, "tell me you are free. You would do me great honor if you would grace the floor at my side."

Dorrie's lashes twitched, but she had set him in motion.

Lady Iddesford turned her gaze on him. In her copper dress, surrounded by her copper hair, her eyes deepened into the color of sherry. The stunning effect took his breath away. Then her words dumbfounded him.

"I have not that much honor to give, my lord. Has my daughter-in-law not told you?" With a tight smile she swept away, but not before Benedict saw the pain in her eyes. It hit him with the force of a blow. Dorrie, too, looked stunned.

"That woman is the outside of enough," the countess said through clenched teeth. "How did she come to be here?" She made a grotesque attempt at a smile. Then she fanned herself vigorously. "Do be a good boy, Fitzhugh, and get me some wine?"

There was nothing for it but to bow and murmur that he would be delighted. He felt no few qualms about leaving Dorrie to the old harridan, however, and on his way to obtaining wine, located his aunt and told her what was what. Aunt Bourre smiled at him and patted his cheek in the fond way she had employed throughout his childhood. Her expression nonetheless reassured him she would not permit the current countess of Iddesford to molest her daughter.

Benedict obtained a glass of wine, as large as he could find, and glanced about in the mirrors with feigned casualness for the lovely dowager. What mischief was she wreaking now?

He saw neither her nor a telltale clutch of gentlemen. Her graceful form had not joined either line of happy dancers. Lady Jane Compton blushed vivaciously across from Letellier.

A flash of copper was all the warning he had before Lady Iddesford took the arm not carrying the glass of wine.

Benedict felt as though someone had spilled cold water down his back. "Have we not said all that needs to be said?"

"Do you not remember that you wanted to question me more thoroughly about your friend and his plans?"

The tapping of her fingers against his arm summoned any number of disturbingly vivid images. "Your maneuver just now has answered all my questions. Do excuse me. I have promised this glass of wine."

"You cannot believe Augusta requires *that* much stimulant? Why, she has not had a delicate moment in her life."

"That little display of yours—"

"Suited her to a tee," the dowager said. "She thrives on loathing me. She always has. So I give her what she wants."

A group of gentlemen had noticed Lady Iddesford and converged. Benedict became aware that he received searching looks not only from mamas and their charges against the walls, but also from gentlemen wondering why Iddesford's Folly had her arm linked through his.

One of them begged for the next dance. The lovely dowager smiled and shook her head. "Not this time, sir. I am afraid Lord Fitzhugh has already asked me." And she turned those sherried eyes upon him.

He nodded because it was ungentlemanly to disagree with a lady. That was what he told himself, anyway. "I will come back in a moment for our dance, my lady," he said.

"Oh, yes, that glass of wine. Or are you more worried about the companion you left her with? Who is that girl, anyway? The famous Miss Bourre, perchance?"

Benedict nodded.

Lady Iddesford glanced over toward Dorrie, smiled. "I should like to meet her properly." She held her fan before her face. "Hurry over, so you may hurry back." Then she made a little shooing motion, and accepted a compliment on her hair from one of the other gentlemen.

Benedict tried not to resent the man giving the compliment. But he had to pause a moment and straighten his back at the burst of laughter behind him. Why did she torment him?

He traversed the ballroom as quickly as one could without looking like one was traversing it quickly. There he found the countess of Iddesford fanning herself, and Aunt Bourre speaking soothingly to her. Dorrie, at least, did not appear so overcome.

"There. My wine, at last." Before Benedict could extend his arm, the countess took the glass and swallowed its contents. Then, in a neat move, she plunked the empty glass down on the tray of a circulating footman.

"As I was saying, my lady," Aunt Bourre said, "it may be the merest of coincidences that *that woman* and Mr. Letellier were in such close proximity when the dance began."

"And pigs don't stink, Mrs. Bourre," replied the countess.

Aunt Bourre blinked.

"Your daughter likes her," Benedict said.

The countess glared at him, then sniffed and said, "They have eight years' difference in age. Jane is but a scrap of a girl, and impressionable. Besides, my late father-in-law encouraged a friendship between them."

Hm, Benedict thought. *Impressionable.*

Aunt Bourre came right to the point. "Doubtless you will remind Lady Jane, as I remind Eudora here, that she does not dance without my express permission. Young ladies these days . . ."

Benedict bowed and excused himself. Dorrie stepped a pace away with him. "Where are you going?"

"The dowager snared me as I was coming back with

the wine," Benedict said. "I am promised to lead her out."

Dorrie glanced over at the large knot of people surrounding Lady Iddesford. Gentlemen had fallen into the first ranks, then, gradually, mamas and their hopeful daughters had gravitated toward them, hoping to catch someone's eye. "She chose you?"

Benedict bowed.

Dorrie flushed. "Benedict, I did not mean to imply that—"

"Do not trouble yourself." But her assessment hurt. It hurt more than her rejection had. "Likely the invitation merely continues her little digs at Lady Iddesford. Current, that is."

"You will be back by the seventh dance? You are promised to me, then."

"I have not forgotten," Benedict replied.

Again she flushed.

"Of course," Benedict said, more gently. That brought a fluttering smile, and he wended his way back through the crowd.

Gillespie had joined the thickened throng around Lady Iddesford. Only reedy Smith-Jenkins separated him from her. Seeing Benedict, Gillespie's eyes narrowed.

Lady Iddesford turned the same look of entreaty upon Benedict she had the night before, although she also maintained her society smile.

Hell, Benedict thought. Whatever *she* was, *he* had to err on the side of caution. If only there were not so many gentlemen between him and Gillespie.

Benedict pretended someone had bumped into him, shot a glance of annoyance behind him, and stumbled against some of the gentlemen in front of him and into the inner circle. He apologized to their affronted looks and protests.

"And this is the man who won a fencing match this morning," Gillespie announced, which brought general laughter.

Benedict accepted the barbed ribbing on the chin. "And this is the man I advised not to use the matter of a hundred pounds—owed!—to renew an acquaintance."

Thin color crept up Gillespie's neck and into his face.

The men around them guffawed and made comments about Gillespie's prowess with the fair sex.

Then Lady Iddesford silenced them by saying, "Does that mean I must congratulate you, Lord Fitzhugh?"

"I had thought that was why you favored me with a dance, my lady," Benedict said. "You wished to let me know you did not resent me for depriving you of the aforementioned hundred pounds."

"So long as I lost it in a good match, sir."

"Indeed, you have it, ma'am. It was quite the brilliant match," said Smith-Jenkins. "I saw it all. We did wonder, there, for a while, whether Fitzhugh would pull it off. Indeed, ma'am, it was one to one, and then two to two. Then, quick as lightning, Fitzhugh took the last point."

"Quick as lightning?" she asked, looking beyond Smith-Jenkins to Benedict from hooded lids.

"I do believe no fewer than ten gentlemen said they could not see his sword move before Monsieur Marguillier called the point and match," said Smith-Jenkins.

"The eyesight of English gentlemen is not what it once was," Gillespie commented.

Smith-Jenkins looked hurt.

Lady Iddesford smiled at Smith-Jenkins. "I am grateful to you, sir, for a précis of the event, for I have learned enough of Lord Fitzhugh to believe he would admit he had won under only the most dire of pressing. So, gentlemen, do I gather three touches is the charm?"

The gathered gentlemen grinned appreciatively.

Benedict gritted his teeth at how easily she played them. He found himself saying, "Only in fencing matches, ma'am."

"Ah, now we know the source of the modesty," Gillespie said. "Fitzhugh is a puritan."

Most of the other gentlemen looked surprised and wary. A couple barked laughs.

Then Lady Iddesford said, with a light, teasing smile, "And yet I have promised him a dance, sir. Do not ruin it, I beg you. Dread is so . . . dreadful."

Letellier came up to them, alone. "What could you possibly dread, my beautiful countess?" Letellier drawled.

"Your friend Mr. Gillespie here has told me your other friend Lord Fitzhugh is a puritan, and I have already promised him a dance."

"You did?" Letellier said.

Lady Iddesford shrugged ever so slightly, but the interesting ripples the motion caused in her décolletage created a sympathetic ripple of excitement among the gentlemen. Nor did Benedict consider himself immune.

"He asked me," Lady Iddesford said, "when I was all alone." She did not look at Benedict, daring him to contradict her. When Gillespie was near, Benedict would not have contradicted her to save his immortal soul. Why he should still feel that way, after her behavior last night and this evening, he did not know.

"Hard to believe *you* all alone," Letellier said.

Lady Iddesford smiled, but her eyes did not enter into agreement with her mouth.

"Do permit me to have the dance after Fitzhugh's," Gillespie said, bowing.

"No, I, my lady," clamored a gentleman.

"Would you do me the honor?" Smith-Jenkins said simultaneously.

Lady Iddesford shook her head, saying, "How could I possibly choose? Lord Fitzhugh?"

Benedict took the proffered hand, not unmindful of his rather primitive feeling of triumph, however temporary, and however she might perplex. He led her to the floor just as the music began, aware that they were very much on display. Fans raised around the room, eyes sparkled above them, and their immediate partners began whispering. Benedict caught sight of Dorrie, her chin high. Of the older Lady Iddesford and her daughter, there was no sign.

"You would tell me if there were a target painted upon my coat?" he asked.

The lady laughed, not the thrown-back laugh of the hoyden, nor an overrefined titter, but a natural chuckle that lifted Benedict's spirits from an abyss he had not known he was in. "No, sir, no target." Then she sobered. "Merely the stigma of dancing with a lady notorious. In time, you may become used to it."

Pain hovered at the edges of those beautiful eyes. He had not imagined it before. But was it real, or just another allurement? "Only used to it?" he asked.

"There is another option?"

"I had thought you rather proud of it," Benedict said. "You surprise me."

"You think I am not proud of it?"

The figures called for them to step together, and as they did, Benedict made an experiment. He whispered, "No," against her cheek. He caught a whiff of exotic frangipani, thoroughly intoxicating, before he stepped back.

"Having surprised you," she said, as they circled each other, "what may I expect?"

"It would help if you filled in those missing pieces of

information about my friend." *So I can know how you fit
into this puzzle.*

"Oh," she said, in a slow exhalation, then, flatly, "him."

"Well, yes."

"You do amaze me, sir, the way you can discuss my reputation and yet be immune to what likely caused it."

"Did you want more pretty compliments upon your
eyes?" Benedict asked. He was not about to admit how
deeply she affected him, how much he wanted her, despite his suspicions.

"Not from Lord Perriweather, nor Mr. Smith-Jenkins,
no."

They danced in silence, and not even the people they
passed along the line seemed to dare conversation.

Then Benedict said, "Your reputation does not reach
your eyes. There is only pure, starry brilliance there."

She looked away, and chewed her lip.

Benedict cursed himself. He would shortly lose the
ability to observe her in such proximity did he continue
ham-handed comments like that. He changed tack. "Do
not save your laughter for fear of offending me. I know
I am not one for pretty compliments. I have not a poet-
ical disposition."

"It is too much modesty, sir," she said, protesting, "and
none of it puritanical, unless to be puritanical is to be
kind, which I have never believed." She looked at him,
and the sheen of tears lit those eyes so they were not unlike stars.

He could not comment on her tears, not here in the
middle of a ball, but they touched him deeply, as perhaps
they were meant to do. "I do not care what Gillespie said."

"No, you do not, do you? You make up your own
mind, and stand like the proverbial rock while others
wash over you like the tide."

The question hung implicit between them.

Then Dorrie and her partner, a smart officer of the Horse Guards, who had been working down the line as Benedict and Lady Iddesford worked up, became their partners. The ladies inspected each other covertly. Neither would meet Benedict's eye.

But it was the officer who prevented Benedict from seeing what conclusion each reached. "Heard about this morning's match, Fitzhugh. Well done."

Benedict thanked him, and then they were past.

"Does everyone know I lost a hundred pounds this morning?" she asked.

"Whether everyone knows about the bet, I cannot say. Jeffries there is an avid swordsman."

She laughed. "That put me nicely in my place." Then, as the figures called for them to come together again, she said, softly, "Thank you."

"For what, ma'am?"

"For letting me be part of the tide."

She was not the tide, but a violent storm blowing off the ocean. She overcame his normal cautions, his usual desire to leave others to their own business. By fulfilling his father's request to get close to Letellier, Benedict had found himself in waters he had never expected.

He wished desperately that he had some guide to help him navigate the strange twists and currents of their meetings. He was not unaware of the irony of his position. Many men had wished for the very same thing over the ages. Did every generation have its Helen? Did he dance with her now?

The wealth of feeling she provoked in him—pity, mirth, disquiet, exasperation, suspicion, protectiveness, appreciation, and above all, desire—would require a month's quiet contemplation to unravel.

Benedict did not have a month. He had minutes, seconds, sometimes, to react. Almost he understood why his father espoused living from moment to moment. It was a heady feeling, but Benedict did not want to live like this all the time.

"I hesitate to ask what you are thinking," she said, tilting her head in that enticing way she had.

"I hesitate to think it," he replied.

That brought raised brows and a contemplative pucker. It was so unlike the coquette that Benedict thought a cold tide had truly washed over him.

The dance ended with a trilling triumph of violins. Benedict and the lady bowed and curtsied. Then Lady Iddesford, eyeing the crowd of gentlemen gathering on the dance floor fringes, waiting for her to walk off, took out her fan and said, "Would you escort me outside for a moment? I quite feel the need for fresh air."

Helen, tide, or force of nature, Benedict allowed his fascination with her to take the fore. "It would be my pleasure." And he led her in the opposite direction of the gentlemen.

Chapter Seven

Lord Fitzhugh continued to surprise, amaze, and intrigue. So little expression crossed his face as she had acted the veriest she-devil, been beset by Gillespie, and then made no secret of her appraisal of the woman he had professed to want to marry. So little expression, true, but Esme decided he was not being miserly with his face. No, deeper emotions ran freely, but he possessed the control to keep them from erupting.

Perhaps it was this element of control that made Esme look so closely at him, enjoy the illusion of commanding him, and depend upon him.

The night air had cooled a trifle more than Esme had expected. Still she considered the large balcony, which extended fifty feet from the house toward the garden, infinitely preferable to the throng of gentlemen inside. No other couples had found their way outside yet. *All young misses supervised by careful mamas,* Esme thought. Not that anything below-board could happen here, not with the lanterns on poles scattered about.

They illuminated his face, which became more handsome to Esme each time she looked at it. His left brow ran fractionally longer than his right, she decided, and he had once broken his nose. Not badly, but here in profile, she could see the slight dent. A small scar also ran an inch along the very corner of his jaw, testimony to many a stick fight as a child. On a dark-haired, dark-bearded man, it would be readily visible all the time. But on fair-haired Lord Fitzhugh, it took direct lantern light and the eyes of someone who would like to see every inch of him.

These little idiosyncrasies of his face endeared it to her.

She should not be thinking that way. This same gentleman had tested her the night before, and given her a failing grade.

He had also again come to her rescue.

"It will not take long before they find you," he said.

"Take me into the garden?" she asked.

He considered her. "You do not want to be found?"

"Not yet."

"And not by Gillespie."

She shivered. "Never by Gillespie."

He did not ask, but continued leading her down the stone stairs that ran off each side of the balcony and into the garden. Torches appeared along the paths at random intervals, but it was certainly darker here than on the balcony.

"Your dress does not lend itself to stealth."

"It was not intended to," Esme replied.

"Come to this side," he said as they passed a stand of rosebushes, blossoms tightly furled against the night air. He handed her around him, as deftly and gracefully as when he danced, so she walked farther under a sheltering line of dogwoods, also in pale bloom.

"You think me odd to dress to be noticed, and desire to escape notice. Would you believe me if I said I was attempting to think of your reputation as well?"

"It is an intriguing notion," he replied, and stopped walking.

Esme did as well, and since there was a dogwood behind her, she leaned against its cool bark. She shivered again and straightened.

He took off his black coat and whisked it around her shoulders. The sudden weighty warmth and masculine smell made her sigh with pleasure both simple and complicated. His white shirt and waistcoat gleamed in the dim light. By the quickening expression in his gray eyes, she knew her sigh had affected him.

"I kissed you last night because I was grateful to you," she said.

"I admit that in some circles, the ability to boast of having kissed you—for whatever reason—would have been worth a high price."

He spoke with detachment, but thus prodded, Esme said, "Would everyone have as much meat to make their boasts." He would have said something, but she interrupted him. "You are an attractive man, and I *was* grateful. More than you know. Now that I know Gillespie is here, and I must be here, I can handle the situation. I wanted you to know that. I owed it to you to know that. It was not prudent to say such things inside, however. Your friend Miss Bourre might overhear and take it badly. That is all I meant by saying I thought of your reputation. I should not want to be the cause of her heading into the arms of the duke of Breshirewood. You deserve whatever woman you desire."

"Come now, you cannot expect me to believe your actions derived from prudence."

"They did."

"Then you view our being out here as different in kind than singling me out to dance?"

Esme was shocked. "I did. It is not?"

"No. Not to Dor—to Miss Bourre, and certainly not to Letellier."

Esme shook her head impatiently. "Letellier, he

needs some time by himself now. Augusta will be looking about for me, and not paying as much attention to
Jane after a dance or two. Jane will not dance with him
again tonight, but he might be able to get close enough
to her to arrange the next assignation. And if he is frustrated in that effort, he will ask me to."

"And you will oblige."

"I will make arrangements," Esme said, deliberately
obscure. Her arrangements would leave plenty of room
for a slip between cup and lip. But she did need to give
Letellier the appearance of autonomy. His overweening
opinion of himself would not permit any other kind of
handling.

Lord Fitzhugh shook his head, and braced an arm
against a low-hanging branch about the level of Esme's
shoulder. "I wish I could understand you."

"When you do, sir, I beg you, let me know. It would
greatly help me illuminate my character for myself."

"You are jesting with me," he said. "You would have me
quit the subject. Where is the green mask when it is
needed?"

"That was not like me," Esme said.

"Not like the girl who was a hoyden?"

"I mean, not like me anymore. Last night, it was like
entering a time out of time."

"I would like to think so."

"What do you mean?" she asked.

"It would explain my continuing desire to do this."

She saw the kiss coming, had a second to spend either ducking it or anticipating its heady warmth. Esme
chose anticipation, and the feel of his lips against hers
was all the more intoxicating to her for it. From his
coat and his nearness, his scent surrounded her, as
though she lay in his bed with him. The sensation oblit-
erated any resistance she should have had. Esme bent

into Lord Fitzhugh's kiss like she was indeed the tide crashing into his hard, unyielding desire.

One hand twined in his sandy hair, the other across his back and the thin lining of his waistcoat, pressing him as close to her as she could get him. She could feel every muscle limned beneath her fingers as though she had had full say in carving him to her ideals.

Esme had never felt so womanly, and, when he trailed small kisses along her neck, so perfect. Growing up she had taken a great deal of pleasure in her looks. They commanded others' attention, gave her influence over them. Later, though, after her marriage, she had resented her looks, for she could never hide them. She could never run away.

Tonight, however, here, in Lord Fitzhugh's arms, she thanked God for whatever gifts of beauty he had given her. They had brought her this pleasure.

She could not permit it to continue. She knew that, but as each second spun out in thicker ropes of pleasure, she told herself that she would stop the next second. Then the next.

Finally he was the one to draw back, grazing her cheek with his hand, then just holding it there. She pressed her lips against his palm, and the shudder that ran through him rewarded her beyond her expectations. But he did not react beyond that. Esme admired him deeply for it.

"Will we ever know ourselves?" she asked.

"Part of me does not want to," he replied.

"You should listen to that part of you," Esme said. "You should not be here, playing with me, however lovely the game."

"Is this a game to you?"

Again, he did not speak with anger, but with that interesting detachment that provoked whatever guilt or sour feeling Esme had. "No! No, I meant only that I know you wish you were paying court to your Miss Bourre. I am sorry I distract you."

Liar, liar.

"My lady, you distract every man within view. Worse, you distract every man who has the pleasure of hearing your name introduced into conversation. Even my father—" He shook his head and drew back his hands. "I should go back inside."

The criticism of his father intrigued her. Lord Fitzhugh intrigued her. "I will not say anything about this. I have not spoken of last night, either."

"Gillespie knows it was you. Letellier told him."

Were it not for Lord Fitzhugh's coat, Esme would have shuddered. "That explains his rather pointed comments. He does not thank you for the experience."

"I have never regarded Gillespie as anything. He has always just been . . . there. May I ask what matter causes the friction between you?"

"He was kind to me, once, or so I thought. Then he betrayed my trust." She could not talk of it any further. Not with him. She had to bear his believing her capable of bad decisions; she could not bear to have him think of her as damaged goods. "Now I am older, and wiser."

"But still beautiful. He wants you yet."

"He will not have me," Esme said.

"No," Lord Fitzhugh said.

That simple acknowledgment thrilled Esme almost as much as his kiss had. She accepted his arm and they strolled toward the light and gaiety of the ball. She did not want to go back in. All the true light and gaiety lived outside in the dark, under a blooming dogwood tree.

They approached the stone stairs of the balcony. "You should take your coat back," Esme said, and lifted it from her shoulders. He shrugged it on without any seeming effort, but it fit as snugly and neatly against his body as if he had had a valet tug him into it.

"I can still feel it against my skin," Esme said, even though the cool night air was raising goosebumps.

He touched one of the silky curls that dangled down her neck. "Good," he said.

"About Jane and Mr. Letellier, will you hinder me?"

"I shall study the situation."

From anyone else, such a statement would have been prevarication. From Lord Fitzhugh, it was a pledge.

"I will accept that. I must."

"Yes. You go in here, first. I shall go around to the library."

"How do you know it will be open?"

He regarded her gravely. "The Tunbridges are Miss Bourre's cousins. I have been in and out of this house more times than I can count."

"Oh," Esme said. "I see." She wished she did not feel so despondent. *Miss Bourre, you are a fool not to see him as a man.*

"I shall see you inside," she said.

"Across the ballroom."

Quickly, so she could not change her mind, she ran up the stairs into the light. A couple stood in earnest conversation at the rail. She whisked past them. She walked boldly into the ballroom, the night air and the memory of Lord Fitzhugh's coat hovering about her, cushioning her from the hot, heated air.

No sign of Miss Bourre, but Jane was dancing with Mr. Smith-Jenkins and Letellier watched with his cronies toward the mirrored side of the ballroom. Fixing her polite smile, Esme made her way across to him.

"There you are," he said when she was at his elbow. "I wondered where you went after you danced with Fitzhugh."

"I needed some fresh air," she replied.

"He *is* dreary," Letellier replied.

Esme wanted to giggle. Instead she said, "Have you been able to talk to Jane again?"

"We came close, but not yet."

"Write a note for her, and I will endeavor to deliver it."

He leered. "What other surprises do you have this evening?"

"What do you mean by that?" she asked, keeping her voice teasing and light.

"You arrange that very improper dance for me with Lady Jane, you dance with Fitzhugh, you offer to courier notes, and I learn you ducked Gillespie last night, also with Fitzhugh."

"He was there," Esme said with a toss of her curls, "as you were not. And I do not like Mr. Gillespie."

"He said he is an old friend of yours."

"He was. Past tense in every language."

"It is nice to know you may loathe so well. Passion, my dear Lady Iddesford, only adds to a woman's beauty. Ah, there he is," Letellier said, looking over his shoulder. "He has been playing cards to console his frustrations."

"Who?" Esme asked.

"Fitzhugh, of course. He does look grim."

"Do they play for high stakes? Here?"

"No. He is grim because he has likewise fallen under your spell, my dear, and you have dismissed him."

Esme turned a brilliant smile in Letellier's direction. By shifting her weight a little, she had a clear view of Lord Fitzhugh, and he of her, smiling. Even across the ballroom, she felt his strength, and his desire. For now, it was enough.

It had to be enough.

Chapter Eight

"Here you are, hale and unharmed," Dorrie said with a forced cheerfulness that twisted at Benedict's heart. She stood with her mother, Lady Tunbridge, and her son, the Honorable Edmund, no doubt fielding questions as to where Benedict was, and the reason for it.

"It is the seventh dance, Dorrie," Benedict said.

"Is it? I barely noticed."

She was acting the same way she had whenever he had promised her a treat and could not, for one reason or another, deliver it. Benedict felt a pang of guilt, then irritation, then fresh guilt. "I am happy the time has flown so pleasantly that you have lost track."

"Indeed, the last two dances have been excessively pleasant. We have been watching my niece, Miss Tunbridge, dance with Lord Wolleston," said Aunt Bourre, gratitude in her voice that her niece was dancing.

Benedict knew without turning that Lady Iddesford had again attracted a crowd of gentlemen. He could tell by the dearth of black jackets at this side of the ballroom, and the predominance of sparkling jewels and bright colors. Much of the group's conversation must have centered on how the alluring Lady Iddesford had ruined Miss Tunbridge's come-out ball. There would be many angry mamas who would go home from this occasion resenting Lady Iddesford's inclusion, and their daughters' forced wallflower status. It would not matter to Lady Tunbridge, or to many other ladies, that Lady Iddesford had come in under Letellier's aegis and had not been planned. The steam from the scandal broth would rival London's fog.

"Wolleston is a fine man," Benedict offered. He gave Tunbridge a glance, then slid his gaze to Dorrie, and back again. Tunbridge shook his head slightly.

Dorrie had not danced.

"Here they come," Lady Tunbridge said, and smiled.

The conversation became exceedingly polite. Wolleston glanced at Benedict, looked highly self-conscious, then said, "Capital good fencing match this morning, I hear, Fitzhugh. Wish I could have seen it."

Benedict thanked him and understood, even without the darkening frown on Dorrie's face, that he had held Wolleston's interest for another reason than his ability to fence. For a moment that primitive triumph surged through him again. He knew what it felt like to dance with Lady Iddesford, to walk with her in the moonlight, to kiss her.

The feeling wilted. Could he be certain she had not granted the same favor to others? Could he be certain she felt anything when she granted any favor? Could he be certain she was not using him to her own design?

"You are thinking again, Fitzhugh," Dorrie said.

The familiar gambit prompted the familiar response. "I shall try to keep all hazards to a minimum."

Aunt Bourre smiled at them, and Dorrie blushed. Dorrie blushed! Dorrie had not appeared insecure in his presence beyond the first time they had met in London.

He readily offered his arm. "Come, Dorrie. Shall we dance?" As the musicians began, he asked, "Will you tell me what happened while I was gone?"

Dorrie confirmed Benedict's suspicions, added that

her aunt Lady Tunbridge had been quite ecstatic that Lady Iddesford had gone for a while. The gentlemen had pined, and then decided it was better to dance than not to.

"Some of them have mothers who have taught them something of manners," Dorrie declared with her normal spirit. Then she chewed her lip. "Then there were the most horrible things being said about . . . about you, Fitzhugh, and that woman. Where did you go once you left the dance floor?"

"She wished to go outside. I escorted her, then went to play cards for a little while."

"Oh, how much you must have hated this evening, with all these people talking about you. I am sorry I promised you the seventh dance so that you had to come back in here."

"You may never be sorry to call on me, Dorrie," Benedict said, and he meant it.

She smiled, touched. They danced in silence. Benedict again noted that the number of couples dancing had declined, and that there seemed to be a greater number of people at the far side. Lady Iddesford had worked her strange magic on the crowd.

"I said I did not understand the woman," Dorrie said with a tentative, though nonetheless inquisitive, look. "Do you?"

"What would you understand?"

"You would ask that question." Then she relented. "It is very like you not to make assumptions or blanket declarations, while to everyone else here, in London, it is quite common. I have forgotten that one of the things I have always prized about you is your charity."

"I do not think of myself as a charitable man. I am perfectly willing to condemn someone who should be condemned."

"But you do not condemn for trivialities."

"You are finding your Season difficult."

It was a lucky guess. She flushed. "It is not what I expected."

Benedict could not ask her more. "What amusement would you like to try? I would be glad to escort you."

"You are too good to me."

"You deserve to have someone be good to you." The echo, however, of Lady Iddesford's words made him glance toward the side of the room. Uncannily, her gaze knotted with his. He had to look away before her dazzling smile, knowing it was false.

"There is Lady Northam's rout tomorrow evening," Dorrie was saying. "And the race north of Islington. Nor have I seen the Tower or ridden in Hyde Park. Yes, let us ride in Hyde Park. Tomorrow?"

Benedict thought of the woman he faced and the woman behind him. "Nothing should please me more."

They agreed to go riding before the fashionable hour of five o'clock, when the lanes would become jammed with the *ton*'s carriages. It was a sparkling sunny day, nicely warm in the sun but still cool in the shade of new, bright green leaves. *Emerald leaves,* Benedict thought as he and Dorrie trotted under and out of each treed canopy. Green as the stone that had swayed with Lady Iddesford's breathing two nights ago.

"You look very fetching today, Dorrie," he said. She wore a sky blue habit in the popular military style. The color matched her eyes, and blended nicely with the coat of her light gray mare. Her hat was cocked enough to be jaunty, but not flashy.

How would Lady Iddesford have worn it?

"Thank you, sir," she said and laughed.

It felt good to hear her laugh, and, bright emerald leaves or no, Benedict found himself returning to that happy time in his life at the beginning of last summer, before he had proposed to Dorrie, when they had spent so many afternoons riding along the river Barre, following its sinuous paths, picnicking in fields miles away from all cares and considerations.

"Do you remember the inn we found that—" he said.

"The one that served the delectable peach pie? Oh, Fitzhugh, you shall make me hungry!"

A light, trilling laugh with hints of both mockery and frustration in it sounded farther up the path.

Dorrie flushed, and, before Benedict could ask her if she wanted to turn around, urged her horse forward. They passed through the screen of a willow, and beheld two women sitting in a lovely little phaeton painted in yellow with black and red along the wheels, and a groom keeping two black horses standing quietly.

It was Lady Iddesford and Lady Jane Compton.

They were both dressed in the first stare of fashion, Lady Jane in a riding dress of scarlet as suited her blond hair, and Lady Iddesford all in cream except for the emerald that again dangled across her bosom. She held a cream parasol to protect her from the sun.

Dorrie gasped and pulled up, forcing Benedict to as well.

It had been Lady Jane who had laughed. Now she spoke in what she likely wanted to be a whisper. Instead it carried clearly. "It shall not come off now, not if everyone and anyone is about to come down here. Take me home, would you please?"

A martial light came into Dorrie's eyes. She reined her horse forward and said, "Why, hello, Lady Jane. How are you this lovely afternoon? Is it not a wonderful idea to come out to the park before *just everyone* else gets here as well?"

Lady Jane had the grace to flush.

Lady Iddesford's supple mouth flattened in what Benedict recognized as an attempt to hide a smile.

Benedict recognized that this careful scene was Lady Iddesford making arrangements. Another willow screened the other side of the path, a pond ran behind, and a hill rose on the last side. A pretty little box for an assignation. But Lady Iddesford did not seem perturbed by their arrival. Rueful, maybe, but perturbed, no.

Odd.

Nor was the groom walking the horses. They were perfectly cool and content. Either they had walked the entire way here, or, more likely, they had been standing for some time.

Lady Jane Compton recovered herself. "Miss Bourre, how do you do. Yes, it is lovely to be here when it is quieter."

"*Lord Fitzhugh and I* thought just the same," Dorrie said. "One does not always wish to see and be seen. What were you telling me, Fitzhugh? That it was time for practicing your sums?"

"Your sums?" Lady Iddesford asked.

"A game I play, my lady. Whether I can add to within five pounds the value of another's equipage, livery, and horses."

"You do not prefer to hazard a guess and go by general impression?"

"No," he replied, "although I am not insensitive to the charms of that system."

She raised her brows. "How do you know if you have guessed correctly?"

"One way or another, I find out."

She smiled, licked the very inside of her bottom lip. The movement seemed to take a long time.

"Do permit me, Fitzhugh," Dorrie said, "to introduce you to Lady Jane." And she did. Benedict took Lady Jane's hand and bowed over it, while keeping his horse to its manners by Lady Jane's side of the phaeton.

"You must permit me to introduce my step-grandmother, the dowager countess of Iddesford, to you, Miss Bourre," Lady Jane said. And she did.

"I am very pleased to meet you, my lady," Dorrie said. "Formally, that is. Matters proceeded so quickly last night at my cousin's ball."

"Indeed they did," Lady Iddesford said tranquilly. "We were just about to drive back to Lady Jane's home, but should be pleased with an escort, my lord."

"With pleasure," Benedict said, for there was nothing else to say.

"Do you continue on that side, my lord, for I should so like Miss Bourre by me. I would like to talk to her more."

Dorrie hid her dismay with a polite smile, eyes lowered. Seeing it, Lady Iddesford smiled across the phaeton at Benedict. *I would not*, that smile said, *hurt a child*.

And Benedict nodded, although he did not know whether to believe her.

They quitted the park, and the driver took a circuitous route toward Lady Jane's house, and pulled up just before the mews. With an apologetic but winsome smile, Lady Iddesford said, "If you would be so kind, my driver would hold your horse, my lord, while you walked Lady Jane down the street."

Lady Jane, who had conversed with polite punctiliousness with Benedict through the streets, took on a haughty look not unlike her mother's. For a second,

Benedict was tempted to consider her welcome to Letellier. But the right marriage and a few score miles between her and her mother could be the making of Lady Jane Compton.

Thankfully Dorrie did not quibble, although Benedict could tell how much she wanted to give expression to some feeling.

So Benedict saw Lady Jane into the bosom of her household, dropped a card on the salver presented by the butler, declined the formal offer of refreshment that neither he nor Lady Jane expected him to accept, and requested a dance for the next ball. Lady Jane smiled and said she would check with her mama.

That left Lady Iddesford, and Dorrie, to return to. They had not moved, but a strange note lurked in Dorrie's expression.

"Thank you, Lord Fitzhugh, for your kind attentions to Lady Jane. It is so awkward to have a word with her sometimes, and we have always been friendly."

That was for Dorrie's benefit. "My pleasure, ma'am. It is lucky we happened upon you, all alone."

"Yes, is it not?" she said in a limpid, guileless voice. Really, Lady Iddesford could out-Siddons Siddons.

"I am for home now, if you will excuse me. Lady Northam's rout is tonight, and I have a million things to do beforehand."

Benedict took Lady Iddesford's hand to bow over it, and suddenly wished very much that he had not, for by touching her, he wanted to keep on with it. He hoped he had not given himself away. "My lady," he said, and released her hand, and caught her grimace. Because he had held it, or let it go?

Then she smiled for the audience, and signaled her driver to pull away.

Dorrie sighed. "I do not understand the woman." She

sighed again. "But I like her a little better. That is odd, is it not?"

"Come. I shall escort you home."

"Where are you going?"

"Why do you think I have a destination in mind?"

"You have the look you always get when you are determined about something. You may as well tell me, for I will not sit at home and miss all the fun."

Now it was Benedict's turn to sigh. "We are going back to the park where we found the ladies. We must be quick, and when we get there, do not say anything if anyone is there."

Eyes sparkling, Dorrie forbore questioning him. They set off together. Benedict shortly felt grateful to her, for they were stopped several times by acquaintances and Dorrie always knew what to say to extricate them expeditiously.

Reaching the grove, they found Letellier, astride, slapping his roan horse's reins against his gloved palm. Dorrie's brows did not so much as quirk.

Seeing them, Letellier's expression registered annoyance and suspicion, but he rallied and said in his mocking tone, "Fancy seeing you here, Fitzhugh, and riding with the lovely Miss Bourre."

Standing a little off from them, Dorrie smiled.

"We were by here once before," Benedict said, "and thought it a very pleasant place at a canter."

"You have been riding before the fashionable hours?"

"My mount has suffered from lack of exercise," Benedict said. "It would not do for him to incite trouble among the crowd."

"Heaven forefend."

"We are to join the promenade. Do you come, or will you enjoy the peace a little while longer?"

"Thank you, I will stay here."

"As you will." Benedict turned his horse. Dorrie waved, and they trotted under the willow and back up the hill where they had first heard Lady Jane laugh.

Benedict thought of peach pie again. Did Lady Iddesford like peach pie?

Dorrie said, gleefully, "It serves them right, our breaking up their little rendezvous."

So Dorrie had not noticed either the cool horses, or the implications of Lady Jane's petulance. Benedict would not disillusion her. Letellier, however, was a different matter. Benedict suspected that he suspected Benedict of breaking up the party. Well, Benedict had never thought Letellier would tell him anything of substance. Or truth, for that matter.

It did all raise some interesting possibilities, though, and reminded him that he needed to see about those appointments in the City.

"We will not mention this to anyone, all right, Dorrie?"

"I can be agreeable," she said. "Especially since no one was harmed, or compromised." Then she grinned. "Except your poor horse's reputation."

Chapter Nine

Horse races impressed Esme for the way they allowed all classes to mix in harmony. It was not the Oaks, or Newmarket, or Epsom Downs, but enough to induce all manner of folk to turn out along a bluff-shaped hill to watch the fine gentlemen race their horses across the downs north of Islington, over stream and thicket and walls bordering the Great North Road.

The spectators of the *ton* sat astride or in their open carriages, as Esme did, close by where the race would begin with a bolt up a grassy hill crowned in woods. Gentry in serviceable but not-so-pretty equipages joined in here and there, as well as the occasional trap. Others spread blankets along the hill. A few ambitious souls had formed a tight ring farther off, and were fighting cocks with loud, punctuated cries.

They had formed a regular parade through Islington, from the New Road to where Upper Street and High met at the Angel, bustling with the mails and carriages bound for all over the country.

There could not have been a better day for it, either. The weather continued to give more good days than bad. No rain had fallen in the last three days, so the firm ground would present no unnatural hazards to horses or riders, and the sun, while warm, was not at all unpleasantly so.

Esme had expected to see Lord Fitzhugh here. She had thought she had overheard, last night at Lady Northam's rout, that he planned to attend. She could not be certain, however, for she had not been able to get close to him.

She had, however, thrilled when he had raised the glass he held in her direction. Did he toast her for not pulling off Jane's rendezvous? Or did he console?

Letellier had required some expected soothing. Esme had started on the offensive, though, by scolding him over making Jane wait and thus exposing her to gossip. They had argued over what time he should have been there, and Esme had agreed that the time on the note she had passed must have gotten smudged.

Then she had made a point of desiring above all things to see him race. As Jane was not to be here—Augusta not holding with racing—Esme easily cajoled him into escorting her. Esme had hoped that between her hanging on his arm and the race itself, he would burn off some of his spleen.

Her tactics appeared to be working. One could not miss him in his bright green coat—almost lime, by all that was holy—sitting on a fine black mare with the other riders, smirking.

Gillespie had not been around the night before, nor was he expected today. Williams said he had gone out of Town for two days. That alone should have been enough to make Esme dance.

But she could no longer be satisfied so easily. She wanted sight of Lord Fitzhugh, too.

There. There he was, his dark blue–clad back toward her, in an open black landau with the crest of the earl of Hadley. Miss Bourre sat in some overly frilly blue-and-white dress next to him. Esme might not have picked out the landau had not the older woman sitting in the carriage waved to Letellier. As she lifted her head, Esme saw her resemblance to Miss Bourre. A stout, older man with sandy whiskers also sat there. The earl himself, Esme judged. When his gaze touched Mrs. Bourre, his expression softened.

Letellier trotted over to the landau and did the pretty, although he begrudged it.

A handsome, dark gentleman Esme did not know also broke away from the group of racers and began trotting toward the carriages. Esme lowered her parasol a little. She had hoped not to attract an encumbering crowd today, and had even worn a dark yellow dress, a color that did not suit her nearly so well as her customary cream, or copper, or green.

Then she had to laugh at herself, for the gentleman went to Hadley's carriage, not toward hers. There he engaged Fitzhugh, and, shortly, the others, in lively conversation. Letellier took the opportunity to bear off.

Esme wished she could be invited to join.

The gentleman was relating something with wide gestures. He dropped his whip, and, with a self-deprecating laugh, slid off his horse to retrieve it. Objecting, though, the horse frisked sideways, and the gentleman twisted his ankle in his stirrup. His "Oomph!" of pain reached Esme's ears.

Lord Fitzhugh jumped from the landau to assist him, and they clasped arms wrist to elbow. The gentleman held his left leg off the ground. Fitzhugh and Hadley helped him into the carriage, where he took Fitzhugh's seat. He gestured toward his horse, and Fitzhugh took its reins.

The stallion was a fine creature, dark bay, about fifteen and a half hands, and of obviously high mettle, for he continued to dance from side to side, and pawed in an irritated fashion at the ground, pulling up tussocks of thin grass.

More gestures, then Fitzhugh mounted the creature and effortlessly trotted toward the white-whiskered gentlemen who had been organizing the riders.

So Fitzhugh would race. This prospect brightened Esme's day as nothing else had.

Apparently it also brightened the day of the watching gentlemen, for several groups of them bent heads and hats together. The wagering was changing.

Fitzhugh touched his hat to Letellier as he passed. Letellier smiled, then, as Fitzhugh went past him, glared at Fitzhugh with such naked hate that Esme dropped her parasol. She recovered it before it smashed into the carriage doors, but she could not so quickly recover her equanimity.

How ironic that instead of Fitzhugh's questioning her about her relationship with Letellier, she should have been questioning him about his. What could cause such hatred?

"John," she said in a low tone to her groom.

"Milady?"

"The gentleman, there, on the dark bay, in the blue coat?"

"Lord Fitzhugh, ma'am. He's on Lord Reversby's stallion Mercury, that went for seven hundred fifty pounds at Tatt's."

Trust a groom to know everyone's horses. And now she had a name to put to the gentleman in Hadley's carriage.

"Between him and Mr. Letellier, who would you bet on?"

"Milady?"

"Truly. I would like to know. You will not offend."

"Lord Fitzhugh, milady. In a heartbeat. Mr. Letellier

has flash, and his horse looks fine. But Lord Fitzhugh knows his horseflesh. Why, he could tell you the cost of everything associated with a horse, ma'am, and whether it was well valued."

"Indeed," Esme said, much amused.

"Yes, milady. He spends time with horses, and talks to grooms, so's I hear. Does his research, he does. Invests in studs. And Mercury's a descendant of Herod, from the black Byerly Turk, milady."

Esme nodded, and settled back in her seat, watching Letellier and Lord Fitzhugh. Fitzhugh had dropped back a bit to converse with Letellier and a few of his friends, Merton among them, all gearing themselves up with bright talk and barking laughter for the coming race.

Maybe she had imagined that look. Nothing more untoward or unpleasant than usual showed on Letellier's face.

Esme shortly attracted the attention of a few older gentlemen not in the race. They were a welcome relief after the young bucks she had been surrounded by the night before. They flirted, but they flirted with the steadiness of men who knew their own stations. Better, their conversations held Esme's interest, and, when she displayed some knowledge of their speculative investments, became more detailed.

But none of them intrigued her like Lord Fitzhugh.

Esme had managed to keep her attention away from where he sat astride Lord Reversby's horse, Mercury, within the crowd of racers. Then the huntmaster's groom blew a horn. Everyone looked up at that.

Lord Fitzhugh neither startled at the sudden noise, nor faced toward it. Instead he looked directly at Esme, touched the brim of his curly beaver hat, and slowly nodded once. To anyone else, the gesture could be attributed to his adjusting his hat to keep the sun from his eyes.

Esme could not help her small answering smile, or the sudden fluttery beating of her heart.

The riders grouped themselves together along the path they would take up the hill. Another blast from the master's trumpet set them into thundering motion. Several women shrieked excitedly, and one matron had to be revived with her salts.

Letellier's horse sprinted up the hill in the front of the pack. Fitzhugh followed closely behind, neck and neck with three other gentlemen. Then they all disappeared past the crown of trees onto the other side of the hill.

The assembled watchers sighed collectively, then a torrent of conversation and opinion flowed out. The race would range over some six miles of enclosed fields punctuated by woods and meadows. It might take as long as half an hour for the first racers to come into sight below, but there shortly became a great hurry moving carriages and blankets to the other side of the bluff, from which they could watch the last quarter of the race.

Two of the gentlemen who had been conversing with Esme elected to follow with her. Esme was grateful to have them, as they prevented others from sidling up in the press that formed along the crest of the bluff.

Grooms eyed each other with barely concealed distrust, and some of the gentlemen likewise kept their eyes on their mounts. The ladies glanced at Esme with either interest or dislike. Esme had learned to take that as a relative measure of their own strength of character.

So passed a brittle twenty minutes. Then someone cried out, "There!" and everyone was straining forward to see. Three riders burst from a covering wood onto a grassy field. Another two followed closely behind. It was too far away to tell whether one was Lord Fitzhugh, but

Letellier's bright green jacket was readily apparent in the second group of riders.

Excited talk of wagers continued among the men. The thundering of hooves reached her ears, and like everyone else, Esme was riveted.

The riders had one more bottleneck to squeeze through, a narrow channel over a rocky stream. They poured out the other side, galloping tired horses up the last, broad, grassy hill toward the crowded finish line.

A wild grin on his face, Letellier pulled level with the leader. Neck and neck they ran the last hundred yards, then Letellier stretched. His horse gave him the last bit of speed necessary to take the lead, and he sailed first across the line, where he passed his foaming horse off to a waiting groom.

He accepted the congratulations of the crowd, and, if he noticed that they were not as warm as they could be, he did not give any sign. Then he went up to Esme. "What do you think?" he asked. His tone held its usual gloating note, but in victory, it sounded so much the worse.

Esme knew what was expected of her, though. She spoke fulsome praise, and loathed him as he drank it in as his due.

"But what are you looking at? The race has its winner."

"There are others to come in," Esme explained.

"We lost a few over some of the fences," Letellier said. He could not restrain his crowing triumph. "They will straggle in. I must report to the master."

As Letellier passed the earl of Hadley's carriage, he stopped long enough to accept Hadley's praise. Miss Bourre, however, looked worried.

Esme turned away before the girl noticed her looking. During their conversation yesterday, Esme had found herself liking the girl. She did not want to like the girl.

The girl had rejected Fitzhugh, which could only be considered bad judgment.

There. There was Fitzhugh, but not at a gallop. His horse trotted haltingly across the field, was passed by two other riders, carefully picked its way across the stream, and walked up the last hill. Fitzhugh had lost his hat, too, for the sun burnished his sandy hair, and the wind had tangled it.

As he crossed the line, a murmur went through the crowd. Grass and mud clung to his jacket and buff trousers, and a trickle of blood flowed from his temple.

Esme felt as though someone had stabbed her. He dismounted, took the panting horse's nose by the bridle, then murmured something to the waiting Hadley groom. The groom clucked at the horse and walked him away. Fitzhugh walked in her direction, but looked grimly at some point well fixed in the distance.

She understood she could not run to him as she wished to. Neither of them had that luxury. But impulsively she found a kerchief and handed it out to him. "You are bleeding, my lord."

He accepted it, but glanced at her only a second. "Again?" he asked, rueful, angry, and embarrassed.

"Fitzhugh!" It was Miss Bourre.

"Excuse me, my lady," he said.

"Of course," Esme said, frightening herself by how much more she wanted to say.

He compressed his mouth and turned away. She forced herself not to appear to watch Miss Bourre and her mother fuss over him, but she could hear them. Once the exclamations died down, Lord Reversby said, "I cannot believe Mercury threw you."

"It was a hole," Lord Fitzhugh said. "On the other side of a stream. I am sorry, Reversby."

"How could you have seen it?" Reversby asked.

Lord Fitzhugh paused. "I will go check on him," he said and jumped from the carriage. "Keep that foot up, eh?"

Esme watched him, so when she heard someone clear his throat behind her, she was startled. She was even more startled to see Hadley, a pugnacious expression on his face, and her lace-edged handkerchief, folded over so no blood showed, in his hand. Hadley looked nothing like his son. Did Fitzhugh resemble his mother, as she did hers?

"Here," he said without ceremony. "My son needs nothing you can offer."

Dumbfounded, Esme stared.

Hadley thrust the handkerchief at her. "You did hear me, didn't you? And you'd be wise to stay away from Letellier, too."

"I do what I please," Esme said, recovering her hauteur.

"Yes, there will always be men to do your bidding, won't there? That's the way women like you are. Leave my son alone."

"What a fine opinion you have of him," Esme said.

He dropped her handkerchief on the ground, and left.

Cheeks burning, Esme lowered her parasol a trifle. The day was too squinting bright for people to really tell, but still. Letellier came and climbed into her carriage all unasked. "Quite the day, isn't it?"

"Do you know what happened?"

"I just won a race, my dear."

"No, to your friend Lord Fitzhugh. He was thrown."

"Oh, is that what the commotion was?"

"Are you not the least bit interested?"

"Are you?"

Esme had to remember with whom she was dealing. "It looks to be the *on dit* of the day. Do you think I should want to be told what happened by someone who was not here?"

A smile slithered along Letellier's mouth. "Who would have thought that the delicious Lady Iddesford could ever imagine herself capable of being trumped?"

"I prefer to know what there is to be known. It does level the playing field."

"By tilting it entirely in your direction."

Esme shrugged. All she could think of was the handkerchief, lying in the dirt.

"What, my lady, no rejoicing? Think of what news of my victory will do to Lady Jane."

Esme had forgotten Jane, and she cursed the girl for being susceptible enough to be attracted to such a one as Letellier. She cursed herself, too, because she was susceptible to Lord Fitzhugh, who did not act consistently.

"It will certainly make an impression," Esme said. She gave Letellier her most winning smile, the smile that promised things Esme had no intention of ever giving. Even things she did not know she promised.

"That is what I like so much about you, my dear."

"And what is that?" Esme asked.

"You are single-minded in your purpose. That in a woman is a delight." He saved her the effort of a reply by jumping down from the carriage. He bent down, then held Esme's handkerchief to her. "You dropped this."

Esme took the leaf- and grass-covered handkerchief. Her sole consolation was that it remained folded, Lord Fitzhugh's blood and her churning emotions hidden inside from Letellier's questions.

Chapter Ten

A bare week ago Benedict had been highly conscious of moving through a London ballroom for no other reason than his eligibility. Since then, however, Lady Iddesford's attention had made him an object of interest to other gentlemen, and his cachet among the ladies had not decreased. Naturally the story of his spectacular fall at the race rippled through the *ton* like an error in a balance sheet.

Naturally.

Right.

Could he but hide behind one of the many potted palms decorating this gilt-and-red ballroom. Instead he stood by one, along a short line of steps that ended at the balcony door, looked toward Dorrie dancing with the Duke of Breshirewood, and saw instead low stone fences and creeks, swollen with the spring rains, and broad fields that skirted woods waking to life and leaf in the warm spring sunshine.

He had seen the stream coming, remembered standing in the stirrups and patting the stallion's foaming neck, marveling at the animal's power, and heard the rider behind him. Never would he have imagined the bump that sent Mercury so far to the side, where the ground lay wet and uneven.

Then trees had grown upside down, clouds dusted

blue, textureless grass, and a face presented itself before him, lovely in all its lines, framed with intense copper hair, green-hazel eyes a rival for any of the spring-gowned trees around him.

You are not Dorrie's face, Benedict had thought absurdly. Then, *I am sorry, my lady. I have failed you, too.*

If only he had had time that afternoon and evening to sit and wrest the image from his mind. But Dorrie and Aunt Bourre had insisted on fussing over him. Dorrie fussing over him should have constituted a dream come true. Instead he had wished he knew how he had lost the handkerchief Lady Iddesford had given him. When he had come back from seeing to Mercury, it had disappeared.

"Here you are, Fitzhugh," said Reversby, limping. "Are you trying not to look like you are hiding behind this palm?"

"Am I succeeding?"

Reversby grimaced.

"As bad as that?" Benedict asked ruefully.

"Trust me, my friend, I know all about the desire to hide oneself away. It works for a little while, but 'tis like stuffing yourself on bread without any meat. You come back twice as hungry in half the time."

Benedict had to smile.

"I know why I would do it, but what is your excuse?" Reversby asked.

"None so good as yours. Anne was the best of women."

Reversby appeared to be looking very far away. Then he smiled. "She was."

"I should like to make you an offer for Mercury. He'll carry an ugly scar, and I—"

"He is a wonderful animal. I will not begrudge him the scar."

Benedict nodded, much relieved.

They watched the dancing together. "I had hoped to see Lady Iddesford here tonight," Reversby said. "The dowager, I mean."

Suddenly tense, Benedict merely lifted his brows.

"Over the past day and a half that I have been in Town, I have had no fewer than eight ladies complain most bitterly about the way she has disrupted balls. I shudder to imagine the conversations around the tea tables these past few days. Which hostesses have been forced to invite her because of some favor owed Lady Howard, and which invite her just to enjoy the mêlée?"

Lady Howard, hm. But Benedict said, "*Et tu*, Reversby?"

Reversby laughed and clapped him on the shoulder. "That is more like it. I had thought you lost to all humor. Truly, though, you are the only one she seems to favor, other than Letellier, which does make one excessive confused."

"Compliment, or criticism?" Benedict asked.

"Compliment, my dear man. Only compliment. So, do I take it the specter of Lady Iddesford has you hiding behind the potted palms? If so, my dear Gawain, you should do better to flee. From what I hear—too late."

Smith-Jenkins and one of his friends who had paid court to Lady Iddesford had come up. They bowed, and Smith-Jenkins said, "My lord, would you do me the honor of crossing swords with me tomorrow?"

"Have we quarreled, sir?" Benedict asked, bemused.

Reversby hid a snigger in a pretend cough.

"No, sir, of course not," the young man said, flustered. "I have had the honor to see your skill and wish to test mine against it."

"The honor shall be mine, then," Benedict said. "Eleven o'clock?"

"Eleven o'clock should be perfect," Smith-Jenkins

replied. "And do permit me to introduce you to my friend, Mr. Lloyd."

After Benedict and Mr. Lloyd bowed, Mr. Lloyd said, "Would you do me the honor of engaging me at noon, sir?"

Benedict had to ignore Reversby, whose shoulders were twitching, to say, "With pleasure, sir."

The two young gentlemen bowed and left with jaunty strides.

"Tell," Benedict said.

"It is the notion that since you defeated Letellier at Monsieur's, the lovely dowager has paid you attention. They, naturally, think . . ." Reversby rolled his hand suggestively.

That they are less confused than I am. Benedict sighed. "How many?"

"I heard of five."

"You have been busy."

"I would attribute it all to my winning countenance," Reversby said, "but I fear people want to talk. Had I known you were to be here in London and providing this much fun, why, I might have come to Town sooner."

"I shall be all day tomorrow at Monsieur's *salle.*"

"They might not all find the backbone," Reversby said with an encouraging smile totally belied by his glee. "Then again, they might. And five is all I have heard of. Doesn't mean that's all there is."

"You are a sadist."

"It is possible," Reversby said, pretending to study his well-manicured nails. "Care to help me in my vice? Introduce me to the lady in question. I promise you I shall not fence you, not you and your ruddy strong arm. No, indeed."

"She is not here."

"Not yet. But Letellier has arrived, and Lady Jane

Compton, with Lady Avondale. The great forbidding countess-mama has some ailment, but they heard Breshirewood would attend, and so she sent her sister-in-law to mind the heiress."

"You *have* been busy. A veritable fount of information."

Reversby shrugged. "Remember, right after we got out of school, how you insisted I jump in that damnably cold lake and get the shock over? What is Town but a damnably cold lake? Never have forgiven you for the lesson, though, just so you understand me."

Of mutual accord, they made their way to Aunt Bourre, stopping to let some matrons lament his and Reversby's inability to dance that evening. Benedict let Reversby make most of the conversation. Words flowed from Reversby, and it was a treat to listen to him.

They were greeting Aunt Bourre when a sudden lifting of chins and glances told Benedict all he needed to know.

"Immediate, or leisurely?" he asked Reversby.

"Immediate, surely, for otherwise we shall have to fight our way through a thicker thicket. If you see what I mean."

"I do," Benedict said.

Tonight Lady Iddesford wore a green dress that rivaled her eyes. With an overslip of net that moved half a second behind her, and her hair piled in high curls, she resembled a creature of Faerie. She smiled at the crowding gentlemen, and those privileged to be close to her chuckled at something she said.

"Anne, do not strike me dead for thinking it," Reversby murmured.

The crowding gentlemen parted before Benedict. Cold, green-hazel eyes greeted him. "My lord Fitzhugh, such a surprise."

A murmur passed among the gentlemen.

Highly conscious, Benedict said, "My lady, do allow me to present Viscount Reversby to you."

Lady Iddesford said, "Lord Reversby, I was very sorry to hear about your wife. I met her, you know, in Calais. Together we managed to persuade a very crotchety band of lighters to row our baggage out to meet a ship bound back for England."

"She told me. May I request a dance. Ahem. While I may?"

"I have not yet decided whether I incline to dancing. But thank you, sir." She turned cold eyes upon Benedict.

Not knowing what it meant, Benedict bowed and took himself off, with Reversby following. "Well," Reversby said, "what did you do to the woman?"

"I have offered no insult, if that is what you mean. Maybe that is my crime. I know no other."

"Take heart in the fickleness of women." Reversby snorted. "Perhaps Lloyd and Smith-Jenkins are regretting their haste in challenging you."

Lord Fitzhugh looked pale.

Esme wanted to escape the crowd and explain. Gnarled prudence held her back.

Tonight Augusta did not accompany Jane. John fulfilled all expectation by sitting in the card room like the lazy, self-indulgent sot that he was. And Lady Avondale would not resist the crowd of gentlemen Esme would shortly surround her with.

Effectively detaching Jane.

The surreptitiously passed notes, the whispers in the ears, the baiting and switching upon both Augusta and Letellier, these Esme understood. But Letellier's flashiness, his reaction to her clever maneuvering around the meeting in Hyde Park, signaled that he would pursue the quick campaign. Worse, he would shake off all her attempts to slow him down. Then there would be no helping Jane. At least now Jane trusted her.

Lord Fitzhugh distracted her, pure and simple. Besides, would it not be better if she bowed out of his life now? Hadley's words had stung, but she accepted them. She could not offer Lord Fitzhugh anything. She could not offer anything to any respectable man.

At least, nothing she wanted to give.

An hour later, her plan was working flawlessly. With secretive smiles and careful promises, she employed her gentlemen in distracting Lady Avondale. She strolled off with Jane toward the balcony, gently rebuffing other gentlemen who thought this an opportunity. Then she signaled Letellier with a glance across the ballroom. Of Lord Fitzhugh there was no sign.

Letellier joined them on the balcony. Someone had blown out the lanterns, leaving a spill of light from the ballroom that did not reach the stone balustrade. A crescent moon provided the only other light. Still, Jane was discernibly blushing.

"Mind," Esme said, "you do not go off the balcony. I shall stand over there." She indicated a section shadowed by an out-jutting room, darkened beyond its glass doors to signal it was not open for guests.

With an oily smile, Letellier made his promise. He took Jane by the arm, and led her over to the balustrade, with Jane saying, "I heard about the race. You won! How very exciting!"

Letellier laughed in a low, triumphant tone.

The snake.

It would soon be over. Then she might retire to relative obscurity, go back to Yorkshire and tend to dear

Lady Howard, who became frailer with each passing month.

Esme listened to the faint sounds of their conversation. Nothing untoward, nothing too urgent.

She was satisfied.

Esme leaned back against the house, her hands behind her to protect her dress from the cool, bumpy stone.

But then someone was beside her, taking her arm. "My dear Esmeralda." It was Gillespie.

"Let go of me this instant."

"Or what?"

"Are we not past childish exchanges?"

"There is nothing childish about what I want from you."

"You will not get it."

"Who will stop me?" he asked in his braying voice, his mouth so close to her that she could smell the brandy on him.

Esme looked over to where Letellier and Jane stood. Had stood. They were gone.

"You want Letellier? Let us find him together, in the garden."

A click behind them gave them a half-second's warning. "I think the lady wants to be left alone," said Lord Fitzhugh.

Esme thought her legs would give out on her in relief, except that Gillespie tugged her around to face Lord Fitzhugh.

"We have had this conversation before, as I recall, Fitzhugh."

Lord Fitzhugh sighed. "It *is* tiresome of you, is it not? Let her go. Now."

"She will not scream," Gillespie said, "or she will tell all and sundry that Lady Jane is in the gardens being compromised by Mr. Letellier."

"She does not need to scream," Fitzhugh said in that provokingly reasonable voice of his. "My rendering you quite unconscious need make no noise."

"I am not the boy of sixteen you could intimidate."

"No, you are the man of thirty who appears to have become more of a bore than he was then. I never thought of thrashing you when we were younger, but I am sore tempted to thrash you now."

"And ruin your pretty face?" Gillespie said, sneering.

"*My* face is not at issue," Lord Fitzhugh said.

Gillespie flushed, but abruptly he released Esme's arm. She darted behind Lord Fitzhugh.

"Does Letellier know that he is sharing her with you?" Gillespie asked.

"Does Letellier know that I must protect her from you?"

Gillespie might not have noticed the anger seeping into Fitzhugh's tone, but Esme did. She shivered.

"Get you gone. Now," Lord Fitzhugh said. "I am losing my patience."

"I am not done with—"

"Quiet," Lord Fitzhugh said, in a tone, which, if anything, was more chillingly reasonable. "Not another word."

"You are welcome to her, the—"

But before he could say the dreadful word, Fitzhugh shut Gillespie's mouth. His teeth and jaw clicked together. "Not. Another. Word," said Fitzhugh.

Gillespie shrugged him off, glaring, but retreated into the ballroom, tugging at his coattails. It did not save his dignity.

Esme was about to thank him, but he said, "Let us find Lady Jane and Letellier." Taking her by the arm, more gently than Gillespie but not without some force, he led her down the balcony stairs and into the garden.

"Thank you," Esme said.

"If we find them quickly, we may all return to the ball-room and lend each other countenance."

Emotions flashed through Esme as they walked quickly along the garden path. Appreciation for his quick thinking. Stinging hurt that he could be so abrupt. Acknowledgment that she deserved no consideration from him. She had embarrassed him in public and caused him no end of trouble.

They looked down side paths, found nothing. The main path led through a lofty grape arbor about ten yards long. On its other side stood a vine-encrusted gazebo. Just on the inside of the arbor, Lord Fitzhugh stopped walking, and perforce Esme stopped as well. He held up a hand to prevent her speaking.

Esme heard a baritone murmur, followed by a so-prano giggle, coming from the gazebo. She released her pent-up breath, and started forward.

Then Lord Fitzhugh gathered her up in his arms and pressed her back against the arbor's edge. She gasped before his lips descended upon hers.

Chapter Eleven

From the entrance to the arbor, Mr. Smith-Jenkins said, astonished, "Fitzhugh?"

His companion said, "By all that's holy."

Lord Fitzhugh held Esme's gaze and pitched his voice low. "I shall see you tomorrow, at eleven o'clock, sir. Do go away now, there's a good man."

Retreating footsteps gave him his answer.

Esme ached to have him kiss her in fact. She ached so badly she went up on tiptoe, her breasts grazing his chest, her hands twining in his hair.

He took her hands from him, although she had the satisfaction of knowing how fast his heart beat. "Now they will talk about us, and not Lady Jane."

"You are awake on all suits, sir," Esme said.

"What else would you have me do, my lady?" Then he shook his head. "This is not the time for this discussion. Come." He raked fingers through his crisp sandy hair as he strode up to the gazebo. He did not look inside. "Lady Jane? Lady Jane?"

The soft talking inside ceased. "Lady Jane, you have been missed. Lady Iddesford is here to take you back."

Jane's face when it appeared at the gazebo doorway looked so like her dear grandfather's whenever he had been caught imbibing something his physician had urged him not to imbibe that Esme required all of Letellier's annoyance not to laugh.

"So soon, my dear countess?" Letellier asked.

"I brought them, my dear," Esme replied. "Lady Avondale had to hold them." She did not care to speculate on what Fitzhugh thought of this exchange.

"True," Letellier said after a long pause. He lifted Lady Jane's hand to his lips and murmured something in her ear. Then, "I shall wait here a while, then find out what your dear grandmama has planned for us tomorrow, eh?"

Jane trilled a little laugh, and linked arms with Esme. Lord Fitzhugh said, "The sooner we are back?"

"Yes," Esme replied, and they retraced their steps through the arbor and the garden path.

"Such a beautiful evening," Jane said, swinging her free arm wide. "The stars, the moon, the gazebo . . ."

Esme desperately desired her to stop rhapsodizing before Fitzhugh. "None of which you will mention inside. I have been sewing up your flounce, dear."

"No," Lord Fitzhugh said. "That will no longer work."

Esme stiffened. "No. You are right. It will not."

"Why?" Jane asked.

"Never mind why. You—"

"Sought your father," Lord Fitzhugh said. "But since he has gone off to cheerful nowhere, you missed him. And you found Lady Iddesford when you chanced to look outside."

"That would do, would it not?" Jane asked, missing the questioning look Esme gave him. "I am so happy you are helping, too, my lord. I thought so, the day before. Why, did I not like Mr. Letellier so well, I should fix my cap at you."

Lord Fitzhugh looked grimly amused. "I shudder to imagine the possibilities. Thank you, Lady Jane."

"It is as well you do not," Esme said, feeling waspish, "for he has quite fixed his interest elsewhere."

Jane laughed. "Do you tell me you have indeed succumbed to my favorite relative's charms, sir, as the gossips say? It is too wonderful."

"No," Esme said. "He has not."

That silenced Jane.

Esme wished something could come along and take her from her misery. She strolled not ten inches from him, and he might as well have been back in that arbor, kissing Miss Bourre. The irony of it smote her.

He led them along the side of the house, to that unused room from which he had emerged. From there, he moved confidently along a hallway until he came to a back stair. "The ladies' withdrawing room is at the top, ma'am. May I suggest you visit it and then come back downstairs by the closer staircase?"

"You do seem to know all these London houses, my lord," Esme said.

"Houses are not names, ma'am, and I have eyes. Your servant." He bowed and strode away toward the ballroom.

"Does he not like you, then, Cousin?" Jane asked, using the name they had agreed upon when they were alone.

"He is a mysterious man," Esme said. "I do not understand him, but I can rely on him to do what's right. You may, too."

"What good is that? I want one that excites me."

"Sometimes, in rare, rare sometimes, the same man may do both. Think well on that, dear Jane."

Jane tilted her head, considering, as they entered the ladies' withdrawing room. Esme followed, resenting that missed kiss.

* * *

Benedict found Dorrie, Aunt Bourre, and Reversby standing together by a rose bouquet fresco. The musicians were setting their instruments down in preparation for a break, and many clumps of friends and acquaintances formed all over the ballroom. There was no mistaking Dorrie's pained expression, nor Aunt Bourre's confusion.

Benedict tried not to look harassed, but he could not slough his feelings of annoyed irony. He had kissed Lady Iddesford twice before. The time he did not kiss her, however, was the time he informed and delighted the gossips.

Worse, the time he did not kiss her was the time he had most wanted to. He had to exorcise the woman's spirit from his soul. She made him feel disloyal to Dorrie. Surely she had enough men on her string. She did not need him, too. Surely she was only toying with him because of his association with Letellier. Her dropping him earlier had told him that. He was a candidate for Bedlam did he think he could try to influence her relationship with Letellier and their plans for Lady Jane.

"Dorrie, may I speak to you a moment?" he asked, holding out his hand.

Either his straightforward approach or long acquaintance worked in his favor. Dorrie glanced at her mother, took his hand, and allowed him to lead her a few yards away.

"I do not know what you have heard—"

"Hmmha. Excuse me, my lord," said a brown-haired gentleman of about twenty-five at Benedict's shoulder. "May I have the pleasure of—"

"We are not acquainted, sir," Benedict said.

The gentleman bowed. "Sommers, sir."

"Pleased," Benedict replied. "One o'clock, Monsieur Marguillier's *salle*."

"Very good, sir. Excuse me."

"What was that, Fitzhugh?" Dorrie asked.

"Nothing," Benedict replied. He took a deep breath. "Just as what happened in the garden was nothing. I know *you* can keep a confidence, Dorrie."

"Excuse me, my lord," said a mousy gentleman come up to them. "May I have the pleasure of crossing swords with you at your convenience?"

"It is Brimley, is it not?"

"Yes. We met at school."

"I thought so. Two o'clock, then. Monsieur Marguillier's."

"I shall be honored."

"What have you to tell me?" Dorrie asked, her expression one of amused apprehension. "Best be quick about it as well, before you must commit yourself to three o'clock."

Benedict had to smile. Dorrie grinned back. Benedict squeezed her hand. "Thank you, Dorrie."

"For what?"

"For being Dorrie."

She blushed, but said, "Tell?"

"It is this. I did not kiss Lady Iddesford in the garden this evening." Enough qualifiers made it true in letter, if not in spirit. "I made it look as if I did, though. Do you remember how we found her and Lady Jane in Hyde Park? Lady Jane found herself needing a diversion. Lady Iddesford and I created one."

"And 'tis very diverting," Dorrie said. "The entire ballroom is abuzz. Poor Fitzhugh. I am glad you helped them. It is too bad, however, that you have had to draw this attention. Your father, I know, will not be best pleased."

Benedict grimaced his assent as they went to rejoin the others. Would it make any difference that Letellier had been Lady Jane's partner in the gazebo? Probably not.

He wished that his father had never asked him to befriend Letellier. Then he could . . .

Then he could what?

Then he could kiss Lady Iddesford with impunity? No, there was Dorrie, whom he wanted to marry. Besides, nothing relating to Lady Iddesford could be free of consequence.

"I wish I could stand by you during the dance after the interval," Dorrie said, "but I am promised to Breshirewood."

Her kind gesture wrapped the hurtful admission in tissue. Very Dorrie. But Benedict did not feel as hurt as he thought he should. Only a week ago he would have suffered excessively. "I shall quite shamelessly make use of your mother, then," he said, which made her laugh.

Then she chewed her lip and said, "You do not mind?"

"I have wanted, above all things, your happiness." His feelings might resemble a murky evening fog, but that much he could say for certain.

She searched his face with an odd expression on hers, then a brave smile twitched.

"All is well?" Aunt Bourre asked.

"All is very well, Mama," Dorrie said, which mollified Aunt Bourre.

But Reversby lifted his brows. He bided his time until Aunt Bourre and Dorrie went down their own conversational path, then said, "Did those pups—?"

"I am fencing from eleven until three tomorrow."

"Serves you right. You must not have had enough exercise of late. My mother always told me lack of exercise led to any number of ills."

"It is not what it seems."

"Everything is exactly as it seems, Fitzhugh. Whether

it is true, that's another matter. You know that. Especially in London. For instance, one could regard Lady Iddesford standing so stolidly next to Lady Jane and Lady Avondale as though she hoped some of their respectability might rub off on her."

"You believe that?"

"What I believe is as much use as a torch in hell. She is looking at you, you know."

"She is angry at me," Benedict said, wanting more than anything to meet her eyes. Would they be as smoky and stormy as they had been in the arbor, when he had felt her silky skin, and drunk in her alluring scent mixed with the roses?

Reversby snorted. "Then Gillespie must be actively loathing you. By the punch bowl. I think he's been augmenting his. Getting wobblier and wobblier. Sneerier and sneerier, too."

"I am not worrying about Gillespie."

"Fine," said Reversby, unconvinced.

The musicians assembled for more dancing. His Grace the duke of Breshirewood approached them, and Benedict studied him while introductions and politenesses went around. Benedict judged the dark-haired duke as a few years older than himself, a few happy inches shorter, and not unhandsome. He was possessed of a loquacious, but more or less charitable, disposition.

"Fitzhugh," he said jovially, as though Benedict were not of interest, "I understand you are holding an open house at Monsieur's tomorrow. Does your schedule allow any room?"

Benedict's expression must have said, *Not you, too,* for the duke said, "Purely for the honor of the lesson, sir."

"Likely he has given too much time between Mr. Lloyd and Mr. Sommers," Reversby said, studying his nails.

"Do you believe so?" Benedict asked.

"Oh, yes," Reversby said. "Lloyd is quite dreadful. Sommers, though, will give you a run."

"Then it is either half past noon, or three o'clock, Your Grace," Benedict said.

"I shall come early, sir, and watch, if I may."

"My pleasure," Benedict said.

"Are you really fencing the better part of tomorrow, Fitzhugh?" Dorrie asked.

"It does appear that way," Benedict replied.

She pursed her lips, but allowed the duke to lead her off, as the musicians were striking up in earnest. They made a nice couple, Benedict thought, and hated it.

"I should send a letter 'round to Monsieur this evening," Benedict said.

"Do not worry yourself there," Reversby said. "He will appreciate being the event of note tomorrow."

"Is there nothing else happening in London?"

Reversby shrugged. "So far it is a dull Season. Prinny is not in any greater debt than usual. Princess Charlotte has not committed any *known* indiscretions. Nor has Cumberland, for that matter. Heh. The Government continues to churn and debate our commitment to Spain, but no one here cares about that. The Americans are fighting us, I hear. Otherwise there has only been the affair of Miss Maria Lovington, who eloped to Gretna Green with Haverstock."

"You must be joking."

"Devil a bit," Reversby said.

"Join me, back at Hadley House, after?" Benedict asked.

Reversby promptly accepted.

Thus it was that when the note arrived from Lady Iddesford, Reversby occupied the same studded maroon wing chair Benedict's father had a few nights ago.

"My lady's footman awaits a reply," said Donaldson as he handed the note to Benedict, bowed, and left.

"It's one o'clock," Reversby protested mildly.

No witty—or adequate—answer rose to mind. Benedict settled for a shrug, and broke open the seal.

> *Dear Sir,*
>
> *I would like to continue the discussion we began this evening tomorrow at your earliest convenience. Would you do me the honor of suggesting a time and place?*
>
> > *Yours, sincerely,*
> >
> > *EI*

Benedict handed the note to Reversby.

Reversby raised his brows, then said, "A lot of women in her position would threaten, or demand."

"What do you consider her position?" Benedict asked.

"Don't cut up stiff, Fitzhugh."

"Stiff?"

"Stiff. You have that rather forbidding expression on, and I do declare, I have not earned it. Apology accepted."

"Thank you," Benedict said. "May we view this question objectively?"

"I can be objective. Better than anybody, I do declare."

"Does that strange bobbing of your head indicate sarcasm?"

Reversby grinned. "But I can be serious, too, Father."

"You think I cannot be objective. Here is objective: What position does she have? She has confirmed her reputation and either tarnished or polished mine, depending on the eye of the beholder."

"So you were listening to me before," Reversby said.

"I had learned the lesson already, thank you." Benedict sat down, smacking the letter absently against his palm. "The trouble is, the lesson may obtain, but it does not satisfy."

Reversby looked at his tented fingers and said, "When I married Anne, I thought she was a sweet, mild girl. Her father and mother said she was a sweet, mild girl. Everyone who met her thought her a lady who would never set one foot out of place. Well, I discount utterly what her mother said. *She* knew better, but then, she and Anne were extraordinarily close, and Anne wanted me. God knows why. Her father had no idea. But let me tell you, after we were married, she was no longer the sweet, mild girl I had thought she was. She was no virago, do not let me lead you astray. She was a lioness, eager to hunt and explore. That is what I miss the most, her driving spirit. I have been wandering around some time without a compass."

Benedict poured them both some fresh Madeira. A gust of wind whistled through an open window, sending a light curtain spinning. "To Lady Reversby," he said, and held up his glass.

Reversby smiled and clinked glasses. They drank. "I do not mean to be maudlin. I do not see her everywhere, in every other blond woman about five feet tall, with a figure . . . . No, not anymore. But I think I do see her in Lady Iddesford, if I may be so bold."

"I am not sure I understand," Benedict said, uneasy.

"There may be a lioness inside the lovely dowager, but I do not think her lacking in a moral compass. Anne once told me she would have had to do something completely shocking to change people's idea of her. You put the pieces together."

Benedict wondered how Lady Reversby had first shocked her husband into thinking she was not meek and mild. "On what is your impression based?"

"Are we back to objectivity?" Reversby asked.

"We must be. For I say to you and believe it: I know no

way to separate what she truly feels from what she claims to feel. If you can, how do you do it?"

Reversby raised his brows. "I suppose I must rely on instinct."

"I distrust instinct," Benedict said, "particularly my own where the lady is concerned."

"Like that, is it?"

"There is no future to it," Benedict said.

"Now I would say, who cares about the future?"

"I am not sure I want there to be a present, either, except that my father wishes me to stay close to Letellier."

"And by staying close to Letellier these days, one brings oneself in her sphere. Lot of speculation over that, and none of it flattering."

"She has added an unexpected element," Benedict said.

Reversby nodded, accepting that Benedict had said all he could on the subject. "You have to meet her tomorrow."

"Yes. I need to know at least what she would profess. Whether there is aught to truth in it . . ." Benedict shrugged.

"I do not envy you tomorrow, Fitzhugh."

"Hopefully I may find an end to it, know where she fits, and understand what Letellier is really up to."

"Then what?"

"That would depend, would it not?"

Reversby smiled, a trace of pity in it. "Feeling as you do, you would do better to say to Hades with Letellier, ignore the lady, and throw yourself into making Miss Bourre fall under your spell. She could, you know, despite His Grace."

"Do you think so?" Benedict asked.

"Yes, although for God's sake, try to sound a little happier about it."

Chapter Twelve

Esme paced about by the willow and the pond, in Hyde Park where she had set up the sham meeting between Jane and Letellier, her carriage and driver to the other side of the little hill. Another mild day spread itself over London, with the westering sun gently bronzing the tops of trees and roofs of distant houses. Esme thought she should feel relaxed out here, in this beautiful setting, but twice circumstances had ruined that pleasure.

Lord Fitzhugh's reply had asked her to meet him there, at five o'clock.

I do apologize for the late time, my lady, but it appears I have engagements until past four.

He was ten minutes late. Did Esme not believe Lord Fitzhugh would sooner cut off his arm than tell a falsehood, she might have believed him capable of putting her off to increase her agitation.

Esme tugged at a knobby branch, pulling off some young leaves, then felt guilty.

She paced again.

Farther from the tree.

She had questions, questions that had kept her up far too late the night before and plagued her as she had gone about her day. The trouble, however, was that asking any of them presumed a connection she did not think he felt, nor would expect her to build on so slight a thread as two kisses. Her reputation indicated otherwise, and she could not yet have him question her reputation.

What matter that those two kisses had made her feel more alive than she had ever felt?

Maybe she should leave now.

"My lady," Fitzhugh said, taking choice from her.

It was not fair that he should appear so quietly and look so handsome, when his expression told her that speaking to her ranked last on his list of enjoyable activities.

"Lord Fitzhugh. You startled me."

"I am sorry. I was detained."

"No matter. It is a pleasant day, is it not, to be in the park?"

"Very pleasant."

Drat the man, Esme thought, *he will not ask me.* "You seemed to enjoy the rest of the ball, last night."

"When one is being gossiped about, I find it essential to enjoy a ball." He spoke calmly. "Do you not agree?"

Esme said, "I hope my arranging to have Lady Jane dance with His Grace worked to your advantage with your friend."

"Thank you, but as I have spent the last four hours with His Grace, answering his not-so-veiled questions about my friend, I must say it does not, particularly."

"Can you not accept that I would like to do something for you to thank you?"

"I do not want thanks, thank you."

"You will not be satisfied, will you?"

"You want me to be satisfied?"

The sudden change from defense to attack flustered Esme. "I want . . ." she began, but did not know what to say.

"With what should I be satisfied? Your obvious if inexplicable desire to aid Letellier in his pursuits with little thought to the consequences of ensuing events? Your giving Gillespie chances to take whatever he likes? The reputation that leads him to believe he could offer such insult? Your apparent desire to put me in situations where I have only the choice of playing the cockerel or the fool? The pain such appearances give to those who hold me in some slight regard? I ask you, with what should I be satisfied?"

Embarrassment and impotent rage flashed through Esme. She knew her face flamed. "That is quite the longest speech I have yet heard you make."

He bowed.

"If you feel that way, why are you here? Another test?"

"No."

"Research, then. Do you have me down to the closest five pounds?"

"Not at all. I do not understand anything about you."

"Because I am the wicked Lady Iddesford, sometimes called a lady notorious, sometimes called Iddesford's Folly, many other sobriquets I would as soon never have heard, and likely some I am glad I do not know?"

The expression on Fitzhugh's face suggested he had heard a few of those. "Tell me you did not earn them."

She wanted to with every hot pulse of her heart. She knew she could not with every scrap of wit she possessed. Even if she had not made her promise, Hadley's words had their own power. She intended to tip her chin and say nothing. Instead she tipped her chin and spoke. "You said my reputation was not in my eyes."

"It was in mine."

"Even when you said it?"

"Yes."

That cooled her. She had assumed that his decency had prompted him to be fair. Why else had he helped her the night before? She said, slowly, "I had considered you a friend."

"Do you treat all friends so, you are fortunate to have such a beautiful face."

"You are cruel."

"No, I am honest. I will not be moved by tears, either."

"You would expect them to be crocodile tears, most likely," she said, losing her composure.

"To everything good I know of you, there is evidence to give it the lie. Nothing is consistent about you, my lady, except your ability to entice and perplex. How do I reconcile the lady who would gag a statue with the lady who would allow a relative to be compromised in such fashion, or with the lady who could converse gently on the subject of her eyes? Or with the lady who would snub someone for no apparent reason? Or with—"

"I beg you, sir, stop."

He bowed. "A fitting conclusion to our discussion."

"No, not yet."

"Not yet?"

Esme gathered her wits. "Your friend, Mr. Letellier, what do you do about him?" she asked.

"You must be more specific, ma'am," he replied carefully.

"Do you still wish to hinder him from pursuing Jane?"

"That is my business," he said.

"May I ask another question, then, sir? Have your actions regarding Mr. Letellier been *to* him, or *for* him?"

He raised his brows. "That is an interesting question, ma'am."

So, someone else *had* asked Lord Fitzhugh to watch over Letellier. Hadley?

Esme felt better that Fitzhugh continued on with Letellier from obligation, rather than simply the bonds of friendship. "You do not need to answer it, sir."

"Just what do you believe to be true?" he asked.

"That you are not your own man in this matter," she replied airily.

That pricked him. "We all have our duties. Who among us may claim each and every one is self-imposed?"

"You have it precisely, sir."

"You are the most maddening creature," he said, amazed.

"Am I? Truly?" Esme asked. "Would you have me insensible of any obligation other than my own whim?"

"You cannot deny you have been insensible of some obligation to me."

"I have thanked you for all you have done for me. I deny utterly that I owe you more than that. You are over twenty-one, sir, and if you did not want to have anything to do with me, you had that option all along."

"Truly one cannot wonder at . . ." He shook his head.

"At what?"

"At how so many men have fallen under your spell. Here I am, telling you I find your inconsistencies maddening, and yet I still stand here trying to puzzle them out. Is that your skill, that you become every man's mystery?"

"You must be the judge of that."

"I believe I have. Ma'am, becoming acquainted with you was an accident of circumstances, not an act of will on my part, and our ensuing conversations and actions were likewise. Should circumstances throw us together again, I intend to act as I have."

"For the sake of consistency," Esme said.

"For the sake of no longer experiencing the curious desire to throttle you and kiss you, maybe throttle you while I kiss you."

"If I got into trouble?"

He paused. "If I saw it, I would help you. But I shall not be watching over you, my lady."

He could not be plainer. No ambiguity, no shilly-shallying.

She searched him for some flaw. She wanted something she could remind herself of when she wanted him. She found no flaw, other than his belief in her detour from the straight road of propriety.

No flaw, only the desire to be held safe and secure by his strong arms, and kissed by his mobile, intoxicating mouth.

"I regret any pain I may cause you," he said formally. He bowed and strode away before Esme could draw breath in protest.

Her heart beat quickly within her. Now she did breathe, long gulps of the sweet spring air. They steadied her, but she still felt shaken by the power of his emotions and the answering feelings they had stirred in her.

Before meeting Lord Fitzhugh, Esme had thought she had lost the ability to feel desire for men. Gillespie had taught her too good a lesson. Had the feelings lain dormant, waiting only for the next kind, available man to awaken them? Or did those feelings exist for Lord Fitzhugh and only Lord Fitzhugh?

Esme thought about that while she climbed into her carriage and asked her driver to take her home, avoiding as much traffic as possible. The green of Hyde Park gave way to the ornate, gated houses of London's wealthy. Could some other gentleman, possibly residing in the blue house with white stone garlands she passed, conjure the same exquisite feelings?

Esme hoped so, for all indications painted a gloomy picture for any future between her and Lord Fitzhugh. He had been right about being dragged into her troubles, although it stung to have him think that her actions painted a true picture of her character.

At Lady Howard's house, she dragged herself up the

front stairs, feeling the very epitome of dejection. The front door opened without her having to pause, letting Esme know Williams waited just inside. She handed him her parasol, then took off her gloves, slapping them palm to palm together before passing them on.

"The conversation did not go well," Williams said.

"No, it did not." Esme tipped her head in the direction of the library, and Williams followed her in and closed the door. "I did not expect my return to society to be painless. But I did not expect to take casualties other than myself."

"You regard Lord Fitzhugh as a casualty?"

"He does, the victim of my oh-so-pernicious reputation coupled with a complete lack of sense, which forces him to have 'only the choice of playing the cockerel or the fool.' Yes, I do believe those were his exact words."

"Indeed?" Williams said, his voice frosty.

Esme shook her head. "Do not think it, sir. The devil of it is that he is right. The whole *ton* perceives him that way, and will continue to unless he gives me the widest possible berth. What other choice is there for him?"

"Suitor?"

Esme allowed her burgeoning anger at her reputation and her promise to dry her tears. "There is the earl," she reminded him. "And his Miss Bourre. So you see, there is no future to it. A moment's dalliance—how would that help him? No, nor would it help me, do I want to convince the next gentleman that there is more to me than my reputation."

Williams looked thoughtful, but not yet convinced.

She smiled, hoped he would accept it. "I shall be fine. I am not heartbroken. Now, have you learned anything useful?"

"Maybe. Gillespie entertained Letellier this afternoon. The footman I placed could not hear all the conversation, but he did gather that Gillespie had offered Letellier references to bankers, of dubious repute. Gillespie asked how much he had been able to borrow so far. Letellier said in excess of fifteen thousand pounds."

Esme's brows rose.

"Just so, ma'am."

"What could Letellier offer as collateral for such a sum?"

"I recognize some of the names mentioned, ma'am. These are not the kind of gentlemen *you* would do business with. They do not get overly nice on the subject of collateral. Were I to speculate, however, I would posit Letellier has talked up . . ." He rolled his hand to encourage Esme to supply the answer.

"Jane's dowry," Esme said flatly. She sighed. "Now I must sit down." She suited action to words, resting her forehead on her hand, and waved at Williams to sit down opposite her, in a green satin chair.

"Lady Jane's dowry would more than cover the amount in question," Williams said, "and Gillespie did congratulate Letellier on winning the race yesterday. He was not favored to win, I understand, so he made quite a bit of money from the betting. Not more than ten percent of what he currently owes, but enough to encourage. These kinds of men demand quick repayment. If Letellier were able to give them something back, he would not only have enough to encourage, he would have enough to get more."

"More?" Esme asked. Her breath came more quickly, and thus she realized how angry she was at Letellier's making money off Lord Fitzhugh's blood. Then she brought herself up short. She had neither the right nor the luxury of worrying over Fitzhugh.

He had taken those rights away, and Williams' news stripped away all luxury. She understood him perfectly.

Letellier would have to move quickly to secure Jane's dowry.

"More. Letellier is not at the end of his borrowing. He and Gillespie speculated on how much more they thought they would have to pay for Le Maitre des Brouillards."

"The Master of Mists?" Esme asked. "Who is that?"

"I am trying to find out the answer to that very question."

They regarded each other, two unlikely friends. Then Esme said, "I am sorry so much of this burden has fallen to you, sir. You never made a promise to Iddesford, but—"

"It does not need to be said."

"But I should not like to assume."

"I never believe that you do, ma'am."

Esme smiled.

"There is one more thing Letellier and Gillespie discussed, ma'am."

Williams' steady but troubled gaze told Esme whom they had discussed. "Me."

"And Miss Bourre and Lord Fitzhugh. They are neither of them happy with what they consider his inteference."

"Do they suspect me of sabotaging Letellier's pursuit of Jane?"

"No. From what our man understood, Gillespie's reward for putting Letellier in contact with those questionable gentlemen was that Letellier leave you exposed for Gillespie."

She should have known Letellier would work all the angles. "How does Miss Bourre come into it?" Esme asked, then drew in her breath sharply.

"Yes, ma'am, just so."

"Did he really say he would try to draw in Miss Bourre so that he could draw off Lord Fitzhugh?"

Williams nodded.

Esme pressed her fingers against her lips, thinking hard. "I was not going to go out tonight. Jane is promised to a private dinner party, and Letellier not invited. Could you find out where Miss Bourre is to go tonight? I have a sudden strong desire to deepen my acquaintance with her."

Williams nodded, a sparkle entering his expression. Then he sobered, said, "And Lord Fitzhugh?"

"Since Lord Fitzhugh already despises me, his despising me a little more will not kill me." At least, Esme hoped not.

Chapter Thirteen

Benedict had hoped that Lady McDonald's musicale would lift him from the black cloud he had spent the late afternoon within. His conversation with Lady Iddesford had left him frustrated and annoyed. He had wanted to know what she would profess. She had professed nothing directly, nothing with which he could contradict her. Nor had he learned anything new about Letellier.

But he had taken away an important lesson. She could be consistent in her inconsistency.

He had made the right decision to let her know he would not be taken in by her.

At least, that was the way all the sums in his head had resolved themselves. Trouble was, he had the disconcerting feeling he had recorded the wrong sums.

Lust, he told himself. *It is only lust, and lust comes and passes like the tides.*

Tonight, Benedict would hear different sums. Tonight he would give over to the passion of thought-provoking music. Tonight he would sit next to Dorrie and listen to Haydn's "Le Matin" and Mozart's Jupiter Symphony. Lady McDonald never stinted on the music, but hired a full orchestra.

The refreshments, however, were another matter entirely.

He happened upon Reversby coming into Lady Mc-Donald's.

"Ah, Fitzhugh, there you are. We are almost late together. And how did it go?"

"No more of that tonight, please," Benedict said.

Reversby withdrew a silver flask from his black coat's inside pocket and handed it to Benedict. "I have not been to Lady M.'s musicale in three years, but I remembered to come fortified. At least, fortified for you."

Benedict took a polite sip of the smooth brandy. They passed into the next room, painted a deep blue with white trim and molding, where rows of chairs filled with the chattering *ton* formed broad arcs before another grouping, empty as yet.

"Not as late as I thought," Reversby said.

"Miss Bourre promised us a seat next to her." Benedict walked up the center aisle, looking for her.

"Ah," Reversby said. Then he put a restraining hand on Benedict's arm. "I see Miss Bourre, Fitzhugh, and her mother. And Lady Iddesford, sitting between them."

Benedict felt himself go cold, then hot, then cold again.

"Have a care," Reversby said.

"Of course," Benedict replied.

All three ladies stood when he and Reversby came up. Dorrie gave Benedict her hand, and he bowed over it nicely, as though he were completely unsurprised to find her sitting next to someone she did not understand.

"Do look who has joined us, Fitzhugh. She was quite all alone." Dorrie's tone expressed disbelief and concern, bless her.

"My lady," Benedict said, and bowed. He permitted the intercession of chairs as his excuse not to take her hand. He resented her for his feeling what he felt now. He had walked away that afternoon lest he give in to his impulses and kiss her. It would be like her to try to challenge him that way. It was like her to challenge him again tonight.

She looked different, but it took him a moment to understand how.

She wore cream again, not the embroidered cream, but an unadorned thick silk. A matching shawl circled her shoulders, creating an echo with the understated headpiece that circled her hair, concealing all of its fiery splendor except for a few waves around her face. She wore only her emerald pendant for jewelry. No more than one woman in a thousand could have worn such a style to advantage.

This woman was impeccable. By simplifying herself so, she rendered herself more beautiful than any other woman Benedict had set eyes upon. Even herself previously. And as with those other, fancier clothes, she appeared to have left her ambiguities behind. Nothing but a pure, unencumbered spirit could appear anything but ill at ease in such clothes.

No, that was fantasy. Her very appearance denied the illusion. She had some connivance in motion.

But it upset him that he could no longer remember what color dress Dorrie wore, for looking at Lady Iddesford.

"My lord Fitzhugh," she said in that lovely voice which caused him to hold his breath. Then, as easily as breathing, she released Benedict and said, "And my lord Reversby."

"My lady."

"And Your Grace," Lady Iddesford said, with less warmth. She glanced at Benedict, who struggled to conceal his annoyance, both at the duke's joining them and Lady Iddesford's awareness that he would resent it.

"Good evening. Good evening," the duke said, beaming. "What a lovely evening Lady McDonald has planned."

"Do say you will join us, Your Grace," Aunt Bourre said.

Dorrie blushed.

The duke said, "My dear lady, I should be delighted, thank you. Most delighted."

Lady Iddesford smiled wryly, but whether from amusement or disappointment Benedict could not tell.

Reversby hid a snicker in a cough. And suddenly Benedict saw the humor in the whole thing. The highly proper but effusive duke served as the oddest linchpin for their company Benedict could have imagined. Their sorting themselves into a seating arrangement proved equally amusing.

"Fitzhugh," Dorrie said, "you promised to sit beside me."

"So I did," Benedict replied.

"And I would be honored if I may sit to your other side, Miss Bourre," the duke said.

"We are three gentlemen and three ladies," Aunt Bourre said. "We may alternate. His Grace, Eudora, Fitzhugh, Lady Iddesford, Reversby, and then I shall sit on the end, for who would imagine a matron such as myself needing the attention of two gentlemen?"

"Why, anyone of discernment," Reversby said, a devilish sparkle in his eyes.

"My lord," Aunt Bourre said, smiling, "I did accuse you of flirting the day before, did I not?"

"Excessive flirting, ma'am. 'Tis never a crime unless it is mere flirting. Mere flirting takes no effort and shows no one to advantage. But excessive flirting is the very thing."

"Give over, sir, do," said Aunt Bourre, chuckling.

"Then I do propose," Reversby said, "so as not to send you into peals during the performance, that you sit next to Fitzhugh, ma'am, with Lady Iddesford on your other side. I will sit on the end and protect you both from my excessive flirting and any mere flirting by interlopers."

Benedict raised a brow, tried not to appear either amused or relieved.

Dorrie brightened, and Benedict wondered at her not wanting him to sit by Lady Iddesford now when he almost certainly would have, even if Reversby and Breshirewood had not joined them.

Lady Iddesford herself had remained a silent observer throughout this conversation. Then the duke asked her, "And you, my lady? Have you a preference?"

"I am in charity with all the company before me," she said quietly, "and willing to be directed."

A matron in a high blue turban seated in front of them snorted.

Lady Iddesford lifted her chin, although she did not otherwise register she had heard it. Aunt Bourre looked on her with approval.

How well Benedict knew that look. He had spent so much of his childhood swelling with pride and good feeling under it. Without that look Benedict would have been a much bitterer man. As it was, he still hoped to find such a look once on his father's face.

Aunt Bourre's including Lady Iddesford in the same circle of approval shook Benedict deeply. Benedict had not failed to notice Lady Iddesford's lack of women friends. Then he recalled that she resided in Lady Howard's house, and Reversby was likely right that Lady Howard, who had cheerfully earned her reputation as the veriest dragon, was responsible for Lady Iddesford's entrée this Season.

If Lady Iddesford could fool Aunt Bourre and Lady Howard, had Benedict escaped but lightly to date?

Aunt Bourre said, "I commend you for your patience,

my lady. Is there not anything more dreadful than having a tin ear for the nuances of polite behavior?"

They sat down as Reversby had suggested, with the duke on the far right, then Dorrie, Benedict, Aunt Bourre, Lady Iddesford, and Reversby on the end. Reversby waggled his brows above the ladies' heads, and Benedict looked away from him lest he either laugh or mutter something cutting audible to the matron in front of them.

He had to stop thinking about Lady Iddesford.

"I do like your dress, Dorrie," Benedict said. "The pale pink becomes you."

It did, and fortunately there was a dark red pool that was Aunt Bourre's dress between himself and the exquisite cream silk, so he could make no mistake of looking along a line of light-colored dresses and thinking one dress belonged to one he should not be looking at. Benedict shook himself for thinking such convoluted thoughts.

"Indeed it does, Miss Bourre," the duke said. "You look like the roses that grow in rich profusion around my ancestral house. How happy I am every year to see them springing up again. Why . . ."

Benedict stopped listening, watched the musicians come in and seat themselves, and tried not to let his gaze slide down past Aunt Bourre's red dress. He was imagining, instead, that he could smell the faintest tickle of frangipani on the air.

Aunt Bourre moved from side to side. Finally she spoke behind her fan to Benedict, "I cannot see past this dreadful woman's turban."

"Is something the matter, Mrs. Bourre?" Lady Iddesford asked before Benedict could respond.

Aunt Bourre turned to her and likewise whispered behind her fan. The two ladies stood and changed places.

"You're quite sure, my dear?" Aunt Bourre asked.

"Oh, yes," Lady Iddesford replied, "for I usually close my eyes anyway."

Dorrie stiffened, and Benedict's heart beat so quickly he could feel it in his throat, straining against his collar and cravat. He had thought himself escaped. The sudden nearness of her, the soft, but now definite scent of her, the way she looked so different and yet so lovely, and above all, the tranquility of her beat upon his senses.

"You are comfortable, my lady?" he asked, surprised to find his voice level.

She turned that powerful gaze on him, and her emerald winked on her breast with her breathing. "I want for nothing else," she replied, ending on the softest of smiles. Then she looked away as color came into her cheeks.

Even knowing she was manipulating him, that simple betrayal made Benedict miss the first etude in a haze of longing. *Pale pink,* he said to himself. *Pale pink. Not cream. Not green. Not green. Pale pink.*

By the time the orchestra began the Haydn, Benedict thought he had himself under control. He risked an askance look at Lady Iddesford's face. As she had said, her eyes were closed, the lashes thick, smudgy shadows on her milk-pure cheeks. Her lashes were dark, not copper like her hair. How interesting, Benedict thought. And her arched brows split the color difference. He did not know if he had noticed that before.

She sat perfectly still, too, unlike Dorrie, who fidgeted with her hands or head every minute or so.

The music and her delightful fragrance wove together, creating its own unique, exotic language within Benedict. He resented it dreadfully when the symphony came to an end. Lady Iddesford opened her eyes, and clapped. Benedict pretended he did not see the tears wetting the thick lashes. It was unthinkable that such a one as Lady Iddesford could become so emotional over music.

It *was* unthinkable. That was why it was very much like her.

He turned to Dorrie and said, "Would you like some refreshment?"

"Yes," Dorrie said. "Please, although my mother reminded me not to expect much."

"Ah, yes," Breshirewood said. "It is a disappointment for the uninitiated. I remember looking at the table the first time and quite wondering what I had gotten myself into. Someone must have said something to Lady M. after all these years. Do you think she continues it from some sort of tradition? Like the weak punch at Almack's?"

Dorrie stood with Benedict. "Perhaps I should come with you?"

Benedict offered Dorrie his arm, and she took it.

"I think I would like to as well," the duke said.

Dorrie expressed her delight only a beat late.

"Lady Iddesford," Benedict said, "may I bring anything for you?"

"Oh, no, thank you. I think I shall follow His Grace's plan." She stood. "Mrs. Bourre, if there is yet time in the interval when I return, would you tell me about your home? It is Hadley-on-Barre, is that not right? Your daughter mentioned it to me once, and I should so like hear your impressions of it as well. It sounds lovely."

The four of them moved off, leaving Aunt Bourre with a satisfied smile, and Reversby with a highly ironic one. As the crowd thickened, they perforce moved in pairs, and Breshirewood and Lady Iddesford took the lead. Lady Iddesford broke her stride, as one might do to avoid tripping over someone cutting before one, except that no one was there. Everyone was crowded around the table. Benedict followed the direction of her gaze.

Gillespie stood a little apart from the refreshment table, talking to another gentleman, and, to Benedict's newfound intelligence of him, looking utterly annoyed.

Lady Iddesford turned back to Dorrie, and linked arms with her. "It is the most awful crush. Let us not lose each other."

Benedict studied her, but she looked as if butter would not melt in her delectable mouth. Was her newfound camaraderie designed to protect her from Gillespie? If that was the case, why was she here at all? She had apparently come without escort. No Letellier, and no Lady Jane. Benedict did not think she would risk so much for the music, however obviously she loved it. Nor was he convinced she would risk it to torment him. Some other mechanism was working that Benedict did not understand.

They procured some pale punch in quite the smallest glasses Benedict had ever seen and stood aside to let others have at the dubious delight.

"Yes," Breshirewood said, "I do believe she finds smaller glasses every year. She must do it to amuse herself."

"So long as the orchestra is better supplied," Lady Iddesford said.

"You were quite rapt, my lady," Dorrie said.

"Yes. I have always loved music. As a small child, I remember my mother playing and playing."

"Do you not play as well?"

"No," Lady Iddesford said, and however Benedict wanted to ask why, he recognized the finality of that reply.

Into the breach, Breshirewood said, "There is Smith-Jenkins. I am surprised he can stand, Fitzhugh."

"Why should he not?" Lady Iddesford asked.

The duke did not see Benedict's look of warning, for he was watching Smith-Jenkins. "Because Fitzhugh here gave him such a thorough drubbing today."

"Indeed?" Lady Iddesford asked.

"Nothing to the one he gave Lloyd, or Brimley, however, I assure you. Sir, I must say how much I appreciated being part of the experience. To see such a swordsman! And unflagging, too. Why, I do not think I have learned as much since I was a lad."

"You spent the day fencing?" Lady Iddesford said.

"He was challenged, my lady, by no fewer than four gentlemen eager for the sport, as was I."

"When were these challenges issued?" Lady Iddesford asked, so casually that Benedict felt a chill shiver down his spine.

Dorrie likewise understood what was what, but she was too late to prevent Breshirewood from saying, "Only last night. Is Fitzhugh not admirable to indulge them so quickly?"

"Admirable indeed," Lady Iddesford said. She had been engaging Breshirewood with those enticing eyes, keeping him talking. Now she turned her gaze on Benedict, and it resembled the one she had first directed upon him.

"How excellent to find you all here. Together," Gillespie said.

The barest shudder ran through Lady Iddesford. Benedict would not have known it at all did he not stand next to her. She said, her chin high, "Yes. Together."

"Miss Bourre," Gillespie said, "I have a connection to the primary violinist. Through my valet, oddly enough, as it happens. He is a cousin of some sort. Should you like to meet him?"

Lady Iddesford would have spoken; Dorrie would

have agreed. But Breshirewood said, "I do not believe there shall be time, Miss Bourre, before the interval ends. Let us delay such an excursion until they have concluded."

And, strangeness of strangenesses, Lady Iddesford smiled so warmly at Breshirewood that His Grace forgot to elaborate upon his sentences. "What a sound idea, Your Grace. Yes, let us return to our seats, for I did want to hear of Hadley-on-Barre from your mother, Miss Bourre."

Dorrie looked confused, but good manners prompted her to say, "Yes, of course, my lady."

"Well, then," His Grace said, "later, eh, Gillespie? Awfully kind of you."

"Your Grace," Gillespie said, brow darkening.

"Your arm, Miss Bourre?" the duke said, and tucked Dorrie's arm neatly through his own.

A smile curved one corner of Lady Iddesford's bow-shaped mouth. "Good night, Gillespie." She turned and followed Dorrie and Breshirewood.

Benedict wasted no time catching her up. "What was that?" he asked, mystified and furious. "What is all this?"

"I am not the only one crossing lines," she said, only a pace or two behind Dorrie and Breshirewood, "but when I do, I endeavor to draw new ones."

"You cannot take refuge in being cryptic."

She answered him with an achingly beautiful smile.

"I tell you, it will not help you," Benedict said.

"Mrs. Bourre, you see, we have returned early," said Lady Iddesford. "Please, do tell me of Hadley-on-Barre."

Aunt Bourre took in Lady Iddesford's too-easy manner, Dorrie's frown, Breshirewood's grin, and, no doubt, Benedict's anger, and decided to play along with the request. Lady Iddesford sat down next to her again, and listened to Aunt Bourre describe the countryside. Listening to Aunt

Bourre describe his own home, and hers—his surrogate home—to Lady Iddesford, who was so alien to all he had grown up with and knew, felt disconcerting in the extreme.

"Not good, Fitzhugh, that face you are wearing," Reversby said with high interest.

Benedict tore his gaze away from the winking emerald. "The woman does not exist without a scheme."

"You knew that."

"Yes, and I could not stand the not knowing. I thought I had put a brake upon my curiosity."

"But?"

"But—every time, the outlines of her schemes change, and I am back, wondering. It has to stop." He shook his head. "Excuse me later?"

"You will be paying a call," Reversby said.

"Yes," Benedict said, and let his gaze drown in cream.

"Lord Fitzhugh," Lady Iddesford's butler—no, *majordomo*—said as he opened the door on Benedict and the night air, "were we expecting you?"

"No," Benedict replied.

"Then I shall ask you to wait in the library, if you will, sir, while I determine if my lady can see you. Do help yourself to brandy from the sideboard. Your hat and gloves?"

Benedict handed them over. He and Williams, that was his name, observed each other in identical black and white. Williams quirked a brow.

"I know the way," Benedict said. "Thank you."

"As you will," Williams said, but he waited while Benedict crossed to the library and entered. Then he closed the door behind Benedict.

The fire burned low, but there were two large braces

of candles flanking the desk. Benedict turned away from the advertised sideboard. He needed nothing else fogging his senses. Lady Iddesford's presence all evening long had accomplished that little task nicely.

As he prowled about, passing the enormous clutter of open ledgers and papers on the desk, he almost stepped upon a letter lying loose on the floor. He picked it up, intending to drop it with the rest, but the writer's large hand forced some words to his notice.

" . . . must thank you for all the invaluable advice. Had it not been for your ready ear, your patience for my studied ineptitudes, and your wealth of contacts in the community, I and my sister would even now be living in a barn."

Benedict had read more than he should. He knew that, and dropped the letter as if the paper had fired in his fingers. But as he looked at the ledgers, he realized they were written, not in some clerk's masculine hand, but in a lighter, feminine script nonetheless confident. The notes, too, were mostly in the same sort of hand, with the occasional small note in a heavier, more crabbed hand.

Letters to Sir D, Mr. L, and Mr. A re investment in Boston must go out end of this week.

Messieurs Marston thank you for referring Lord Alphonso Dunsmore. They sent a basket of fruit. I have distributed it to the staff, per your standing orders.

And here was another mystery.

Benedict well recognized what the sums in her ledger represented. Could she afford those speculations, she could afford them at least five times over. That made her an immensely wealthy woman, likely with a fortune far exceeding Lady Jane's dowry.

The ledger revealed the notion of Letellier's investing in Lady Iddesford as ludicrous. The better question became why Letellier did not marry Lady Iddesford for her fortune.

Benedict swore softly. Yes, here was another pretty puzzle to explore with his contacts in the City when he met with them. Thank God those meetings would not be long delayed. The pressure of not knowing grew abominably.

The library door opened.

Chapter Fourteen

"You must pardon my dishabille, sir," Esme said, touching the thick braid that lay heavy on her shoulder, "but I did not want to leave you waiting while I repinned my hair. Doubtless you have a few pithy things to say and want them said so you may be gone. *Quantotius.*"

He moved away from the desk, toward the fire. "Kind of you to leave the door open."

"The front door is open, too."

"*Quantotius,*" he repeated. "As soon as possible. I thought I felt a breeze. You may close your front door. I am certain Mr. Williams will help me find the knob, should I need it."

Esme sat down on a green settee, adjusted a cushion behind her back. She was blessed if she would continue sitting up so straight, corset or no corset, this late at night. Despite the music, despite the bittersweet joy of sitting so closely to Lord Fitzhugh for so long that she could smell his spicy scent, drink in the sight of his immobile profile clear-cut against the dark blue walls, despite all that, it had been a long day. Gillespie's attempt, even forewarned, had robbed her of some priceless internal commodity that she had not yet had sufficient time to replenish.

Having him here in her borrowed library provided not even bittersweet pleasure, for he was only come to ring a peal over her. "Please, sir, say what you will and have done." She glanced pointedly at the grandfather clock in the corner.

He surprised her by sitting down opposite her and leaning his elbows upon his knees. "I suspect I owe you thanks."

Unexpectedly, unreasonably, Esme trembled. But she said, "That was hard for you to say."

He grimaced. "I shall not pretend it was easy."

"Because it is so late at night, I will be blunt and ask why you believe you owe me thanks."

"Dorrie—Miss Bourre, I mean—and Gillespie."

Esme considered what to tell him, decided on as much of the truth as she could. "Mr. Williams learned that Gillespie would try to . . . scare . . . Miss Bourre a little."

"Why?"

"Gillespie did not know you had quite written me off this afternoon," Esme said, and held her breath, lest the tears tickling within her nose would use air as an excuse to come to full life.

"He thought to divide my attention," Fitzhugh said.

"Yes," Esme said.

"That is heinous."

"Yes."

Lord Fitzhugh looked into the fire, and the dull flickering light played weirdly upon his face. Then he looked back to her. "He must still want you very badly to do such a thing."

Esme compressed her mouth. She did not want to think about how badly Gillespie wanted her.

"Why?"

"Really, sir, is that not obvious?"

"Not anymore."

His answer could have lifted Esme's spirits, but she

know where this would lead. He would again ask her why she stayed in Town when Gillespie was there, why she clung to her apparent revenge despite all the pain and consternation it brought to others, and why she had lived her life as he thought she had.

She could no more answer such questions tonight than she could have this afternoon. He would never believe it, anyway.

"I accept your thanks, sir, but they were not necessary. I was in your debt."

"You said that once before. In this very room. Are you always so sore interested in balancing your books?" He gestured to the desk.

Esme looked there, sharply. She had been working there that afternoon while waiting to make her appointment with him in the park. Williams had not put her ledgers and accounts and correspondence away. That was right. She had told him to leave them out, that she would finish tomorrow when she felt more the thing.

"No one else does them for me, sir," she said.

"Not Mr. Williams, the former don?"

"Of history, remember?"

"Historians often search through old accounting ledgers to measure importance by how people chose to spend their money."

"Mr. Williams had a friend, a fellow don, who helped him with that aspect of his research, although since his study was classical warfare, he had not the same need. Now, when he needs something, he asks me. And why are we speaking of Mr. Williams, when I should be asking why you spied on me?"

"I did not mean to. I picked up a letter on the floor, and some things caught my eye. You have quite a few irons in the fire, my lady. Have you had any success in recouping the money you spent in Europe?"

Esme smiled thinly. "Yes, that is one of the rumors about me, propagated, no doubt, by my daughter-in-law because she wants to think it so. It would please her no end to believe that I must borrow this house from dear Lady Howard so that I may spend my last few hundred pounds on my dresses."

"You lay the blame for all gossip upon the countess, then."

"Of course not. She has not the imagination."

Lord Fitzhugh's lips quirked. Then he frowned.

"But we are not talking about my reputation tonight," she said. "I have had quite enough from your family on the subject of my reputation."

"My *family?*"

"Your august father, sir, told me in no uncertain terms that I should not lash my dreadful talons into you."

"Did he?" Lord Fitzhugh asked, very still.

"You did not know?"

"No. I did not. When?"

"After the race. He gave me back my handkerchief."

Lord Fitzhugh nodded as if one puzzle had been solved.

"You should thank him for looking out for your best interests," Esme said. "Had your virtue not stood up to mine, he could have been a valuable second line of defense."

Lord Fitzhugh stood, looked like he was not quite sure what to do with himself.

"The brandy is on the sideboard," Esme said, leaning her neck back to look up at him and pointing over her shoulder in the general direction.

"No, thank you," he said, and sat back down. "I am sorry. About my father, I mean. He tends to the impulsive."

"I do recall thinking you must resemble your mother.

But it is of no matter. Impulsive or deliberate, you both came to the same conclusion. So, as it has worked out, I thank him, too, for had I not had that reminder of who and what I was, I doubt I should have taken your speech this afternoon as well as I did. I am out of practice with being dismissed."

"You would have me believe your regard for yourself is the only thing bruised?"

"Asking me anything else presumes quite a lot for someone who has suspected me of any manner of mischief, do you not think? To forestall argument, we may, *temporarily*, dispense with your summations of this afternoon. That done, what do you know of me? Come, volunteer your opinions and observations.

"No? Then I shall provide some." She held up a finger. "I would marry my step-granddaughter to your friend Letellier for sheer spite." She put up a second finger. "I indulge in liberties with gentlemen who are not my near relations." A third. "I inspire young men to desire to accost you with swords. I cause gossip. And from looking over my ledgers, you will have decided I am of a subtle, competitive spirit that would not easily take no for an answer."

She smiled, put her splayed hand down. "Or do I flatter myself? You may strike subtle. Confess, now, my lord, you do not know anything for sure about me, except that I will be true to my purposes, whatever those purposes might be."

"I consider you the most infuriating, maddening, mystifying woman I know," he said, with something like awe.

"*Woman* usually suffices. The adjectives are redundant." Esme was, she realized, enjoying this. She was enjoying clubbing him over the head with her reputation. She did not like who she was very much of a sudden.

"I am sorry," she said, and stood. "You have given your

thanks, and I have acknowledged them. I hope tonight's display will be sufficient to discourage Gillespie from continuing in this line. You will inform your friend Reversby, if you have not already, so I do not think I need worry about Miss Bourre."

He had stood with her. "You do not need to worry about Miss Bourre. How," he said, then broke off, compressed his mouth, and resumed, "how did Mr. Williams learn of Gillespie's plans?"

"Mr. Williams is a very resourceful man."

"Even though he cannot balance a ledger."

"Even though."

He took a step closer to her, and Esme thought that if she took too deep a breath, her breasts would graze his white waistcoat. "Did you but treat me honestly, you could trust me to do what is right," he said, almost in a whisper.

"I know," Esme whispered back. "That is the problem."

She knew he would kiss her. His intent desire showed plain. Esme held her breath as his hand set aside her heavy braid to stir the tendrils at her nape. Trembling, she allowed it. Desire coursed through her as his lips gently brushed hers, desire that would not lie quietly. Her sigh was all the encouragement he needed, and his mouth buffeted hers with the sweetest of gales.

Esme gave in to her own desire, kissing him as she wanted to be kissed in return. Her greedy hands explored his back, then pulled him closer to her. She wanted him closer to her.

His indrawn hiss of pain made her pull back. "What is it?" she asked.

He shook his head, would have kissed her again, but Esme stepped back, her arm extended and braced against his shoulder. "No more. *You* cannot have any more. Which one of the ones you fenced with today did that to you? Gave you that bruise?"

Fitzhugh collected himself, straightened his shoulders. "Sommers. It was my fault, really. I tripped over my own feet and fell against Lloyd's boot."

She ran her fingertips down his cheek, felt its dear, firm roughness. "No. It was not your fault. It was mine." She drew her hand back before he touched her. "I shall try to stay out of your way from now on. Any further interference will be unintentional."

"Must it be like this?"

"Yes," Esme said.

He accepted that with a bare nod. At the library door he paused and said, "I wish things could be different."

Esme nodded, fearing to speak, and let him go. The front door closing gently behind him sounded with the loud finality of fate.

Benedict, groggily following the clink of cutlery against china toward the breakfast room of Hadley House, stopped abruptly and put his hand out against the dark-patterned wallpaper for balance.

"—beautiful causes all kinds of troubles for one—" That was Aunt Bourre.

His father's voice rumbled indistinctly in reply.

"But Mama, look what she has done with it." That was Dorrie. "She can be charming, true, but her reputation cannot be built on air."

Benedict closed his eyes and took a deep, calming breath. They were indeed discussing Lady Iddesford. After leaving her, Benedict had walked the London streets for some time, knowing he should not sleep. Indeed, he had not fallen asleep until dawn, but he did not resent his dry eyes and general befuddlement.

Benedict had the unsettling feeling that he had seen Lady Iddesford as she truly was, not just as a beauty, or a lady notorious, but an agile, honorable intelligence. Benedict knew what it took to research and manage the speculations she was engaged in, because compared to her, he was a dabbler.

Maybe he had seen only what she intended him to. Maybe she wanted the bare form of her argument against herself, as she had held a finger up for each point, to indicate a reflection of someone who thought as long and hard as he did himself.

Likewise she had told him of his father's opinion, as though knowing that would absolve Benedict of his angry words of the afternoon. She had all but spoon-fed him his excuse to leave. And, although he flattered himself by thinking so, he did not believe she had wanted him to leave.

Maybe.

The question remained, however, why such a woman involved herself in Letellier's plans. Her lack of pretense had not prevented her from reticence. She would not say why his doing the right thing should so worry her.

She had something up her sleeve, some part of this game that she had not revealed.

The notion had inflamed him, made her more desirable to him. He had not thought it possible, but as he had kissed her, he had felt himself connecting to her, body, mind, and soul. He had meant every word when he had said he wished things could be different, for he could not bear the thought of another gentleman having had the same feelings he had had with her as a willing coparticipant.

I hope you have not gulled me, my lady. I wish I did not have to hope.

His father's voice rumbled into the hall. "Fitzhugh will be held to account. Don't you worry there."

Benedict pushed off the wall and went into the breakfast room. Three faces registered various amounts of surprise, chagrin, and annoyance. Benedict took time pouring himself coffee and adding sugar. He sat down, said pleasantly, "What must I be held to, sir?"

"I'll have none of that tone from you, sir," his father began in rising accents.

Aunt Bourre touched Hadley's wrist, her blue gaze on Benedict. "You were seen, Benedict. Last night. Outside Lady Howard's house. And, I am told, it was not the first time."

Dorrie looked away from him.

"Yes," Benedict said, controlling his hurt. "I went to thank her."

"Is that what gentlemen call it these days?" his father asked.

"No, sir. It related to that other matter."

His father and Aunt Bourre exchanged an uneasy look.

"Dorrie," Benedict said. "Dorrie? Will you not look at me? Well, then, continue to believe the worst of me if you want to, but do heed my words. Do not allow yourself to be alone either with Mr. Gillespie or Letellier. Stay close to Reversby or Breshirewood, I beg you."

"All these years I thought I knew you, Benedict," Dorrie said and fled the room.

Into the shocked silence, Benedict said, "I mean it, Aunt."

"Do you not offer yourself as well?" she asked him.

Benedict's smile twisted. "Did I not think she might as well upbraid me as listen to me."

"You truly think Alexander could be a danger to her?"

"I think, witting or unwitting, Letellier is a danger

to everyone around him, ma'am. I am sorry to pain you so, for you tried to take him in as you did . . . . But there it is."

Aunt Bourre nodded. "Excuse me, Hadley. I shall see to Eudora."

When they were alone, his father drew out his watch chain. It clinked through his fingers. "Well, now, speak plainly."

Benedict poured himself another cup of coffee, added milk with the sugar. "Lady Iddesford learned that Gillespie would attempt to scare Dorrie some way."

"Some way?"

"She was not specific, but the more I have seen of Gillespie lately, the less I have liked of him."

"His father was a horse's arse," Hadley said, "and a bully. Do you link him and Letellier?"

"Regretfully," Benedict replied. "I am not at all certain I will be able to continue the task you asked of me, Father. I have never seen Letellier so . . ."

"Well?"

"Extreme, sir, for lack of a better word."

"Because of Iddesford's Folly?"

Benedict flinched from the name, but said, "I do not think so. He seems to regard her as a piece of jewelry, or someone who can do things for him, rather than a person in her own right. Yes, that is very much like it. They are business partners."

"And the business is Lady Jane Compton."

"And I wonder . . ." Benedict put his coffee cup down, and sat up straight. An idea came to him, so startling, and yet so obvious now that he knew what he knew of Lady Iddesford, that he could scarce credit himself for not seeing it before.

"What do you wonder, sir?"

"I am the biggest idiot," Benedict whispered.

Hadley thumped the table with the flat of his hand, making the crockery dance. "I said, what do you wonder, sir?"

"I wonder why Lady Iddesford has not been the best, most organized partner Letellier has ever had."

His father harrumphed. "She's a woman, ain't she? Pretty to look at, but—"

"Excuse me, sir," Benedict said, standing. "I have to go. There's something I have to find out straight away, appointment or no appointment."

"What, before you've thought for a quarter hour on what to have for your breakfast? Never seen you—"

"Sir," Benedict said, and left his father spluttering.

"You have not done for me what you promised you would do, my dear," Letellier said with one of his nasty smiles.

"Do not, pray, be more specific," Esme said under her breath. "We are in public."

Every ball seemed to be getting larger, the decorations more elaborate, the dresses more ornate. She and Letellier stood with their backs to a wall, and she could not see halfway across the room for the press.

"You, my dear, are very public. Naughty, naughty Lady Iddesford, caught leading a respectable man astray. Only look at how Lady Wells-Stokes gives you the gimlet eye."

"Lady Wells-Stokes has been cross-eyed all her life. Regardless, such looks no longer bother me."

"I daresay they do not."

No, Esme thought, but her hostess's comment had as Esme had come in and thanked her for the invitation. "I did not need to trade in a favor from Lady Howard," Lady Tolling had said with a sly smile. "I detest Augusta

Iddesford, and I do not launch my daughter for another four years. Do your worst, my dear."

Esme shook off the memory, said, "And did I actually believe you felt as you represent, I should be quaking."

"Oh?" Letellier asked, amused.

"Indeed, for it would mean one's black character could be redeemed, and then mayhap *I* would have to start attending church."

Letellier laughed, but Esme could not ignore the edge to it. "It is taking too much time," he said.

"Do I not remember telling you it would take time for the *family* to recognize the inevitability of your suit?"

"You remember everything, I am sure, my dear, but I think we both know where we were headed."

Yes, you snake. She kept her voice cool, though, and played absently with the fan upon her wrist, as she said, "I would have preferred their going to the expense of a wedding, rather than your heading North. Gretna Green is so . . . passé."

"But quick, and cheap." He kissed her gloved hand. "One week. Do you think it can be done?"

"I could do it," Esme said, trying not to shudder. "If I did not have to worry about Gillespie following me about."

"What's the matter with Gillespie?"

"He lacks the basic intellect of your friend Merton, for one," Esme said.

Letellier snickered. "Gillespie does well enough for himself. He's very good with money."

Esme shrugged. "Whenever Gillespie gets involved, your friend honest Fitzhugh does, too, and that does tend to force me to change my plans from true. And so we have Lady Wells-Stokes and her gimlet eyes."

Letellier's eyes glinted. "I will ponder the matter. Gillespie is, after all, his own man."

"We know what we are about, then."

"*I* know. I hope you do, too."

Esme moved away from him, heading toward the punch bowl. Soon she picked up a train of gentlemen, Mr. Smith-Jenkins and Mr. Sommers among them. Although she wanted to dislike them for causing Fitzhugh such a bruise, it was a pleasant enough way to spend a few dances until Jane arrived. Hard to imagine anyone else fitting into the ballroom, but there it was.

The crowd, always parting and resolidifying, gave Esme a glimpse of Miss Bourre speaking closely to Letellier. "Gentlemen, pray excuse me," she said quickly, and hurried across the floor, not oblivious to the looks of dislike or admiration that followed her.

"Why, Miss Bourre, fancy seeing you here, talking to Mr. Letellier. Of course, you are childhood friends, too, are you not?"

"Think on what I have said, dear Dorrie," Letellier said. Then he gave Esme a wicked smile. "My lady." He slunk off.

Miss Bourre looked like she would cry.

"Miss Bourre, do come with me," Esme said, for the sake of the crowd. "Your dress has a tear, but we may fix it in a trice." She linked arms with the girl, who started to resist. "Control yourself," she said between clenched teeth and a smile. "We're being watched."

"You would know about that, would you not, Lady Iddesford?" the girl asked bitterly. "Do you not know that you are the very last person I wish to see?"

"I did not know it, but if you do not be still, the entire room will know it."

"And why should I care?" Miss Bourre asked.

"Because *your* reputation has nowhere to go but down."

They progressed to the hall off the ballroom, where

one could either go out the door, proceed right to the card room, or go left to what was likely the ladies' withdrawing room and another door. A drawing room?

Yes, dim except for a low fire. A private room, for the family, with family portraits occupying all available wall space. Between the pictures and the absence of light, Esme was hard pressed to make out the room's colors.

"We will wait here a few minutes, then go back to Lord Reversby. Why did you leave Lord Reversby, anyway?"

"I do not need to be minded like a child."

"If you will insist on speaking to Letellier right now, you do."

"You do."

"True," Esme said. "But when he speaks to me and I do not like what he says, I can keep my temper. Did he offer you insult?"

"No," Miss Bourre said. "But I would wager that what he said *would* make you lose your temper."

Chapter Fifteen

"Such provocation, Miss Bourre. You may consider yourself asked."

"Very well," the girl said, tossing her head. "Alexander told me you have made Fitzhugh a laughingstock. He was seen coming from your house last night—oh, excuse me, *Lady Howard's* house—and once before."

"Yes, Letellier told me that. He was not the first one, either, so I was not surprised. Nor, I think, were you."

"No, but that does not matter. Do you not have one shred of decency? Do you not care that until he met you, Fitzhugh was never the object of gossip or speculation?"

"He is a grown man, Miss Bourre, and capable of making his own decisions."

"He is the very best of men. Did you know we grew up together almost like brother and sister? It was the rare day indeed that he was not in my house before breakfast and not leaving it until well after dinner. I know him better than any other woman. Just because he does not speak in long, grandiloquent sentences does not mean he feels less. To the contrary, he has the most heightened sense of feeling of any man I know. He is honorable, noble, and not to be sullied by the likes of you."

Her heart beating rapidly, Esme said, "And if he proposed to you tonight, would you reject him again?"

"He told you that?"

"He did not have to." Esme forced herself to sit down on a settee. Miss Bourre would not run back into Letellier's arms again, not while she was on this subject.

"Then how did you figure that out?"

"Why is it so important to you to know?" Esme asked. She felt a disconcerting internal twinge, like she was reaching too hard and too far for something out of reach.

"I had no idea how he felt . . . last summer. He surprised me. Then he left and we had little word of him until his father asked him to come to Town this spring. He has not seemed uneasy to be about me. We resumed our friendship. Then he began being with you, and I . . ."

You realized someone else might like to play with your toy, Esme thought and upbraided herself.

The girl lifted her chin. "Alexander told me it was too little, too late. He told me about last night. He said you had Benedict quite wrapped around your little finger."

"Letellier is nothing if not kind."

"I have never liked him," Miss Bourre said with distaste, "for all Mother and the earl said we should pity him for his father dying and him and Madame Letellier having to leave France. But I thought that if what I felt was so obvious to Letellier, that it might be as obvious to Benedict—"

"Lord Fitzhugh?"

The girl blushed. "Yes. But I do not know how to tell."

Esme wanted to throttle the girl. Did Miss Bourre not notice the difference between Fitzhugh's frowning from anger and frowning from puzzlement? His lips quirked up when he was merely puzzled, although both times his brow looked as dark. Did she not recognize his true smile, the one that started slowly, deepened, then left a lopsided dent in his right cheek? Did she not register the glimmer and glitter of desire in his warm eyes, the way he could surround her with his body, make her feel protected and powerful and wildly weak all at the same time, even when yards separated them?

Maybe she did not.

And likely something of what Esme had thought had shown on her face, for Miss Bourre said, "So you might as well stay away from him, because he's going to be mine. His father would never let him have anything to do with you if it were not for Le—" She clapped a hand over her mouth.

"I perfectly comprehend the earl's feelings on this matter," Esme said, to salve her pride. Once she had Jane safe from Letellier—by Jane's own decision—she would leave London to rejoin Lady Howard in the North. Fitzhugh would propose to this girl and live happily ever after. It was what he wanted. It would help heal the breach she suspected existed between father and the perfect son.

"Well, then?" Miss Bourre asked.

"I have already warned Lord Fitzhugh of my vile nature," Esme said. "What he does about it is his business."

"You would do nothing more?"

"I cannot do everything."

"What do you mean by that?" Miss Bourre asked suspiciously.

"If Lord Fitzhugh yet labors under the impression that you would not accept him, then he will be more inclined to pursue other interests. Even interests that have no future."

"You do not know Benedict very well if you can say such a thing."

Esme shrugged. "The next step is yours, Miss Bourre."

"But how does a woman go about declaring her feelings like that? I am not you. I do not crook my little finger."

Esme realized she should be exceedingly annoyed. She had never appreciated presumption or pushiness. She had certainly never appreciated her reputation. Nor had she ever appreciated the sloppy way it made people make assumptions about what she was and how she thought.

But she was not annoyed. Well, maybe the tiniest bit. Mostly what she was, was sad, and tired. For the life of her, she could not understand why.

"Then find something else to crook," Esme said.

The girl gasped.

Esme's spirits lifted a little. "That can be taken metaphorically, you know."

"Do you know, I thought I might like you. Once."

"If disliking me prompts you to do what you consider necessary to your future happiness, by all means, dislike me. But do not disregard me."

Miss Bourre tipped her head, and a frown of perplexity replaced her frown of anger. Then she nodded once, curtly. "Very well. I will do as you say."

"Good. That is settled. Now until you find Lord Fitzhugh, do stay away from Mr. Letellier and Mr. Gillespie."

"Benedict would not tell me why, either," the girl said.

You make very free with his name. "Doubtless he does not want to alarm you. It may all yet come to nothing." Esme stood. "Let us return to the ballroom. We have fixed your flounce."

Each wrapped in private thoughts, they returned to the ballroom to find a greater throng than before. The heat of dancing and candles smote Esme. Miss Bourre took out her fan and applied it. But fans could do nothing against the clattering noise. It was an interval between dances, for no music played.

Esme smiled and nodded to Miss Bourre, looking about her, and striking off on her own. She had to see whether Jane had arrived, to assess the likelihood of dear, steady Charles's impetuous grandchild rushing off to Gretna Green to elope with a snake like Letellier.

But before she made it more than five steps, Miss Bourre gasped. Esme looked back over her shoulder, beheld Fitzhugh.

"Fitzhugh, how I have looked for you this evening!" Miss Bourre exclaimed, stepping close to him.

But Fitzhugh was not looking at Miss Bourre. He met Esme's gaze instead. Did Esme imagine it, or was there also a rather triumphant, knowing expression in his gray eyes? Then he took his childhood friend's arm, and one of those rare, complete smiles spread over his face, ending in that lopsided dent in his right cheek.

She could not hear what he said over the crowd. She did not need to.

The combination of Miss Bourre's happiness and Lord Fitzhugh's expression made Esme freeze like any startled animal. Realization washed over her colder . . . and with more driving force than any winter rain.

What had she done?

She had told Miss Bourre how to pursue the man Esme herself loved. She loved Lord Fitzhugh. She loved his lopsided smile, his quiet authority, his questing lips, even his suspicions of her.

When had the heady combination of desire and appreciation for a worthy opponent changed into love? Had it changed, or merely deepened? Admixed? Grown? Transmuted? Had it happened only because she had seen him happy, as he was with Miss Bourre? Did love reveal itself only in self-pity?

Only years of self-control kept her from turning back, taking the steps toward him, crooking the finger that might still induce him to come to her. As she walked through the crowd, she cursed every experience that had made such control part of her. She cursed every time she had listened, with no expression on her face, to her father berate her. She cursed every time she had stood in public

and known women derided her behind fans and colon-
nades. And she cursed every time she had stood on
Charles's arm and let the rest of the Iddesford family
sneer at her.

Why had she made it so easy for the girl?

Rhetorical question. She knew why she had made it
easy for the girl. She had made it easy for her so it would
be easy for him. He needed to forget Esme. It would be
better for him, and better for her to leave this glittering,
transitory world of hostility and pettiness.

The musicians were tuning up. Esme needed to find
Jane. It did not matter that loss made her hollow and too
much thought made her dizzy.

Then strong arms were behind her, almost pushing her
onto the dance floor. She knew it was Lord Fitzhugh before she looked back, and a satisfaction so deep it
bordered on joy welled up within her. But no matter how
sweet the feeling, she could not give in to it.

"We were done, you and I," she said.

"We were, but—"

"Where is Miss Bourre?"

"She is promised to Breshirewood."

Esme could not contain the tremulous twitching of her
lips. Still, she managed to say, "We *are* done, and I must
find Lady Jane and—"

"And sabotage your own plans some more?" he asked.

She looked as startled as she looked beautiful. Achingly
beautiful, although she had returned to the gaudier style
she used for balls. A deep green dress, cut low across perfect, creamy breasts, and the barest of hair coverings,
topped by a net shimmering with emeralds, such were the
stuff of desire.

Such was Lady Iddesford.

The dreadfully stuffy room did not appear to bother her, but it bothered Benedict readily enough. No matter how he might try to breathe, he found it difficult. Or maybe that was because he was near her and desire clotted his brain.

Eventually he would work past this desire. With Dorrie, he felt comfortable. She was every memory of his childhood, every striving after approval. With Lady Iddesford, he felt invigorated, overstimulated. But now Benedict had learned enough to realize that it was the seeking restlessness of her, as much as her beauty, that drew him.

Being so close to her burned. He already burned to know the names of every gentleman she had ever been with, to seek them out and challenge them. He recognized these as visceral feelings, the kinds of feelings his father would have, and completely at odds with his own character. Still, he could not stop feeling them.

The musicians began playing a waltz, and he pulled her into it. Startled or not, she moved with grace, her skirts swaying against enticing ankles, her hands light and firm. She was his to be led, at least for this little while.

And she gave herself over to him. As his hands crossed her back, she sighed, looked as entranced as she had during the musicale.

It did not last long, perhaps half a circling of the floor, and then she tipped her head back and said, "What did you say?"

"Oh, no, my lady, you shall not wriggle out of this by pretending ignorance."

"Of what am I ignorant?"

He grinned. "You are the mistress of misdirection, so it did take me until this morning to puzzle it out."

"Really, sir, you are not being kind."

"No, my lady, it is you who have been unkind. You would tempt me with your very luscious self and try to run rings 'round me. Why, even now, when we attempt a conversation, all I can do is marvel at how gracefully you dance, and how neatly you fit within my arms."

"I cannot deny I like fitting here. What would be the point in such protests? You see, I am not always a mistress of misdirection."

"You enchant me." The words came from him without thought.

She stiffened. "It will be temporary, sir. Let us make that quite clear now. I do not form lasting . . . obligations."

Benedict did not like her reminding him. "Very well," he said, "let us return to our original subject. I could wait no longer, so have spent today shamelessly walking into offices of acquaintances in the financial world. Without appointments, may I add. I find we have many acquaintances in common. Rothschild sends his regards."

"You spoke to Mr. Nathan Rothschild unannounced?"

"Yes."

"He never sends *regards*."

"I edited the words to give you the spirit."

"He has a boorish spirit, too."

"True, but he respects you. He, among others, confirmed what I determined this morning."

He had to spin her around so they could promenade.

"Do not keep me in suspense."

"I wondered how any woman who could control the resources you do, who could take the risks you do, all cool-headed, could have made so many mistakes getting Lady Jane and Letellier together. The incident in the park stood out as a particularly stark example. You may not know this, but Miss Bourre and I went back to that glen and found Letellier waiting."

To his surprise, she smiled. "He was mad, wasn't he?"

"Spitting," Benedict said, and they laughed.

"You will not tell him?" she asked, sobering. "I need him

to think me marginally competent for a little while longer."

"Is that what worried you about my doing the right thing?"

"No."

"I want to help you."

"No matter what I am planning?" she asked. "Your father depends on you to stand Letellier's friend."

"How did you—oh. Dorrie."

"She let it slip, not knowing to whom she revealed relevant information. Do not blame her, I beg you. But I mean to separate Jane from Mr. Letellier in such a way that she will never regard him again. She has to be made to see him as I do."

"I did not want to believe you desired revenge, although from conversations today I have learned something about the lengths to which the current earl has gone to contest his father's will."

"He cannot break it. Iddesford worked very hard on it, and he had much more native wit than John."

"Then why?"

"Very simple, really. I promised Iddesford I would look after his granddaughter."

"But from all accounts, he held you in contempt," Benedict said, confused.

Lady Iddesford turned that wonderfully measuring look upon him. "You ask too many questions. It is history now. Answer me mine. Will you interfere? Can you allow me to lead, no matter what you may think of the direction?"

"So long as you do not expose yourself to any danger."

"Then why are we dancing?"

The question caught him squarely in the heart. He did not know how to answer.

She blushed, not Dorrie's kind of blush, from the

throat up, but a rosy glow high upon her cheeks. He had never seen Lady Iddesford blush, and the sight transfixed him as surely as her words had.

"I am sorry. I have embarrassed you," she said. "Do not mind me. The strain of the past week . . ."

"No one looking at you would ever know."

"No," she said, but an inexplicable sadness crept over her.

They finished their dance in charged silence, Benedict unable to ignore the scent of her, the graceful line of her shoulder, her delectable collarbone, the poignant bend of her elbow revealed by the edge of her glove. At the same time as his senses felt overwhelmed, his mind galloped along with questions.

Why had she made a promise to a man who despised her? How had she known what Letellier was without meeting him? And why had his compliment appeared to depress her?

"I must find Jane," she said, when the dance had ended. She let go of his arm, and the world slowed.

"If she is not spoken for, I will ask her to dance. Would that help you?"

This time she did not mask her stark speculation. He imagined he could see her toting up figures in different columns. "Yes," she said after a pause. "Yes, it certainly would. Yes, Augusta will not know quite what to do with you."

And before his eyes, she turned into the sparkling, shallow creature she had been the night of Lady Tunbridge's ball. She looped her hand through his arm, batted her lashes, and said with excessive bonhomie, "The lady of your dreams stands by the far wall, sir."

No, she holds my arm.

Swept up, Benedict soon found himself bowing before

the stout figure of Augusta, current Lady Iddesford, and felt again all the irony of the situation.

"My dear Augusta, only look who I found. You know Lord Fitzhugh, do you not? Yes, of course you do. Do you know he and dear Jane met in the park the other day? They had such a lovely conversation. Dear Jane told me all about it just last night." Lady Iddesford leaned in toward her daughter-in-law. "Now you see, I have saved him for her, snatched him from the very clutches of countless other women." She fanned herself, and lowered her voice even further. "I have quite brought him into fashion, don't you know."

Benedict pretended not to hear this last.

The older Lady Iddesford did not know quite what to make of this, so she settled into belligerent suspicion. Scathing words rested on her lips, but before she could give them form, Lady Jane sailed up on some gentleman's arm. Neither her mother nor her partner saw the subtle communication of eyebrow raises between Lady Jane and Lady Iddesford, but between them, they managed to get Benedict and Lady Jane on the dance floor.

"I do not know what Lady Iddesford has planned," Benedict said as they formed the line. "We must let her surprise us."

Lady Jane's face lit up, but good manners prevented her from saying how much she wished she were dancing with someone else. She conversed about the company and how she found London, and they passed a nicer half-hour than Benedict usually experienced with a debutante.

Then, as the dance concluded, Lady Jane said, "Dear Cousin Esme must be making long-range plans. I half expected Mr. Letellier to cut in on us. I wonder did she learn such underhandedness from dear Grandpapa."

"You call the earl underhanded?" Benedict asked, striving for a light note to cover his interest.

"He snuck me any number of presents and treats that Mama did not wish me to have. He could do it with quite a straight face, too. I miss him." She laughed. "But that was another time. I daresay we all look back happily on our childhoods."

Another time, Benedict thought. *History.*

He returned Lady Jane to her mother, and spent a few minutes in polite conversation. The dowager Lady Iddesford had moved away, having accomplished this purpose and likely needing to accomplish yet another. Then he found Reversby, and said, "Can I depend on you to continue looking after Dorrie? I have a most pressing errand."

"You are the very master of errands," Reversby said. "Righty-ho."

Benedict squeezed his shoulder. Twenty minutes later he stood in Lady Howard's foyer facing Lady Iddesford's Mr. Williams, his hat and gloves taken away by a curious footman.

"My lady is not at home," Williams said.

"I know."

Williams' brows rose impressively.

"I deeply regret to say that history was never my subject, sir. I inclined more to mathematics and natural philosophy. At the moment, however, I find myself quite interested in the subject and thought to discuss some of the finer points with you. If you would be so disposed, sir, that is."

Williams spread his arm, indicating Benedict should precede him into the library. A nice fire was laid, and candles burned brightly. Benedict even fancied he could yet smell a trace of frangipani.

Williams poured two brandies from the sideboard and handed one to Benedict, who accepted it from politeness.

They sat down on the green settees by the fire. "Are you

interested in a particular war?" Williams asked. "They were my specialty, the wars of classical Greece and Rome."

"I am interested in more recent history," Benedict said.

Williams set his brandy down and sat back, spreading an arm along the settee's back. He nodded. "I thought so. As to that, then, my lord, you may not find me much of a historian."

"But possibly a witness," Benedict said.

"You are reputed to be something of a swordsman," Williams said. "That was a shrewd thrust."

Still sitting, Benedict bowed. "Thank you, sir. It is my last, I fear. Beyond that, I do not know what questions to ask."

Williams considered, and Benedict let him. Then Williams said, "Let us imagine for the sake of argument that a man had everything: a respectable, interesting position as a don of classical history, and despite the requirements not to have a wife and family, he yet had a family of sorts, for his sister and her beautiful children lived a street away. Let us further imagine that he lost this family, the only one he would ever have, to a carriage accident. Then let us imagine he looked at his celibate life through the lens of grief, saw it as just more questing after things long dead."

Benedict dared say nothing.

Williams continued. "He would lose his position to drink. Let us last imagine that after wandering the streets of London for weeks he found himself waking up from a drunken stupor to find a woman who could rival Helen of Troy for beauty looking down on him, not with disgust, but with concern."

Benedict twitched a little at the Helen of Troy description.

"This man had, the previous night, snuck into the lady's mews. He would have shambled off, for there was still enough of the man he had been within him to be ashamed, but she insisted he be brought, stinking, inside, for a warm meal. When he had finished his meal, she returned.

"She said if he would promise not to drink another drop, he was welcome to stay in her household. She also warned him he would endure the hardest three days of his life, but it was his choice entirely. When he agreed, saying, *'Etiam'*—for they had been having this conversation in Latin, one of the things he had thought he had abandoned forever—and she replied, *'Bene,'* he made a promise to himself to regain the man he had been.

"He suffered bitterly those next three days, as she had foretold, and he knew not whether it was day or night, but lived for the times when she would sit by him and read Ovid.

"Then he woke that night, not wishing for wine or spirits, but hungry. He was slicing cheese to put on bread when he heard the scream."

Benedict tensed.

Williams looked at the snifter of brandy upon the table before him, then at Benedict. "I took that animal off her, and threw him from the house. Into the very same mews from which she had rescued me."

"Gillespie."

"Gillespie," Williams said. "It did not take me long, sober—and clean, finally—to assess the situation. She proposed she leave, travel, and I agreed with her. It seemed reasonable. Even if her father had been alive, she had no family, and she could conduct her affairs by correspondence wherever she was. That is what we have done, until she met Lady Howard in Portugal, and Lady Howard asked her to come winter with her in Yorkshire. Of course I monitored Gillespie's movements, so we knew he and

Letellier were friends. Then we discovered Letellier's interest in Lady Jane, and my lady would have none of that."

"She said she made a promise to her late husband," Benedict said.

"I cannot be a witness to that, sir. It was before my time. She found me after her mourning was done. But from the correspondence I read between her father and the late earl to arrange the marriage, I would infer he loved her very deeply. Whatever he told the family."

"And whatever she did not."

"My lady learned early to keep her own counsel, I do believe."

Benedict's protest of confusion died on his lips. He remembered her trying to fix the mask on the statue.

"Did your father never beat you?" he had asked her.

"Not as much as he could have," she had replied.

Benedict stood. "Thank you. Sir." He set the glass down. "It is a shame we wasted two glasses of brandy."

"It is not a shame," Williams said, standing. "For I could never drink mine. I poured it against the near possibility of desiring to toss it on you."

"It is easy, is it not, to assume?"

"It would be, were I not a man of reflection."

Benedict accepted the hit with a rueful smile. With a bow, he quit Lady Howard's house. He had not asked the question he had wanted answered. He had not needed to. He knew the secret of Lady Iddesford's reputation. Now the only question remaining was what he should do about it.

Chapter Sixteen

Benedict first, however, had to speak to his father about some other interesting things he had learned that afternoon. He found his father in their library newly returned from an excursion into Kent.

This time Benedict drank deeply from his brandy. "How is Madame Letellier?"

"Not well. There is no possibility of moving her here to London, as I had wished." His father smoothed the maroon chair arm, and Benedict followed the move, slow stroke after slow stroke.

"It may be as well she is away from here," Benedict said. "Sir, I spent some hours today with my associates in the financial community."

His father grimaced. "So that's where you were. When there is so much to be done, you—"

"Sir, you told me—"

"—Eudora upset, her mother anxious. Why, I had a note from her and—"

"Sir, none of that matters."

His father stopped stroking the chair arm. "I beg your pardon. For a while I thought you had become a gentleman a man could be proud of having for a son. A man who could be counted on in a crisis. A man with the proper priorities."

"Could you but listen? Sir."

His father's chin rocked back as though he had stopped short. He frowned, but gestured for Benedict to speak, pulled out his watch chain, and ran it through his fingers.

"Sir. Not only has Letellier asked his mother for the family assets, he has been borrowing money. A lot of money, and from the wrong people. He has borrowed it by promising he will have Lady Jane Compton's dowry as collateral. But he has taken longer wooing the lady than his creditors will tolerate."

"Is that what your financial friends do, gossip about each other's troubles?"

Well, yes, Benedict thought. Knowing who did what, with what, and where had immense value. And he felt no little warmth to have had these people he trusted confide in him. Even Rothschild in his belligerent way.

"How much?" his father asked.

"A little over ten thousand," Benedict said.

The clinks from the watch chain increased in frequency. "What's it for? Do they know?"

"No."

His father sighed. "Keep your eye on him, just as you have."

"I must mention, sir, that I do not think Lady Jane will have him."

"You know something you have not said." His father gestured to him to speak up, but Benedict shook his head. "It has to do with that woman, then. Your mother would weep to hear your name connected with such a one as hers."

Benedict winced, but plowed on. "Sir, what if her reputation were not as heinous as represented?"

"What about it? What about it? Good God, you pose the question seriously. How would you like to know that every gentleman you met would be wondering whether he could cuckold you? And how many gentlemen have already shared her favors?"

All Benedict's thoughts of triumph, of being the person Lady Iddesford had permitted to touch, to dance with, to kiss, rang hollow. His father was right. Even if, as Benedict now believed, she had not bedded the men with whom her name was linked, she had moved away from them, on to other men. Had he not recognized his attraction to her restlessness, her constant questing? That trait had its dangers, too.

How long could Benedict hold her interest once she no longer needed his help with Lady Jane?

"Far better for you the unplowed field," his father said. "Trust me, 'tis simpler."

Benedict remembered Dorrie's face lighting up as she saw him earlier, how she had put her hand on his arm, how wonderful he had felt.

"Eudora was fair upset this morning," his father said.

"I had the impression, sir, last year, that you did not encourage a match between me and Dorrie."

"Wasn't the match, sir, it was your way of proceeding with it. I have always believed faint heart never won fair lady," his father said. "That was how I got your mother, you know. Bowled her right over, poor woman. Stab me if I don't believe faint heart ever didn't win anything."

Was that not always the case? Benedict thought. He should be cheered to find his father and he could agree on the substance, at least, of a thing.

He should be cheered. He should be.

But what he wanted to do was find Lady Iddesford and speak to her about what he had learned from her Mr. Williams.

"So, as far as Alexander and Lady Jane go, we'll cross that bridge later. But that would be as well."

"Sir?"

His father declined to answer, stood, and said, "A game of billiards, Fitzhugh?"

It had been four years since his father had invited him to play billiards. Lady Iddesford was not going anywhere, and maybe it was to his advantage to sleep on the matter. Fresh insights so often came in the morning. "Thank you. I should enjoy that."

Another ball. Esme was heartily sick of them. One assembly here and there caused delightful anticipation and the allure of the extraordinary. Even three balls in a row could constitute enjoyment. But as nights led to nights, she wished for nothing more than a quiet daily routine. In the sunshine.

She chuckled at Lord Perriweather's latest sally on her eyes, stopped thinking about how sick she was of simpering at gentlemen, ignoring glances of envy, and wondering whether Gillespie stood behind her. Mostly she was sick of denying her feelings for Lord Fitzhugh.

She hoped tonight was the very last night.

Jane was ready, primed and floating with enthusiasm, and Letellier's smirk showed across the room where he stood with Merton.

When the dance ended, Esme would have to pull something off, and she did not have all her pieces in place.

Despite her tension, however, she could not miss the ripple passing through her assembled gentlemen. It was her warning that someone interesting to them had come. She hoped it was Fitzhugh.

It *was* Fitzhugh, and she barely contained her happiness. He looked wonderful, severe and appealing, his customary aplomb parted only by the glimmer in his gray eyes. Esme's body reacted with a shiver of awareness that coalesced in a pool of heat. *Do not blush,* she told herself. *Do not blush.*

"My lady," he said, placing a light but unmistakable emphasis on the *my*. The other gentlemen shifted, doubtless debating whether they should protest or merely posture.

"Lord Fitzhugh," she said, a woman who knew her worth. "So good of you to join us."

"Us?" he asked, pointedly.

Esme smiled. "Would you excuse me, gentlemen?"

Unhappy, they moved off a little.

"I called on you," Fitzhugh said. "Mr. Williams told me you were from home most of the day. I want to speak to you about—"

"There is little time," Esme said. "The dance is ending sooner than I thought, and I need you."

"Command me," he said.

"After, well, you will see. You must find Jane. Tell her there is something she must know, and bring her outside, quickly, toward the garden."

"She will not resist?" Fitzhugh asked.

"She will be expecting it, but she will not get what she expects." *Nor will you, but soon you will have the life you deserve.*

He nodded.

Esme slapped him, creating a shocked ripple beginning with Fitzhugh himself and extending to everyone nearby. The livid mark clear upon his left cheek, he bowed with steely grace and turned on his heel. The embarrassed crowd parted before him.

Esme fanned herself vigorously, forced herself to spare no glance toward his retreating back, and stalked toward Letellier.

"My dear countess," Letellier said through his smirk, "such a to-do."

"He presumed what he should not have," Esme said. "I do not like presumption."

"Yes," Letellier said, "Gillespie said you dislike the bold approach."

"Gillespie misstated, as he is so often wont to do," Esme replied tartly, "if he told you he was bold. He was merely incompetent."

Merton sniggered, and Esme and Letellier turned cold glances on him. "Ah," Merton said, "um." He bowed and left.

"Take me outside for some fresh air," Esme said. "We will anticipate our other plans by a few minutes, and I dislike being watched so."

"They are surprised their queen bee has a stinger," Letellier said, giving her his arm, his eyes sparkling with malice and anticipation.

"They should not be. I am no courtesan."

"That would be Fitzhugh's mistake, then," Letellier said. "He thinks in such stark lines. Good. Bad. Nothing in the delightful middle."

"He was fun to play with for a while," Esme said, and breathed in the moist night air. "Oh, much better. Down the stairs, if you please."

"Toward the mews?" Letellier asked silkily, fishing.

"Not entirely," Esme said. "Not yet. We mustn't give it away. Let us wait here a moment." She fetched up against a stone banister that fronted a second stair down to a recessed pond. It was quite a lovely effect, with trees dripping blossoms at the far end, and ducks serenely paddling. More to the point, anyone at the top of the stairs they had just descended could not see them because of the overhanging lip of the balcony railing.

"Yes," she said, after a long pause, "you were quite right about your friend Fitzhugh."

"And there I was, thinking you saw promise in him."

"He was a novelty, and he kept Gillespie away."

"You quite hate Gillespie, don't you, my dear countess?"

"My regard for him could not be described as high."

"So, Fitzhugh was a novelty."

"Like you gentlemen sometimes indulge in."

Letellier laughed. "You have an interesting idea of novelty, and not at all like a gentleman's."

"Oh?" Esme said, all innocence. "Do you mean to tell me the stories I have heard of whores dressing as nurse-maids and nuns are all stuff and nonsense?"

"My dear countess, you shock me."

"No, I do not." She placed a finger on his lapel. "Do not for a moment pretend I shock you."

"Why, my lady, do you regret my leaving?"

"Let us say, hm, that I regret the time I spent with Lord Tedious. It is too bad, too, because—"

"He presumed on lack of skill?" Letellier said.

Yes, Esme thought, *that is what you most want to believe.* How she longed to tell him how wonderful Lord Fitzhugh made her feel!

Did her hope imagine it, or did she hear silk rustling above them on the stair? Heat coursed through her, the sharp lick of desire and the spreading warmth of profound gratitude. Two different feelings, one man. "That was only one black mark against him."

Letellier wet his lips. "There were others?"

"I had to organize so many of my plans around him. When we began this venture of your seducing Lady Jane, we spoke of getting better acquainted. That has not happened."

"I will not be in Scotland long, *ma petite,*" Letellier said, tracing the line of her collarbone. "The girl and I shall travel there, wed, consummate it so no one can gainsay me, then come right back to claim her dowry. Then I shall buy you an emerald to rival the one there."

He touched the spot directly above her breasts. The emerald pressed against her skin.

Esme said, "Do not waste all your skill on her."

"*Ma petite,* what skill would I waste on her when I thought you were waiting? Five minutes and the thing is done. Then . . . then—"

"Then nothing!" Jane said, leaning over the banister, angry and tragic, bosom heaving. "Nothing!" She disappeared in a clatter of shoes upon stone.

Letellier hissed, took hold of Esme's arms. Then he let go and sprang up the stairs.

Esme sagged against the stone banister.

Then a voice cut through the moist air, mixing with the melody from the dance, and making her heart ache. "If you are looking for Lady Jane, Alexander, she said you would only speak to her next her mama."

As Jane had rushed past him, Benedict had the sense also to retreat, on the light, quiet feet that made him a superb swordsman, to the doors leading to the ballroom.

Thus Letellier saw him. "You!"

Benedict bowed as Letellier strode up to him. "What went wrong? I thought to do you a favor, since Lady Iddesford has so inconveniently disappeared. You did not . . . ?"

Letellier's eyes shone wildly in the ballroom's reflected light. "You will not fool me. You have been against me this entire time."

Benedict sighed. "No, Alexander. It is true my father asked me to extend the hand of friendship to you. Otherwise I had no plans to come to London this Season. But I had not resented it. You may not think the form of it friendship, but I assure you, my father and I have your best interests at heart."

"Fine words, and kind of you to think you know my best interests. No, Fitzhugh, nice try, but no. Your father is an old woman who keeps counsel with liars, and you, you let jealousy and what manhood you have steer you. More has happened this evening than you know, more sacrificed, than one little rich wench."

"Suppose you tell me then."

"No." Letellier tugged at his coat, straightening it. He leaned close to Benedict. "But if you want to take to task the witch who humiliated you, look no farther than—" He pointed down the stairs.

Benedict raised his brows, then hoped his surprise at Letellier's advice substituted for what should be surprise at knowing she was there.

Letellier lowered his voice. "She likes it rough, and she does not think you are man enough to give her what she wants."

Benedict wanted nothing better than to sweep Letellier's legs from under him, see him sprawled on the stones. How he had burned to hear her speak so to Letellier. Worse, to see his horror and embarrassment reflected in Lady Jane's eyes.

"How funny," Lady Iddesford said, approaching them from the far end of the balcony. "Do you think to take lessons from Mr. Letellier in the art of lovemaking, Lord Fitzhugh? You may as well let him take lessons from you in planning and executing coups. A more incompetent pair I have yet to meet. It was an elopement, sir, and a matter of what? Yes, that was it: five minutes' work."

Letellier's jaw dropped, then his face mottled with rage. But he was too late to grab at her, for she had passed into the ballroom, all fiery magnificence.

"That vixen! She—"

"Is a woman spurned, maybe?"

Letellier checked, and Benedict marveled that appealing to Letellier's overweening sense of self and sympathy with others' base emotions worked so well.

Letellier chuckled, a low, supercilious grating. "She'll get no more of me. I don't need her humiliating me before a crowd to learn my lesson, eh?"

Benedict swallowed the hard knot in his throat. "I don't recommend the experience. Shall we drink to misfortune?"

"No," Letellier replied shortly, turning away. "I have business to attend to."

Benedict spent several minutes breathing deeply of the night air before he reentered the ballroom. Just as he immediately felt himself the subject of speculation, he knew Lady Iddesford stood surrounded by her greedy admirers only twenty feet from him.

But he could not look. They had covered each other's backs, he and the beautiful countess. Letellier could never know for certain whether Benedict had brought Lady Jane to the balcony from a simplistic desire to make amends to Lady Iddesford. Nor could Letellier be certain whether she had expressed triumph or the defensive sputterings of a woman scorned.

Benedict freely acknowledged that he had said he would follow her lead, but he could not accept as compliment her belief that he could take a public slap on the face. What must people be thinking of him? What did he think of himself?

He wanted nothing more than to be quit of this wretched ball. A small smile hiding his inner turmoil, he made his way through the edges of the dancing, only to be stopped by the most unlikely of people.

Lady Jane's mother.

"I have an amazing story from my daughter," said she. "And if true, Iddesford and I owe you a debt."

So, Lady Jane had not revealed her step-grandmother's

role in the evening's scandal. Benedict wondered what Lady Jane was thinking of her now. Did the girl recognize Lady Iddesford's actions for the way they were intended? Would Lady Jane dislike the dowager for being the messenger, or would she believe that the dowager truly desired to steal Letellier?

"You and Iddesford do not owe me a debt, madam. The service I gave was to Lady Jane."

Lady Iddesford, current, sniffed. "Not hard to see why that trollop slapped you, sir. You are too honorable, and quite bereft of savoir faire. But I shall forgive you. You have not children of your own. You do not know how their pain pains you. Whatever your opinion of me, or Iddesford, I do thank you."

No, Benedict thought, he did not know a parent's concern. His father had never given any indication that Benedict gave him anything but pain. The maternal sentiments softened him. "Your thanks are welcome, madam, and sufficient. How is Lady Jane?"

"Crying, in the ladies' withdrawing room, with my sister, Lady Avondale. She will be back out here once her eyes are no longer red."

Benedict did not know why he felt pressed to determine what Lady Jane would say about Lady Iddesford, but he said, "When she emerges, I should very much like to dance with her."

"I will see to it."

"Ma'am," Benedict said and bowed. He had committed himself to stay, so he set off for the refreshment table.

Dorrie intercepted him, concern writ in fine lines around her eyes and mouth. "Fitzhugh?"

"Do not mother me, Dorrie," he said, quite at the end of his patience. He was instantly contrite. "I am in the foulest of moods, my dear. Do not regard me."

She smiled bravely enough, but unshed tears gleamed. "I would take it as the greatest insult did you not feel comfortable enough with me to treat me to one of your foul tempers."

Benedict put her arm through his. "Dorrie, you are a dear."

"I would like to scratch her eyes out," Dorrie said.

Benedict had to look now, toward Lady Iddesford. "Hell," he said.

"What is the matter?"

"Gillespie." For Gillespie stood close within Lady Iddesford's circle of admirers.

"So what?" Dorrie asked.

He could not go over there. It was impossible. She had made it impossible. But Benedict could not forget the expression on Williams' face as he had described Gillespie's attack upon Lady Iddesford, nor could he forget her own horror at seeing him that first time, and every subsequent time. "Hell."

Then he spied Smith-Jenkins walking near him toward Lady Iddesford. "Mr. Smith-Jenkins, sir. A word, if you please, sir."

Smith-Jenkins obviously felt he could spare the ousted favorite a moment of his time. "With pleasure, sir."

"Do you go over to Gillespie and let him know I would beg speech with him."

"He is unlikely to give up his most advantageous position."

"You will whisper to him that if he does not come, I shall challenge him to a fencing match."

"Oh, very good," Smith-Jenkins said, laughing. "Very subtle. Now I know that should I not deliver the message properly, you shall challenge me to another match myself."

"As you say," Benedict replied, and smiled to let Smith-Jenkins believe it was all a joke.

"What is this all about?" Dorrie asked. "You cannot still be worried about her."

"There is more about than you know of, and not enough time to tell you," Benedict said.

Dorrie huffed but went along. A few moments later Gillespie, faintly sneering, joined them.

"And what may I do for you, Fitzhugh?"

"What are you doing here this evening?"

"I was paying court to a pretty woman while looking for Letellier. Have you seen him?"

"He left. You are going to leave, too."

Gillespie's smile mocked him. "Do not tell me you yet care, Fitzhugh. What an excellent joke."

"Leave, or so help me, I will throw you out and thrash you in the street. I have nothing to lose."

"No, you don't, do you?" Gillespie said. "I know when I am defeated. Your servant, Miss Bourre. Fitzhugh."

When he was gone, Dorrie said, "You were right the first time. You are in foul mood, and however its expression might compliment me, I shall prefer your company when you are a little less inclined to it."

"Dorrie," Benedict asked helplessly, "what would you have me do?"

"She," Dorrie said, gesturing with her chin, "can take care of herself. Has she not proved it to you this evening?"

"It is not as simple as that."

"It is exactly as simple as that. Nothing to lose? *I* am asking for your attention."

"I have to dance with Lady Jane Compton."

"Because she is a relation of hers?" Dorrie asked, tossing her head. "I am beginning to think Letellier was right. Lady Iddesford has made a laughingstock of you. Never would I have thought it possible for anyone to make a laughingstock of you."

"Dorrie, please don't."

But Dorrie made a little curtsy and stalked toward her mother, who stood with a grinning duke of Breshirewood.

"Hell," Benedict said.

Chapter Seventeen

A long, lonely night followed Esme's triumph. She had no rumor of Jane's being compromised, so it was likely the girl had kept her head and her tongue. Letellier's boasting would not be highly regarded. And Lord Fitzhugh would never speak of his part. Esme could count on that.

But he had not come by to offer chilly congratulations or request thanks. Her tactic had worked better than anticipated.

After waking late the next morning with no word from him, she wrote him a note, saying, simply, "Thank you." She did not know if he had received it by the time she had to dress for Lady Dimsdale's picnic. Esme had accepted the invitation, though it had come so late it was almost an insult, because it would be the only daytime function she had attended in London. She would go because she wanted to see Jane.

Williams met her as she descended the stairs, pulling on her gloves. "Lord Fitzhugh has called, my lady. He is in the library, and a grimmer man I have yet to meet."

Thus when Esme entered the library, she was unsurprised to find him looking out the window, casting a long, substantial shadow onto her desk.

"My lord—"

"It looks very different here, during the day. Interesting, is it not, that I have never seen it like this before."

Esme winced. "Lord Fitzhugh—"

He turned. The shadow engulfed his face. "I resign."

"I beg your pardon?"

"I resign. Do not think that I hold you to blame for what happened last night. I do not. You were playing a part and playing it skillfully for a cause I consider worthy. But I can no longer play a supporting role."

Let him say his worst, she thought. *It will be best.* "What do you think I yet plan?"

"I do not know. I have not known from the beginning, have I?" He checked himself, frowned, then said, "I spoke to Mr. Williams two nights ago. No, I did not think he would tell you. I know your reputation is built on air, and after much thought I realized that you have become so used to it that you must believe no one else thinks much of theirs. But the rest of us, we are not so self-sufficient, nor so beautiful that we can command attention wherever we go. Between the four of us, you, me, Letellier, and Lady Jane, we made this situation go away, but of the four of us, I am the only one whose embarrassment is the talk of London."

Despite her resolve, angry tears formed in Esme's eyes, and angry words came to her lips. "You did not complain when the gossips pointed at you for pretending to kiss me."

"I was too busy catching my breath in Monsieur's *salle.*"

"So that is all it takes, then, to make you retreat: a little gossip?"

"You are dressed for Lady Dimsdale's picnic. Mr. Williams told me. Because I promised Miss Bourre, I must also be in attendance."

"How fortunate for Miss Bourre," Esme said.

"You would do me great honor by continuing to avoid

me in public. There is no reason to expose either of us to charges of caprice." He headed for the door.

"You possess no caprice," Esme said. "But blame whatever you need to on it, by all means, if it makes you feel better. No need to drive your horses where there is no road, but follow in the well-worn tracks countless others have made."

He fought for the icy composure she had seen him use when dealing with Gillespie. He did not quite succeed, and she appreciated the space between them. She had never seen him so riled. "And if I decided to be capricious, my lady, like as not you would fault me for that, use that as an excuse to run away as you have so many times. Do not dare accuse me of retreating."

He was too close to the mark, nor could she ever explain that she said what she did for his own good. "Leave," Esme said. "Go. I never want to set eyes on you again."

"Then stay home. Do what you do best. Conduct all your affairs by correspondence. Come into the world only to shock and amaze." And he was gone.

Esme sank against the desk's edge, her hand dislodging an ink well. She hissed and held her hand up as though stung. The ink ran across the blotter, and a large drop stained her gloves.

Williams said, "James is coming to clean that up."

Esme stripped off her gloves. "They are ruined. This ensemble does not work without the gloves."

"Change your clothes," Williams said. "Go out."

"What? From you, too?"

"I spoke to Fitzhugh, told him of that horrible night. He seemed surprised that I had agreed you leave the country, after. That has nagged at me ever since, especially since I know about your mother."

"How dare you!"

"You have always encouraged my research. Your mother ran from your father when you were but five years old, and, given my picture of him from his correspondence, I cannot blame her. But running is not the only solution to a problem. Indeed, I do believe your running last time caused your present situation."

"You would write my biography?"

"No. I am too close. I made it too easy for you to run, because I had run, too, from my life's unpleasantnesses. I needed someone to depend upon as much as you depended upon me. We were each other's crutches, and now we must walk unassisted. Whether you walk in the direction of Lord Fitzhugh or not, it is time to show the world the true Esmeralda Iddesford."

"You do not have plans to return to teaching?" Esme asked.

"No, I like being in the world. I also like being here in London again."

Esme considered. "This was to have been my day of victory."

"How do we measure victory? By the casualties? By the great battles? Or by all the little moments when someone just said yes or no, or appeared on that ridge at that time, or heard one thing as opposed to another?"

Esme snorted. "Just when I thought the don had gone."

"It is the small things that gratify historians, my lady."

Esme's smile faded. "I am in love with him, Mr. Williams. That is no small thing. Nor is my reputation."

"You are right. Neither is no small thing, but then, you are not a historian."

"What should I do?"

"Change your clothes. Go out. I can give no other advice."

"Very well," Esme said, and went upstairs.

* * *

"This picnic should have been called a garden party," said Dorrie in the strident tone she had adopted since last night.

Benedict had to concede her point, even if he disliked her tone. Under a warm sun, footmen circled the extensive gardens and lawn of Lady Dimsdale's Kensington estate, canapés and drinks on silver trays that caught the sunlight.

"Does it matter what it is called," Aunt Bourre asked, her countenance serene beneath her blue parasol, "when it gives us the opportunity to be about on such a beautiful day?"

Abashed, Dorrie looked across the wide green yard where many groups conversed and drank happily. "The trees *are* lovely, Mama. The pink line, there, and the deeper mauve behind them."

"What is your opinion, Benedict?" Aunt Bourre asked him.

That Dorrie's consenting to speak to me at all should be making me feel better. "Yes, I am happy not to be wearing black," he said, indicating his navy coat. He quirked a brow in response to Aunt Bourre's. "And fresh air is infinitely preferable to ballrooms."

Aunt Bourre smiled. Dorrie's mouth relaxed in a half-smile.

But Benedict did not feel better.

He had gone to Lady Howard's house intending to say good-bye to Lady Iddesford. For once and for all. But standing before her, seeing her beautiful face, wanting to touch all of her exquisite figure, and remembering the sting upon his cheek, all the bitter, unrelenting words had spilled from his lips.

He despised himself for them. He had hurt her, for no

reason other than to salve his pride. He had agreed she might use him. He had never imagined she would use him in such a way.

Reversby would have it as a compliment. Benedict felt humiliated. More, he had spent so much time not knowing where she stood, who she was, and where he stood with her, that a further surprise soured his entire view of her. And himself.

What had happened to him since coming to London?

"Has Hadley gone again to Kent today?" Aunt Bourre said.

"Yes, ma'am," Benedict replied.

Aunt Bourre compressed her mouth. Likely she knew more about the sad business of Madame Letellier than Benedict.

"Do look," Dorrie said. "Lady Dimsdale has acrobats here."

A troupe of twelve men or so, colorfully dressed in motley as court jesters of yore, streamed across the lawn, turning cartwheels and flips. Cries of delight reached across the lawn as an acrobat would stop and pull a flower from thin air.

"Should you like to have an acrobat make a flower appear for you, Dorrie?" Benedict asked.

"The flowers you sent me this morning were all I want," Dorrie said, her strident tone disappearing.

Benedict did not miss Aunt Bourre's smile. "I am glad you liked them," he said, but felt no leap of joy.

As he puzzled over that, three acrobats stopped a woman wearing a walking dress of a lovely, muted light gold coming across the lawn. A matching hat shadowed her face, but as she followed the acrobats' movements, the sun caressed a burnished curl lying across her shoulder.

Benedict held his breath.

She had changed her dress. She had been wearing

new-leaf green. Had Benedict seen someone wearing leaf green, he would have given her a wide berth. How many others had she fooled into thinking her not Lady Iddesford by dressing in such a color?

Except for the acrobats, she was quite alone.

"Heavens, can that be Lady Iddesford?" Dorrie asked.

"Where?" her mother said.

"In the dull gold dress and bonnet," Dorrie said.

"I do believe it is," Aunt Bourre said.

The acrobats bounced on their toes, then all three flipped themselves backward from her to tumble in the grass. She clapped, as did others nearby. Then, as the acrobats passed on, Lady Iddesford was no longer alone.

"It must be," Dorrie said. "Her entourage never lags far behind her. They seem particularly avid today."

"I am saddened, Benedict," Aunt Bourre said, "that she treated you so badly. I saw nothing that night at Lady McDonald's musicale that led me to believe her character either vicious or so distressingly erratic. Indeed, at the time I thought her quite the lady. I suppose that is the true nature of such people, that they can fool whomsoever they choose."

The duke of Breshirewood joined them, all bonhomie in a light gray coat. He effused over them, then, taking Benedict aside, said, "You must be overjoyed."

"Your Grace?" Benedict asked.

The duke nodded toward Lady Iddesford, but no more than her hat could be seen through the crowd. "Escaping like that. You have not the rash, wild temper that finds such practices alluring or, as those others, so titillating. For that I am exceedingly happy, for Miss Bourre would not like you to be tarred by the same brush. And what Miss Bourre does not like, I think I may, between us, admit to presuming I do not like."

"I beg your pardon?" Benedict said, alarmed.

"You have not heard? It was all over White's this morning."

"I had other business this morning, in the City."

Breshirewood's expansiveness evaporated. "You do not know what is being said about her?"

"You mean about Lady Iddesford?"

Breshirewood nodded, and regained some of his joviality. "It is really quite vile. That she likes men to beat her, needs . . . More than a few of them are over there—and Lloyd and Sommers among them—for the sole purpose of trying to determine where she hides the bruises. If only by process of elimination."

Lady Iddesford appeared as the gentlemen around her laughed and shifted. She was not looking at Benedict, nor did he want to meet her gaze. He could not help but ache, however, for the sun behind her made her hat glow and lit her creamy skin. She wore gloves, naturally. How many of those vultures wondered if she had bruises around her delicate wrists, bruises that even the softest of silks could cause?

Benedict swallowed hard revulsion, and discovered anger. Such ugliness should not exist here, in the glorious sunshine.

"Benedict? Benedict? Are you all right?" asked Aunt Bourre.

"Fitzhugh, you look dreadful," Dorrie said.

Benedict took Aunt Bourre by the shoulders. "Please, my dearest Aunt Bourre, I would crave a favor of you."

"Benedict, you have only to ask."

"Take Lady Iddesford home. Either tell her I said she should go or not. You be the judge. However you deem it easiest. But I beg you, take her home."

"Fitzhugh," Dorrie protested.

"I am sorry to ask it of you," Benedict began.

"No," Aunt Bourre said firmly. "No, you must not be

sorry." She took a gentle knuckle to his face as she often had when he was a boy. "We will take care of her, never fear. Come, Eudora. Your pardon, Your Grace."

Aunt Bourre gave Dorrie a bare second in which to curtsy to the gentlemen, before she bore them away.

"I say, Fitzhugh—" said Breshirewood.

"None of it is true," Benedict said, groaning inwardly as Lady Dimsdale walked near Aunt Bourre and Dorrie, and they were required to stop and converse. "None of it."

The duke's brows rose. "Never say you are an authority."

At a brisk pace for him, Reversby came up, his expression concerned, and said, "Fitzhugh—you *have* heard, then."

"Breshirewood has told me. Your Grace, do you know who started these rumors?"

"Your own friend, Mr. Letellier. I thought it rather decent of him. Perriweather said later he thought Letellier had held his tongue while she was still batting her eyelashes in your direction. It is now general consensus, Fitzhugh, that your reputation is quite intact. To be spurned by such a one redeems any apparent awkwardness, especially among those mamas who have daughters they care about."

Reversby rolled his eyes.

"My deepest apologies on contradicting you, sir, but none of it is true, remember?" Benedict said.

"But you should still be glad—" Breshirewood broke off. "Except that you have sent Miss Bourre to fetch her away."

"Reversby, would you?"

"Honored, sir," Reversby said.

They excused themselves from Breshirewood, who was spluttering, and extricated themselves from the party.

"I left my horses standing," Reversby said, as they reached the long, graveled drive that formed a semicircle in front of Lady Dimsdale's house, "although my man may have had to walk them. Letellier is at Tatt's. There is Jack."

Reversby's groom spied them, picked them up, then handed over the reins to Reversby. "Tatt's, then?" Reversby asked.

"Tatt's," Benedict said. "Spring them, would you?"

They drove toward the Hyde Park Turnpike in silence, and soon arrived at bustling Tattersall's auction house. Benedict jumped down, leaving Reversby to follow. He barely glanced at the two grooms exercising two bays in the central paddock, circling the cupola containing a bust of Prinny. He searched for Letellier among the gentlemen standing under the high-arched enclosure running along two sides of the paddock.

"Damn," Benedict said. "He could not be in one of the subscription rooms, could he?"

Reversby caught his breath before answering. "He's no member of the Jockey Club, for all he would have it so. Look, there."

Letellier, brilliant in a robin's-egg-blue coat and white breeches, emerged from a box about halfway down the enclosure, Gillespie and Merton in attendance.

Reversby put a hand on Benedict's arm. "Careful, friend."

"I just want to talk to him," Benedict said. "My father the earl would have my head did I anything else."

"Just talk. Um hm. Right. So, just talk."

Letellier did not hide his smirk when he saw Benedict approaching him. Gillespie, too, had a nasty little scrunched smile. Only Merton betrayed any nervousness. He swayed.

"Do let me show you the mare I was just looking at, Fitzhugh," Letellier said. "She's a fine, feisty one. Then again, maybe not your sort of thing at all."

Gentlemen were forming a circle around him and Letellier. No one could mistake Letellier's animosity. How many of them were surprised by Benedict's appearance here, confronting Letellier? Benedict wanted to know exactly how many of them understood all of what was occurring. That one man would repeat one word of Letellier's slander against Lady Iddesford, that one man could think . . .

Benedict punched Letellier square in the jaw. Gasps mingled with Letellier's thump as he hit the dirt. "Consider that a challenge offered, sir," Benedict said. He was breathing as heavily as if he had just ridden a race.

Letellier scrambled up, wiped his mouth with the back of his hand, leaving a smear of blood. He smiled, and lunged.

Merton caught his right arm, but even Merton's bulk would have been insufficient to restrain him. Another, older gentleman grabbed his left as the rest of the crowd backed up.

Then Reversby grabbed Benedict, said, "Ho!"

"What is this, gentlemen? What goes on?" asked Richard Tattersall, bustling up.

"A disagreement, sir," Reversby said, letting go of Benedict. "And soon settled."

"If you say so, milord," Tattersall said, and the crowd parted to let him leave.

Letellier held his tongue until Tattersall was well away. Then he again wiped his mouth and brushed at the satisfactory smear of dirt on his white trousers. "Challenge taken," he said. "I look forward to this. Swords. It will be swords."

Gillespie smiled, which gave Benedict his first twinge of unease, despite his confidence in his own ability. "Dawn," Gillespie said, "at Battersea Park."

"The terms are acceptable," Reversby said, after meeting Benedict's gaze. "We're all done here, now, gentlemen. Just look at those bays. Beautiful, are they not?"

"Aye, son," said the older gentleman, who had let go Letellier's arm, but remained close by.

"She has made the complete fool of you," Letellier said, sneering. "Not that it is a hard thing to do."

Benedict swelled with angry breath.

"Enough of that, lad," the gentleman said to Benedict. Then to Letellier, "Off with ye."

Letellier snorted, but backed away some twenty yards, taking Gillespie and Merton with him.

"Walter Abercrombie, son. Pleased to meet you."

"Fitzhugh."

"Don't take it too hard, now. Wait until tonight, when your blood cools, then you can have your second here talk it all out. A woman like that, she's liable to make a fool of many a man."

"There are fools, and then there are fools, Mr. Abercrombie, and most of the time, one does not recommend himself any more than another. This is not most of the time." Benedict took a deep breath. "But thank you, sir, for your counsel, and your arm."

Abercrombie shrugged and went off.

Reversby fell into step with Benedict. "Whither away?"

"Back home. Have you forgotten?"

Reversby grimaced. "You promised to take Miss Bourre to Vauxhall this evening. Good Lord."

They had come out of Tattersall's. Reversby's groom and carriage stood directly where they had left it. Had the entire encounter taken so short a time that the horses had not required walking? Five minutes? Ten?

Benedict put his hand on the edge of the carriage, leaned into it. The cutting anger was fading, but a grim determination fueled him. "There is no possibility of an apology, Reversby."

"I know it, but I will sit in White's this evening anyway, in case Gillespie should come to me."

"Won't happen."

"Likely, so long as your father learns nothing of the matter. He will not regard it with a friendly eye. It is the sort of thing he would do, though, isn't it?"

Benedict reared his head back. "It is. My God."

"Don't take it to heart. We all have to learn something from our fathers."

Esme had letters to read and compose, but she was neither reading, nor composing. She was watching the sunlight fade on Upper Brook Street, turning the white stone facings a pale, rosy gold. It looked so serene, so peaceful.

How many serene facades concealed animated people discussing the slander Letellier and Gillespie had put about?

"How is this rumor different from any other rumor about me?" Esme had asked Mrs. Bourre. Mrs. Bourre had just looked at her. Esme had known it was a rhetorical question. Not different in kind, maybe, but so different in degree that she could barely raise her head in the carriage. Nor had Miss Bourre's smoldering gaze contributed to Esme's degree of comfort.

"May I recommend, Lady Iddesford, that you remain at home tonight?" Mrs. Bourre had said kindly, when the carriage had pulled up.

"Did Lord Fitzhugh ask you to say that?" Esme had said, regaining some of her bravado.

"Fitzhugh would want only what is best for you."

"I appreciate your attempt at sparing my feelings, or at least not riling them further, but truly I tell you, Lord

Fitzhugh would not care if I quit England tomorrow and never returned."

"Fitzhugh is exceptionally loyal. It is a family failing."

Unconvinced and uncomfortable, Esme had thanked her, said, "Good day to you, Miss Bourre," and went into the library.

The rosy glow faded, and in what felt like a heartbeat, the street turned ashy gray. Soon after, Williams knocked on the door. "Will you want dinner in here, my lady?"

"Had I not already said . . ." Esme broke off. "What is it? What have you learned?"

"With regrets, I have from the maid in Mr. Gillespie's house, some rather alarming news. It seems Lord Fitzhugh has challenged Mr. Letellier to a duel, set for dawn tomorrow."

When Esme could breathe again, she said, "What weapon?"

"Swords."

"He will win it, then."

Williams nodded, once. Carefully.

Esme did not have to be told what he was thinking. They had discussed warfare, Williams' favorite subject. Who could guarantee an outcome when men clashed with sharp weapons in their hands? She stood. "How dare he do this! How dare he? He has no right!"

Williams bowed. "Sometimes gentlemen do not consider such things in the heat of emotion."

"But Fitzhugh thinks. He plans. He does not give in to rash folly. The most upset I have ever seen him was this very afternoon, and even then, his temper could not be considered anything less than controlled."

"I was a don for sixteen years. I thought. I planned. And I never gave in to rash folly until something broke suddenly within me."

"Mr. Williams. Dear sir. We may no longer offer that

premise. He himself told me I should come into the world only to shock and amaze it. He has no right to fight for me!"

"You will not convince him otherwise, I fear."

"Please tell my maid to attend me."

"He asked you to stay home, my lady."

"Would you have stayed home if you could have prevented that carriage accident?"

"I could not have prevented it," he said stiffly, then sighed. "But I would give all to have kissed them one more time."

Tears spilled down Esme's cheeks.

"Do you know where he is to be this evening?"

"Yes," she whispered. "Miss Bourre said he had promised her a visit to Vauxhall Gardens. I need a domino. Mine is missing its mask."

"I will send James out for one directly."

Chapter Eighteen

Waiting in the well-lit box he had reserved, Benedict entertained no maudlin sentiment. This night at Vauxhall Gardens would not be his last. He expected to give Letellier a fine drubbing, no more, no less.

Gillespie's smile yet bothered him, but there could be any number of reasons for it. Benedict declined to speculate. The mere thought of Gillespie—

"Goodness, Fitzhugh, you do look grim," Aunt Bourre said.

Benedict stood, swept his black domino back to invite her and Dorrie, also wearing dominoes, into the box, and said, "My apologies. You ladies must be in want of refreshment."

Benedict signaled to the waiting servitor, and seated the ladies, one to each side of him.

"Will the ham really be sliced so thin we can see through it, Fitzhugh?" Dorrie asked.

"I will be interested to see, myself," Benedict replied. "The last time I was here, I had cold beef. The carver did manage to slice it very thin, but we could not see through it."

"Ham has a different texture," Aunt Bourre said.

Dorrie's mouth pulled to one side. Aunt Bourre studied the carving along the outside of the box.

Benedict placed a hand on each of theirs. "What is wrong?"

Dorrie would have spoken, but Aunt Bourre, giving her a pointed look, said, "It has been an overexciting day, do you not agree? But now we may relax and enjoy ourselves. It is nice to be *en famille*, as it were, although I would wish your father were here, too."

"He was not returned home," Benedict said. "And I have always been grateful to have you both regard me as like family."

Dorrie chewed her lip.

"Dorrie, I did not mean to embarrass you."

"Of course not," Dorrie said, and smiled brightly. Too brightly.

Trying not to be alarmed, Benedict directed the waiter in serving the ladies. The ham was indeed paper thin, the punch acceptable, and the bread surprisingly tender.

"But the cost, Fitzhugh," Dorrie said.

"We pay for the experience, not the food, Dorrie."

Shortly after they had finished their repast, some ladies strolling by managed to recognize Aunt Bourre, despite her domino, and stopped to converse. Although they regarded Benedict from behind masks, nothing could hide their inquisitive eyes. Aunt Bourre did not deign to introduce him, either, which caused Benedict thankful but grim amusement.

"Come, sir, let us walk off our thin dinner," Dorrie said. At a nod from her mother, they escaped the pavilion and into the gardens themselves. They strolled down the walk, its boxwood walks and recesses lit by warmly colored globe lamps. Stars glittered above, and murmured conversation and laughter intertwined with the orchestra playing in the center.

"That was well done, Dorrie. Thank you."

"Old busybodies," Dorrie said. "It is pretty out here. One hears such things, but it does not seem at all threatening."

"We are not upon the Dark Walk, or the Lover's, or the Druid's. Those are not for you." They passed under a large arch, then, shortly, another.

"There is a bench, over there, to the side," Dorrie said. "Such a delightful little arbor, too."

"Would you like to sit?" Benedict asked.

"Please." But no sooner had they than Dorrie was twisting her hands in her domino, pulling it back to reveal a white dress.

Benedict took Dorrie's hands. "Dorrie, I have never known you to hold your thoughts so close. Do, I beg you, tell me what has you so upset before you make yourself ill."

She took a few moments to come to a decision. "I know, about tomorrow, that is. I know you and Alexander are to duel."

"My dear, you must not be worried about me. Letellier chose swords. When have I not been able to beat him at fencing? Come, do not be upset."

"I have confidence in you, Benedict. You know that I do. It is the reason you fight him that upsets me so."

"What do you mean?" Benedict asked, chilled despite the mild night.

"Why will you insist on making this difficult for me?" she asked. "Can you not imagine how awkward it is for me to know you fight over another woman?"

"She is not another woman. There is no first woman. Oh—" Benedict broke off. She looked miserable. "Oh, Dorrie, is there?"

Tears glimmered in her eyes. "I was supposed to be in London to find a husband. Why did you think I wanted to spend so much of my time with you?"

"I had ascribed it to loyalty."

"You would, would you not? It is why you stood with me, even though I was fool enough to reject you last summer."

She would not ask, nor say, anything further. Nor did she need to. Only two weeks ago, Dorrie's hinting she would marry him would have filled Benedict with great happiness. His father and Aunt Bourre would have rejoiced. Now he regarded marriage to Dorrie as a curiosity, and from a distance.

He did love her. He doubted he would ever stop loving her. They had shared their childhoods together. Still, the urgent edge had gone from his love for Dorrie.

But nothing would last with Lady Iddesford. She had seemed willing enough to kiss him, but otherwise she reacted very much like a deb who held her virtue dearly. Her experience with Gillespie certainly made that reasonable.

She would either back away, or lose interest after a while. She was too splendid a woman to stay interested in simple him.

And then there was her distressing tendency to run away.

Wild fulfillment for a moment, or contentment for life?

"You *were* a fool," said Lady Iddesford. Her rich, low voice pierced Benedict with a sweet, painful joy. In a dark domino with the hood drawn far forward, she resembled the shadow she cut across the short path to their arbor as she approached them. "I have said so on more than one occasion."

Dorrie gasped. "What are *you* doing here?"

"You were a fool, Miss Bourre, but not so large a fool as you, Fitzhugh, for what you would do tomorrow."

"You make an indiscriminate use of the word 'fool,' my lady," Benedict said, rising.

"There is nothing indiscriminate about it. As clearly

as Miss Bourre did not accept your proposal last summer, you should not have issued a challenge over virtue that is not debatable. Am I not right, Miss Bourre?"

Dorrie did not answer except to clutch Benedict's arm as though Lady Iddesford would spring at her.

"She knows I am right, my lord," Lady Iddesford said.

"I do not," Benedict said. "She does not know, as I do, that you are not your reputation. I fight for what I believe in, not what can be proven. Dorrie, you must believe that what I am doing is right."

"What I think you are doing is throwing away your life for this . . . this wicked whore." And Dorrie seemed so startled by her own language that she put a hand over her mouth, tears brimming in her eyes, then pushed past Lady Iddesford to run up the path.

"Dorrie!" Benedict said, but he did not chase after her.

Lady Iddesford's gaze upon him also shimmered with sudden tears. "You *are* a fool. But *I* could not leave you like that. Not tonight. Would you please take me home?"

"Yes," he said. One simple word, it almost undid her. She accepted his arm with trembling fingers. A few paths and fragrant box-hedges away, the orchestra played a lilting dance tune. People murmured and laughed, sometimes raucously. Esme did not worry. Fitzhugh had her by his side. He pressed her hand between his arm and his body, so even through the fabric of shirt and waistcoat and jacket and glove, she could feel his heart beating.

Nothing bad or wrong would touch her. Nothing bad or wrong *could* touch her.

Nor was she surprised when he plucked, as if from thin air, Smith-Jenkins. "Do me a favor, sir? Mrs. and Miss

Bourre are in the second box from the left, ground. Offer them your escort, then come back here and let me know if that should be acceptable."

"Getting right back on the horse, aren't you, sir?" Smith-Jenkins said, smiling and trying to look inside Esme's hood.

"Mind your manners, sir," Fitzhugh said with a tone that bridged threat and ease.

"Yes, sir." He sketched an *en garde* before hastening away.

"I am sorry—" Lord Fitzhugh began.

"No," Esme said, thinking her heart would burst from loving him, wanting to touch much, much more of him, and bitter regret that he yet worried over Miss Bourre. "Never be sorry."

"I am frequently sorry."

"Why are you doing this?"

"To what, specifically, do you refer?" he asked, touching her cheek, then lightly under her jaw.

Esme drew a ragged breath. "I cannot speak of it with you touching me like that."

"Good." His hand trailed down her throat, crossed the cord that bound her domino, and rested at the top of her bodice. The weight of his hand, the power it controlled, thrilled her. Before him, she was vulnerable and happy to be that way. All the while, he held her gaze, asking a question.

"For you," she answered, "only for you."

"Smith-Jenkins returns," he said softly, drawing her hood full forward.

She growled, and his answering short chuckle made her feel curiously proud of herself. For all her reputation, for all her easy attraction for men, she had never let anyone close enough to her to indulge her body.

"All arranged, sir," Smith-Jenkins said. "Although Miss Bourre is . . ."

"Not happy with me," Fitzhugh said. "A matter of the morning."

"Womenfolk," was Smith-Jenkins' sage, male response. "Now that you say so, sir, I do hope you will give him a good pummeling."

"The lady's honor matters to you, sir?"

Smith-Jenkins eyed Esme, although with her head turned slightly away from him, he could never know who she was. Then he must have come to the conclusion that Fitzhugh either did not consider his companion bothered by the subject or not worth bothering about. "I never believed any of it. She does not have it in her."

"Blinded by beauty?" Fitzhugh asked, a taunting note in his voice Esme had never heard before.

"She has not the cruel eye," Smith-Jenkins said. "You *are* doing right, doubly so since you are obviously out of favor."

Fitzhugh said, "Thank you for seeing to the Bourres."

"My lord," Smith-Jenkins said.

"You did not thank him," Esme said.

"For what?" he asked, taking her arm again and drawing her toward the gate.

"You will not speak of it, will you?"

"No."

They passed the gate. Lord Fitzhugh took her by the waist, as he had that night a week ago. It felt like an age. They passed several standing hackneys before Lord Fitzhugh hesitated. Esme felt the check through his body, tight and tense.

"Would you mind the cigar smoke?" he asked. "Or, that one there has the top down."

"It would return me more quickly," Esme said.

"It would get a roof over your head, and a door."

"A door sounds an excellent idea, doesn't it?" Esme asked, grinning.

"I hope I know how to treat a lady," he replied, and snapped his fingers at the open hackney. "Upper Brook Street, if you please."

The West End streets presented no trouble to their driver, and he had them before Lady Howard's house in a few minutes. Esme and Fitzhugh held hands under the folds of their dominoes, his finger caressing the delicate inside of her wrist where her glove buttoned. Esme's world reduced to that small pressure.

Fitzhugh handed her down from the hackney and flipped the driver a coin. "Here we are," Esme said.

"I have visited here before, I think," he said.

"But all you have seen is the library."

"There is more."

"I hope there is more," she said softly.

He swept her up in his strong arms. Her hood fell back. The night air grazed her neck, making her shiver. Or maybe the shiver came from feeling how neatly she fit against him, how her body seemed so contradictorily insubstantial and dense with feeling. He pounded twice on the door.

It swung open to reveal an astonished James. "My lady!"

James backed up as Fitzhugh headed for the stairs.

"Tell Mr. Williams I am home. I do not need my maid."

"No, you do not," Fitzhugh said, for her ears only.

"Yes, my lady."

"What is so amusing?" Fitzhugh said.

"That of all households in London, this one should be used to such sights. I have failed to train them adequately."

"A little shock is good for the system. It tempers the steel. Which door?"

"On the right. There."

He pushed open the door with his foot, kicked it shut behind them. Only then did he let her down. He did not let go of her, however, but with one hand holding her close, undid the tie to her domino. A kiss on her neck, and its silk slithered from her. She untied his domino, let it fall, pooling on the floor and gleaming faintly in the low firelight.

He lifted her mask, threw it to one side. "Sensible woman," he said. "No elaborate coif to tangle upon." And like that, he removed the pins that held her hair in its chignon. The sudden soft weight, augmented by his fingers combing through it, almost drove her mad.

"Sensible?" she said in an anguished, amused whisper.

"You can put a halt to this now," he said. "You may put a halt to this any time you want. But I confess that I am feeling far from sensible."

"Does this mean you forgive me for slapping you?"

"This means that I have also done something to make me the laughingstock of London. I am no better than you."

Esme gathered his face in her hands. "Dear Fitzhugh, you are much better than I. You are the best person I know." Gently she kissed him. His shudder gave her the courage to say, "I did not want to need you."

He tugged on one of her curls. "And now?"

"Now I want to touch you. I want you to touch me. No duty. No obligation. I just need you."

"Can there be honor?"

"Mine," she replied. Then she lost herself in his kiss. He tasted of wine and sweet butter, laced with his own heady warm scent. Her greedy fingers pushed off his coat, worked at waistcoat buttons, then froze as his equally greedy fingers released her from her dress and petticoats and stays and finally her shift to expose her breasts. She stood naked before him, and did not need to be told he found her beautiful, desirable.

She melted before the delicious heat of his gaze. He laid her across the bed, and then gently, oh so gently, touched the tip of his tongue to her breast. She gasped with pleasure, and laughed.

He smiled the full smile she had seen so infrequently, then his pulling his shirt over his head obscured it. "Too many clothes," he murmured. "Stay where you are."

She rolled onto a hip and watched him hop up and down a little while he tugged off his tight boots. "I have never laughed," she said. "We have not laughed much together, you and I. I never laughed, with Iddesford. He could barely . . . Why do I laugh?"

He pulled down his trousers.

"Oh. That is not why. And do you know," she continued as he lay down next to her atop her gold coverlet that she would never again be able to think of as *just* her gold coverlet, "I do not know."

He ran his hand down the curve of her waist to her hip and then down her leg. "You said you wanted to touch me?" he asked.

She did. She ached to touch him, trace with her fingers instead of her eyes the muscled chest and arms and back and legs, see whether the blond hair on his chest sprang back against her hand. She began, deliberately, holding his gaze, but soon, all too soon, that was not enough.

He knew it, for he drew her quickly close, his mouth covering hers in a hungry, questing kiss. Again she lost herself in him, reveling in his weight against her, her fingers exploring him without any direction, his hands stirring her to a greater and greater urgency.

Finally she could stand it no longer. She pushed at his

shoulder. He stiffened, drew back enough so that she could push him all the way onto his back.

"My lady?"

"Shh," she said, and, kissing him, impaled herself on him. He gasped into her kiss, and she carried them both into shuddering ecstasy.

Chapter Nineteen

Esme lay atop him for some minutes, both of them recovering their breath, his hands caressing the small of her back and the cleft of her buttocks. Finally she sat up and said, "I *am* a wicked woman, to have enjoyed the act in such a way."

He sat up with her, holding her straddled on his lap. "There is nothing wicked about you, except the way you make me feel." He stroked her hair. "I like feeling wicked with you, my lady."

She chewed her swollen lower lip. "Kiss me, quickly, before I—"

"Before you what?" he asked, kissing her neck instead. Then he met her gaze. "Tell me."

"Would you apologize to Letellier if I asked it of you?"

"No, not even if you asked it of me."

"Then I will not ask. But I am no different from Miss Bourre in my wishes. Should something unthinkable happen—" She wrapped her arms around his neck and buried her face in his warm shoulder that smelled of soap and their lovemaking.

"It will not."

"You think I doubt you, but I do not doubt you. I despise myself. I thought, when there were the first whispers about me, that the people who would believe such things sight unseen were not the people I cared a straw for. Nor did it matter. I played the way I wished to play. I was treated always with deference. I liked that. But I have read enough Greeks and Mr. Newton to know that I may not have everything I want without some price. That price became my reputation, and I grew accustomed to it, stopped regretting it even. Indeed, I thanked God for it when I had to inveigle myself in Letellier's scheme for Jane. No, I never regretted it. Not until I met you. Who gave the Fates the right to—"

"Stop, sweetheart," he said, putting a finger over her lips. "Nothing will happen to me, and my meeting Letellier will put paid to all the gossip."

"You cannot be sure. And I know it will anger your father."

"My father will never hear of it."

"He will afterward, surely."

"So long as it is afterward, when I know all I need to know to defend myself."

"What do you mean?"

"There must be a reason I have not discovered, for my father the earl to ask me here to London to befriend Letellier, and for his sudden desire to marry well and wealthy. Have I told you how beautiful you are?"

Esme shivered with pleasure. "I think not," she said, even as she recalled all the things Williams had said about how Letellier and Gillespie discussed what they must pay for Le Maitre des Brouillards. So Fitzhugh had investigated Letellier as well.

How perfectly wonderful. How she loved the way he thought.

Then all thoughts flew from her head except the feel of his lips and hands upon her.

Afterward Esme snuggled up against Fitzhugh and said, "Now I know why all the tabbies of the *ton* consider me a walking sin. I enjoyed that too much."

"You do force a man to excel."

She wanted to tell him he should excel at coming back to her tomorrow. Instead she ran a light hand over his chest and said, "Good."

"Now I have some unfortunate news. I must see Reversby. He is my second and might have matters to discuss."

"It is two o'clock."

"So it is." He rose smoothly from the bed, all beautiful hard planes and angles limned in the firelight. Esme ached with love for him.

He pulled on his trousers and tossed his shirt over his head. Esme drew on her green silk wrapper, and, inspired, took her green emerald pendant from her jewelry case. "Here," she said, stepping close to him, the ends of the necklace unfastened. "I would have forgotten to take it off, before, when I left for Vauxhall, such was my haste. My maid reminded me it would have given me away. Would you wear it?"

He took a deep breath. "It would give me great honor."

With shaking fingers she fastened it around his neck. The emerald flashed like cold fire. "It was my mother's," Esme said. "The only thing I ever had of her, except my name and my temper."

"You have no temper," he said, smiling.

"Liar," she replied, gathering up his cravat and waistcoat and jacket from the floor. She stood with arms crossed tightly while he dressed. Then, "I will see you out."

Either Williams or the servants had thought to lay extra candles out downstairs, although no one was in attendance. Esme put her hand on the large front door, said, "Be well." She forced back any hint of tears.

Fitzhugh kissed her long, and sweetly. "Never fear for me." Then he was gone.

Esme hugged herself, trying to recapture some of his

warmth. Then she crossed the room and pulled the call bell. Williams joined her so quickly she knew he had been waiting for just such a summons.

"He has gone?"

"Yes, to confer with his second."

Williams nodded.

"Is Percival awake?"

"Yes, my lady."

"Good. I need to be dressed immediately. I am paying a call on the earl of Hadley."

Williams could have made any number of protests. Esme braced herself for them. Instead he said, "I will accompany you."

The mist coming off the Thames trailed over a wide Battersea Park greensward, stuck itself in the trees, and dripped down, faintly stinking, on anyone unlucky enough to wait beneath them. Benedict and Reversby both had their arms crossed and their greatcoat collars up. Few of the thirty or so other gentlemen waiting in the predawn had such protection, appearing to have come from whatever evening entertainment they had enjoyed. Their discomfort may have been why they did not talk boisterously. They used their breath to blow into their hands.

"Where did they all come from?" Benedict asked Reversby in an undertone. "Is a duel often spectator sport?"

"Dashed if I know," Reversby replied. "But word certainly spread somehow. Devillefort's coat is spotted by the mist, and Perriweather has ruined his shoes on a dung pat. Such are my consolations. Don't know which kind, though."

"I thought you liked Perriweather."

"He's a silly ass." Reversby rocked back and forth on his heels. "He always drooled over my wife."

"Keep a lookout for constables."

"As well as dung pats of indeterminate origin? Why?"

"This many gentlemen, coming over the bridge, at this hour?"

"Point taken."

"Where is Letellier?"

"We may get lucky yet."

Benedict grimaced. "I do not think I believe in luck. This has a nasty little feel to it, Reversby."

"That it does. That it does. But you'll do fine." Reversby clapped Benedict on the back, grimaced at his hand's getting wet, and flicked the water away.

"Good luck," Benedict said, and smiled.

"For that, I'll challenge you after you've done with Letellier. Speak of the devil . . ."

Letellier arrived in a low carriage with Gillespie, Merton, and two others. Like the other party-goers, he was in evening attire. Benedict hoped he was the worse for wear.

"Duty calls and all that," Reversby said. He left Benedict to confer with Gillespie, who had drawn away from the crowd, toward the greensward, as was right and proper.

Letellier, however, dove into the crowd. Between the dampening mist and the distance, Benedict could not make out the specifics of what he was saying, but he was laughing, too. Did some of the gentlemen act like they wished him well in a futile effort? Benedict hoped so.

He touched his shirt below his cravat where Lady Iddesford's emerald lay. As he had accepted the token, he had realized that the attraction he had long felt for her, an attraction that he had half hoped would dissipate in the reality of flesh against flesh, had deepened into love.

He loved her, every shining tress framing her beautiful

face and shoulders and breasts, every fervent look, every delicate but strong limb, and above all, the way she made him feel entirely natural despite the wild, uninhibited way she had made love to him. As she had rolled him over, he had not been able to help himself from wondering if at least some of the tales of her were true. But her wonder had banished the thought immediately.

He loved her even though there was no future to it. By sheer passion, she had forced him to give more than he had ever given. He had thought her mind would be his only challenge. Now he feared she would tire of him in bed long before.

But he loved her. He pressed the emerald into his skin until it hurt. He loved her, and he would defend her.

Then she would be free.

With a motion of his chin, Reversby signaled to him. A rustle passed through the crowd as Benedict walked over to Reversby and Gillespie. Letellier loped over. He sported a bruise on his jaw.

Good, Benedict thought.

Reversby and Gillespie went through the ritual of announcing that they had agreed upon the swords and then giving each duelist the opportunity to test them.

"Remember," Reversby said in an aside, "the wet grass." Then, "Gentlemen, are you unable to be reconciled?"

"*He* may apologize," Letellier said, sneering.

"You may take that as a yes," Benedict said, drawing laughter from the crowd, which had formed a broad arc between the trees, on an incline up the greensward.

"I never believed your protestations of affection," Letellier said in a low voice.

"At least one of your instincts may be called unerring," Benedict replied, unruffled. "Are you going to salute me, Alexander? It is to you to start. You would have yourself the injured party."

"The patient boy, the good son," Letellier said. "You have no idea what I have sacrificed, what she made me lose."

"And I don't care," Benedict said. "Your own weak, lustful character betrayed you."

"Stop! Stop this immediately." It was Hadley.

Benedict heard his own groan echoed by Letellier. They exchanged suspicious, distasteful looks, then turned as one to Benedict's father, who parted the crowd on his favorite dark gray hack.

"Not a constable," Reversby said to Benedict.

"Nearly invisible in the mist," Benedict said, and frowned. Where had he heard something about mists lately?

Hadley dismounted. "Reversby, and Gillespie. You're the seconds? Fine. Have they saluted? Have they started?"

"No," Reversby said. "But I assure you, sir, this meeting has proceeded with all the niceties observed. The parties refuse to be reconciled any other way but the field of honor."

"I have something to say to Mr. Letellier that may change his mind."

Letellier stared hard at Hadley, eyes narrowed. He put a heavy hand on Gillespie's shoulder.

"You may say it to me," Gillespie said.

"To all four of us," Reversby corrected.

"All four of us," Gillespie said.

"Let us step away, then," Benedict said, realizing he was quite amazingly annoyed. He was no longer of an age at which his father could or should call him on the carpet. He had feared such lambastings as a child, resented them as a young man, and continued to make his actions conform so that he should avoid them as a grown man.

What had that course gained him? Nothing but tacit

permission to his father to continue his hold over Benedict's actions.

"You are excessive bland, sir," his father said.

"If you compliment my calm, sir, I thank you. If you seek to criticize the weight I give this situation, you may consider it rendered."

"And ignored," his father said.

"Not ignored. Redundant."

His father snorted.

Letellier said, "What have you to say?"

"It is just this," Hadley said. "We know the state of your finances. We know what you owe, and to whom. And looking around at this fine assembly, I may make a conclusion about how you intend to get yourself out of debt."

Benedict and Reversby exchanged a glance. Reversby rolled his eyes.

"Of course," Benedict said and sighed.

Hadley's mouth twisted in exasperation. "It is as plain as a pikestaff."

"Some pikestaff," muttered Reversby. "Some of them are still so drunk they might be eels."

"But Alexander," Hadley said, "the only way you could make money here is by winning this duel. Who would take a bet on Fitzhugh to win, eh? But to lose? Sweets from a baby, that. There's a reason for that, you know. Fitzhugh's skill is much superior."

"Maybe no one here knows that I have spent the week practicing for just such an occasion," Letellier said smugly.

"How like you to press years into a week," Hadley said. "Would it were that easy."

Letellier's face worked. "When I want advice, my lord, I will ask for it. You are no father to me, however you tried."

Benedict started. He had never suspected his father wanted to marry Madame Letellier. The notion that

Madame had refused him, however, gave him some uncharitable satisfaction.

His father said, "No, Fitzhugh, I have not wanted to marry Madame Letellier." Hadley turned to Letellier, who clenched his jaw. "But because of my respect and admiration for her, Alexander, I will offer to settle your debts. It must stop here, though."

"Respect and admiration," Gillespie said in mock amazement.

"I beg your pardon, Gillespie. When gentlemen talk, consider remaining silent."

Reversby choked back a laugh, and Benedict had to work his jaw to keep from smiling.

Hadley glanced at Reversby, who shrugged, unrepentant. Then Hadley again addressed Letellier. "I did not bring you and your mother from France to gratify myself, but because she and Mrs. Bourre's late husband were cousins. But that's neither here nor there. Have you labored under the misapprehension that I wanted to marry her?"

"Is it a misapprehension, or doth my lord protest too much?" Letellier asked.

"Good God, sir," Benedict said.

"Do stay out of this, Fitzhugh," his father said bitingly.

Benedict framed something equally biting, and refrained.

His father spoke to Letellier. "Your mother and I have become good friends over the years, beginning with the gratitude she felt for me, but nothing else. But all this is smoke and mirrors on your part. It is not your real grudge, is it?"

"It is enough. Your visits, they have raised speculation."

"Rubbish," Hadley said. "And if you cared enough about your mother, you would have been the one visiting her. It has been months, sir, and she is poorly."

Letellier was breathing deeply, and Benedict realized that although his father was unarmed, he and Letellier retained their swords. "You may speak of it as the veriest nothing, *my lord*—"

"Don't pull that aristo-republican nonsense on me, boy," his father said to Letellier.

"—but—"

"Your real grudge with me concerns my concealing that your father is alive, imprisoned. Did you learn of his fate the last time you visited your mother? She was afraid you had seen the correspondence. And close your mouth, Fitzhugh."

"No, sir, I will not. You left his father?"

"I beg your pardon, sir," Hadley said, "but I do request you acquit me of having left him there were he not imprisoned for very real crimes. There was nothing of the *distastefully* political about his imprisonment. The Letelliers are bourgeoisie, not aristocracy. No, Monsieur Letellier is also Le Maitre des Brouillards, the Master of Mists, an exceptionally notorious smuggler."

Letellier's mouth tightened. Gillespie's gaze darted here and there. What he thought, Benedict did not want to know. What Benedict thought himself, he had no idea.

"Monsieur Letellier smuggled anything, anywhere, and Robespierre cared little, for he had aristocrats to behead. But when the Revolution turned on itself, a broker in secrets became not only a liability, but an embarrassment."

"What do you know of it?" Letellier said.

"I care little for the politics of France, but I know what state your mother was in. How he treated her, and you."

Letellier's chin jerked back, but he compressed his lips.

"Why do you think I took you here, to England, and tried to raise you next to my own son until your mother found her way?"

"She rejected you, and you forced her from Somerset."

"She preferred to live where she would not feel burdened by gratitude," Hadley said. "You and your toady Gillespie will not succeed in ransoming your father from prison. We are at war with France."

"It can be done. I will do it. Then we will—" Letellier shook his head.

"By God," Hadley said, "she was right."

"My mother guessed?" Letellier said.

"No," Hadley said with contempt. "No, your mother is far too sweet a creature to think you would take to a life of smuggling alongside your father. No, I refer to the woman you two are fighting over. The dowager countess of Iddesford."

Letellier looked ready to boil. Gillespie licked his lips. Benedict considered planting him a facer. But there was a more important issue now.

"How did you come to receive information from Lady Iddesford?" Benedict asked.

"So she had something else to sell?" Letellier asked. "How novel."

Reversby's hand on Benedict's arm kept him from lunging at Letellier, but only just. "Let me go," Benedict said.

"Be still, sir," Hadley said. "There is an offer before Alexander."

"And what do I pay in return," Letellier asked, "other than giving up my ambitions?"

"Recant what you said about Lady Iddesford. There is no longer any need for this spectacle of spleen. There will be no duel."

Letellier stepped back from their circle, turned to the waiting gentlemen, who grew silent. "I stand by everything I said. Let Lord Fitzhugh prove me wrong. Here. Now." And he stood *en garde*.

Chapter Twenty

Hadley squeezed Benedict's shoulder and said, "Do try not to get yourself injured."

Benedict nodded, amazed and affronted. Then he faced Letellier *en garde,* as the others fell back to give them room. They saluted and began circling each other, the grass slick beneath their boots.

"You are a fool," Letellier said, "if you believe an iota of what she said. She knows nothing but lies."

Benedict's very blood hummed. He had no way to judge the accuracy of what had passed between his father and Letellier, or to determine what he should feel about it. Nor had he had enough time to determine what he should feel about Lady Iddesford's bringing his father into his affairs.

"Use your sword, Letellier," Benedict said. "Maybe it will have more power than your tongue. Come on, do you intend to circle me the morning through? Did you tell those betting on you that you might win by walking me to death?"

"You were sent to spy on me. What does that make you?"

"A friend, and a loyal son."

"A dupe."

"Maybe, but I would rather be a dupe than hatch such a plan." Benedict tapped the very tip of Letellier's sword.

Letellier reared back at the clinking, kept circling. "Would you not ransom your father, loyal son?"

There was no reasonable answer to that.

"Of course you would. You would do all in your power."

"Not this way," Benedict said.

"She stole my future," Letellier said in a low, furious voice. "*You* stole my future. What is there now for me here in England? Whatever your father says, everyone thinks my mother has let him make a mistress of her. No one of family will align herself with me. No one trusts a Frenchman with money."

"I am sorry for you, Letellier," Benedict said.

"Were you so sorry, you would call a halt and let me collect my reward."

"Not at the cost of her name," Benedict said.

"It is so easy for you. It has always been so easy for you. You have always known your place in the world."

Benedict could not help but look beyond Letellier, to his father, who stood next to Reversby and Gillespie, his hands clenched into fists.

Letellier took advantage of his lapse to lunge in the low ward. Benedict twisted to deflect the strike, but slipped on the wet grass. He went down on one knee. A gasp echoed through the crowd.

Letellier's smile provided Benedict all the impetus he need to press up. As he did, he drew Letellier's arm high, feinted, then brought his sword around for an upward thrust. Letellier jumped back as the crowd murmured.

"I could have killed you just now," Benedict said. It was nothing less than the truth. Only thoughts of Lady Iddesford had distracted him. This morning he had her token. He needed to fence, not think. "Stop, and admit defeat. My father was right. There is no point to this. Not anymore. You will not win."

Letellier said, "But maybe I can take some of your blood with me," and came on. After the third time that Benedict parried Letellier's attack, the crowd began to chuckle. Someone called out, "This is worth the two hundred I'll lose."

Letellier's already flaming face tightened alarmingly. He made another attempt. Benedict beat it back and sliced open Letellier's shirt, precisely where it gapped between his chest and left arm. The crowd gasped. So did Letellier.

"Stop," Benedict said. "You are making a fool of yourself."

Someone shouted behind him, then a shot rang out. Everyone ducked, then Hadley called, "By God, Gillespie, I'd call you out for that, were you not such a foul, dishonorable coward."

Even as Benedict put two and two together, Letellier lunged again. But Benedict was done with his appeals, and done with pity. He put his sword through the meat of Letellier's sword arm, withdrew it with a sharp motion. Letellier's cry mingled with the roar of anger at Gillespie from the watching gentlemen.

Letellier dropped his sword, went knees down on the grass.

"Enough," he said, panting. "Enough. I yield."

Benedict picked up Letellier's sword. "I *am* sorry for you." He turned, went toward his father, who held Gillespie, one arm twisted behind his back.

Distaste writ large on his face, Reversby held a pistol by two fingers. It stank of freshly fired gunpowder.

Raising his voice, Benedict said, "Let him go, sir. He will never be received again anywhere."

Hadley pushed the offending Gillespie away. The gentlemen who had come to watch crowded in, so Gillespie almost careened into them. To a man, even the half-drunk ones, they showed their disgust.

"Get out," someone said.

"Get out of London before noon, or by God, sir, I'll horsewhip you myself," another added.

"I recommend leaving the country entirely." That was Reversby. "What do you say?" he asked the crowd.

The gentlemen returned a chorus of assent. Some of them pulled swords from walking sticks, and they beat him away, cringing and protesting, with the flats.

Reversby turned away and went to oversee the surgeon who was bandaging Letellier's shoulder.

Benedict and his father were quite alone. Benedict set the swords down on the sword box, took a cloth, and wiped them down. Only when they were both clean did he say, "I failed to befriend him, sir."

"I never thought you could."

The box lid dropped down with a muffled thunk. Benedict stood. "Then for God's sake, why did you ask me to do it?"

"Mind your tone. Since when do you question me?"

"When you send me on such damned awkward fool's errands."

"What? Was it such horrible duty to have to be envied for spending time with a beautiful woman? To go to balls and parties? To have extra time to pursue Eudora? And her mother tells me she may be coming 'round. You've even gotten to prove your prowess with a sword. What horrible duty was there?"

Benedict took a full five seconds to recover his speech. "I will grant you that I enjoyed spending time with Dorrie."

"You see."

"But—" Benedict began.

"We knew Alexander knew of his father, and would not care what mischief he caused. You're a level-headed man, Fitzhugh, so you'll recognize that we had to see what he would do, and scotch it now. He can't have another attempt at this."

"No matter who else he could have hurt?"

"And whom did he hurt? Not a scratch on you, eh? Lady Iddesford? I should think she has done herself more damage just by being herself than Alexander could have."

"What about Lady Jane Compton?"

"What about her?" His father peered at him. "Not interested in her, are you, boy? Is that why you stood up so with the dowager? Lady Jane'd make a fine match for you, that I'd grant, but you'd be breaking Eudora's heart, and that I will not have."

This time Benedict could not speak, choked by the desire to laugh with rage.

His father clapped him on the back. "No. You get on your horse there, and go tell Mrs. Bourre and Eudora that you are quite unscathed. You don't have to mention Lady Iddesford again. Better that way, if you think on it, for the womenfolk. You've proved your point to the gentlemen. Damned if that wasn't fine swordplay, too."

Benedict drew a few deep breaths. "Do you give her no credit for bringing you the report?"

His father shrugged. "Brazen intervention. What can you expect?"

"Sir, I just fought a duel over someone's maligning her."

"Hmph. It's your sword arm, Fitzhugh. You want to feel that way, keep it in public practice. Best inducement not to duel. Get real fine at shooting, too. That way, it won't interfere with or disquiet Eudora, no matter what kind of dalliance you plan."

"You would encourage me to take Lady Iddesford as a mistress?" Benedict asked.

"Since when have you ever needed a pat on the head from me? Always gone your own way, stiff-lipped and all. But I can tell you want a bite of her. Nothing wrong with snacking."

This view of himself from his father's perspective stunned Benedict. He had always imagined the relationship between them as his father fixed in one spot, with Benedict attempting to pull against him. Never had he imagined that his father had been pulling as hard in the other direction. There had never been a center spot to return to. He would never win this contest.

Nor could Hadley.

And his father had recognized that a long time ago.

"I shall consider your philosophy, sir," Benedict said.

"You do that, son." His father took a deep breath and stamped his booted foot against the wet grass. "A fine morning's work. I am well pleased."

"And what of Letellier?"

"I know what to do with him to keep him quiet. He won't like it, but his mother will. And that will make Mrs. Bourre very happy with me."

"Very well, sir," Benedict said.

Reversby joined them, carrying Benedict's blue coat and dark gray waistcoat, which he tossed over. Benedict buttoned it, then shrugged on the coat.

"I'll help you clean up this mess, Reversby," Hadley said. "Fitzhugh here has an errand."

Reversby raised his brows, but said to Benedict, "I'll just walk you to your horse, then?"

Hadley waved good-naturedly at him.

When they were several steps away, Reversby said, "You're not going to the Bourres, are you?"

"No. But do take care not to tell my father that."

"Johnny knows his sums," Reversby said, tapping his forehead. "I'll do you one better. I'll go to them myself, *statim*, when I'm done here. We will either see each other there, or I will make your excuses."

"Thank you."

Reversby clapped him on the shoulder. "You're a damn good friend, Fitzhugh. Couldn't have stood Town without all your distractions. So here's a piece of advice. Do take note of letting her have some coffee before you start burbling. I never got far with Anne before she had her coffee. A moment. Take that back. You never burble."

"I have no idea what to say."

"Take some coffee yourself, then," Reversby said.

Sunshine finally breaking through the mist created a diamond-paned grid on the far side of the dark breakfast room floor, lit the gauzy white curtains, and made the gold-rimmed china on the sideboard gleam. Esme tipped her head, regarded it from the lip of her coffee cup, squirmed a little on her white-on-white covered chair, and tried to guess the time without looking behind her to the large clock.

Did the servants truly believe this morning was as any other morning, or had Williams and Percival warned them all to walk softly around her? Was there a certain solicitousness about the way James served her coffee? She would no sooner drink it down more than a third of the cup than he filled it up. She was wary of putting it down again.

Did he do that every morning, and Esme had not noticed?

So Esme pretended that that was the way things were done every day. Certainly she had never been one to affect the necessity of chocolate on a tray in her room. Her usual routine: She got up and got dressed, although granted not as formally as she was now, for she could not imagine visiting the earl of Hadley in her Vauxhall dress at three o'clock in the morning. No, for that interview, she had worn the severe cream gown she had worn to Lady McDonald's musicale. She would not have him using her clothes against her.

He had not. He had listened and dismissed her promptly, although properly.

"Like a blooming tradesman," Williams had said, fuming.

Esme had not cared. At least she told herself she did not care. She told herself she cared only about whether he would prevent Fitzhugh from dueling, and she was none too certain he would do that.

So nonchalance in the breakfast room served her pride and her servants' complicity. If she betrayed herself by glancing too frequently from her newspaper and out the window at every little noise of London waking itself, well, one had to remember one's servants either knew everything about one, or soon would.

When the sharp knock on the front door did come, Esme started so badly she knocked James's arm as he bent to pour her coffee. The coffee slopped over the saucer and onto the white tablecloth. James jumped back, apologizing, as Esme tried to push her chair back to escape the hot, running liquid.

"Give it no heed, James. It was entirely my fault," Esme said. "Only do help me from this chair. It has gotten stuck."

James wrested her from the chair arms' imprisonment. Esme heard Williams' voice warm in the foyer and abandoned nonchalance. She picked up her skirts and headed for the door.

She collided with a broad chest, reeled back, and was saved from falling by Lord Fitzhugh himself.

Esme wrapped her arms about his neck and pressed

her cheek against him. "You are here. Oh, you are here." She could hear his heart beating, strong and even, smelled the damp of the morning air.

"I told you not to fear for me," he said, hugging her.

She ran her hands over his arms and back and chest. "You are not injured? Not at all?"

"You will see no injury."

That was her first hint that not all was right. She stepped back, shivered.

"My lady's shawl," Fitzhugh said to James, but still looking at Esme.

"No, James, thank you," Esme said. "We shall sit down. Some breakfast for Lord Fitzhugh."

"Milady," he said, and beat a hasty retreat.

"He told you," Esme said.

"Had you asked him not to?"

"In truth, I cannot remember."

Finally he released her gaze. "I see you have had your coffee."

"Yes. Too much, I think. Would you like some?"

"I am awake enough," he replied.

"I do not know what to say," Esme said, feeling around behind her for support and finding a chair back. She dug her fingers into it. "What should I say? You are looking at me like you did right after I had to slap you."

"My father the earl came to the duel and tried to put a halt to it. Before thirty others Letellier had drummed up."

"Oh," Esme said.

"Yes. Oh."

"Is this usual? For duels, I mean."

"No."

"I have embarrassed you again."

"It is amazing how this keeps happening."

"Are you very angry at me?"

"Why did you go to my father?" he asked.

"Gillespie was Letellier's second, was he not?"

Fitzhugh compressed his lips, nodded, and lost his steely expression. "As to that, you showed some perspicacity."

"Fitzhugh!" Esme said, and reached out to him again.

He captured her hand, set it against his chest, where the folds of his cravat tickled her. "I doubt he will be back in England any time soon after that little stunt."

"Are you very angry at me?"

"Not as much as I should be, I am sure."

"Why not?"

"It has been an enlightening morning. Le Maitre des Brouillards."

"Who is that, by the way?"

He studied her before answering. "A smuggler who worked about twenty years ago from France. Also Letellier's father."

"I learned they wanted to pay for him . . . ?"

"To obtain his release from prison."

"Jane's money would have gone to free a smuggler."

Fitzhugh nodded. "Apart from the injury to your family, I understand his motives. It *is* his father."

"Even I would not have done what I did for such a motive."

"The ends do not justify the means?"

Esme looked down, to where his strong hand had captured hers. The abraded skin on his knuckles that she had noticed last night continued red but less raw. "I used to think they did."

"Not anymore? Let me tell you what ends have been achieved by your rather extraordinary means. Dorrie has discovered she would marry me, and Letellier's plans have all come to naught."

"Congratulations. All your wishes are come true."

He quirked a brow. "What I find ironic, however, is

that although neither you nor my father knew it, with respect to Letellier, you and he were partners, working to accomplish the same ends. I was just a spare piece on the board."

"Yes," said Esme, feeling very cold. "Very ironic."

"Yes, it is. It is also most vexing, for I do not care that neither of you wanted me involved. I do believe that is why I am not as angry at you as I otherwise would be."

"What do you mean?"

"My father and I, although our natures might be said to be complementary, do not compliment each other. This morning I discovered that even when we agree on an outcome, we will never agree on why it had to be that way. Or how it would best be accomplished."

"He chided you for dueling, and over me."

"Not exactly. He chided me for upsetting Aunt Bourre and Miss Bourre. It appears that if I had kept the matter more private, he would have been pleased as punch to turn out and watch. And it goes deeper than that."

"I wondered . . ." Esme said, and at his inquiring brow, continued, "about Lord Hadley and Mrs. Bourre. When I saw them together, he had the air of a man very keen, she the air of a woman not as."

Fitzhugh snorted. "That would explain some things. They must agree on my marrying Dorrie, then, or my father would not have brought me to London. My enlightenment continues. I wonder if they have conferred on my father's permission to me."

"Permission?"

"I am encouraged to make you my mistress. Covertly of course, so Miss Bourre should not know."

"Of course."

"It would raise my cachet amongst the gentlemen."

"I should think so," Esme said and laughed, hoping Fitzhugh did not hear how brittle it was. She wrapped her shawl she had refused before around her, and cursed her pride. "There is a problem, however, although not with being covert. In fact, this will ensure our being so covert as to not have an affair at all."

"What is it?" he asked, tight-lipped.

"I have had a letter from Lady Howard. She is poorly."

"I am sorry to hear that."

"I was planning to return to Yorkshire. Tomorrow."

He folded his arms. "I will accompany you."

"Not covert, Fitzhugh."

"I have not explained properly enough, have I?"

"Obviously not, *and* you are being patronizing."

"Let me make this very plain, then. My father would encourage me to make you my mistress, but there is more than his way of having you in my bed and my life. Will you marry me?"

Esme opened her mouth, but no sound came from it. Then her knees buckled, and she felt profoundly, absurdly grateful there was a chair behind her.

He dropped to his knees beside her. "Esmeralda? I am sorry. I did not mean to shock you. I wish it had not been such a shock. I thought, after last night, that you would know how I feel. I thought you understood that I love you more than life."

"I know how I felt." She touched his face with shaking fingers. "And I, Fitzhugh, I love you more than life."

"Then you will marry me."

"No. I will go to Yorkshire. Alone."

"I see," he said, standing. "Running again, are you?"

"Yes. I am running again. But this time, I am running as much for you as I am for me."

"Explain to me how that makes any sense."

"Your father will never accept me, and I will not be responsible for driving a wedge between you. I was the final wedge between Iddesford and his son, and look what that wrought."

"It brought him pain, no doubt, but it brought me you," he said stubbornly. "Esmeralda, I learned something this morning, that eventually my father will come around. He always has."

"You cannot be sure."

"Your 'brazen interference' in his affairs impressed him. He respects strength, and you are the strongest woman I know. He *will* come around. I may never understand him, but now I can predict him."

"Maybe, but listen, love, if you can, to reason. Assume your father is no longer one of our problems. Just because you married me, it would not stop everyone else from talking. You would be fighting any number of other men, do I not sever ties with you now."

"I *am* an excellent swordsman, and not a bad shot, either. I shall practice daily. And it sounds wonderful to have you call me 'love.' Do it again?"

"Fitzhugh! That is not a funny joke. Why do you make this so difficult?"

"It could only be difficult did you truly wish to be rid of me. Come, my dearest, you do not need to be polite. You do not need to say you love me and then excuse yourself for my own good."

An angry retort rose to Esme's lips. Fitzhugh's guileless, playful expression matched his words. Then she realized the expression did not enter his gray eyes, which were shadowed with worry and doubt, and said, lightly, "What need have I of polite methods? I have slapped your face once in public."

"True."

"I love this smile of yours, the one that starts out as a dimple in your cheek." She traced it. "And then spreads out more left than right."

"You like me because I am eccentric?"

"I love you," Esme said. "I do not know why entirely. Maybe because you *are* eccentric. You have been unlike every other man I know. I do not think I could ever tire of you. Not here," she touched his forehead, "nor here," she touched his broad chest, "nor—"

He kicked the breakfast room door shut. "Nor where?" he asked.

She shivered with anticipation and need, which had lain silent while worry had preoccupied her. Now her desire blazed free, recognized, ascendant. Her fingers trembled as she undressed him, pulled off coat and waistcoat with little regard for buttons, before attacking the cravat.

He, too, wasted little time finding pins and laces and freeing her from their confines. The cool air and his touch made Esme ache. When she pulled his shirt over his head and found herself looking at her emerald, she touched it, said, "My champion."

"You are the most beautiful woman. May I be your champion for the rest of my life?"

"Kiss me," she said. "Make love to me."

Fitzhugh kissed her, and pressed her bare bottom against the table, away from the dishes. The tablecloth felt deliciously slippery. His tongue traced chains of fire along her neck, her breasts, her belly, then down until she gasped her need.

"Say yes."

"Yes," she said. "Yes, yes, yes."

Shortly, china smashed onto the floor at the other end of the table.

Esme inhaled, then tried to contain a chuckle, saw that Fitzhugh was trying, too. It was enough to send them both into peals.

"I owe Lady Howard some crockery."

"*We* owe Lady Howard some crockery."

"*We* owe Lady Howard some crockery," Esme said.

"You may tell her you threw it at me."

"What will she think of us?"

"Whatever she wants," Fitzhugh said, his gray eyes serious.

"What will we do now?" Esme asked.

Fitzhugh ran the fringe of her shawl along her shoulder. "You will get dressed and come for a short walk with me."

"But Fitzhugh, we should feed you first. Help me with my clothes. I cannot think where James is with that breakfast."

"James is just fine, if I know your Mr. Williams."

"He likes you, you know."

"I will take your word on that," he said, lacing her up. "Take your shawl. The air outside remains damp."

"Where are we going?"

He smiled, laid a finger across her mouth, and shook his head.

The morning air did remain damp, and sparkled with the rising fog. They walked arm in arm away from the park, into the rising sun, toward Grosvenor Square. For all that the members of the *ton* were asleep, their servants were about. Footmen swept porches and walkways. Gardeners tended plants with sickles and rakes. Maids opened windows and greeted each other. And wagons belonging to milkmen and greengrocers trundled along toward the mews. They tipped their caps or knuckled their foreheads as Esme and Fitzhugh walked by, and Fitzhugh acknowledged each with a touch to his beaver hat.

"You will not tell me where we are going?"

"We are almost there."

They entered the square, turned right to go down to South Audley Street.

"There," Fitzhugh said.

The angel statue stood in shadows from the trees behind it. But a darker shadow covered her mouth. A black mask from a domino.

"Fitzhugh," Esme said, half laughing, half crying. "When did you do it?"

"On my way to you from Battersea Park," he said. "It is daylight, Esmeralda, and she may not talk. Why are you crying?"

"Because you *are* the best man I have ever known."

"You said yes before. You would say it again, here?"

"As many times as I have opportunity."

"I will announce our engagement, privately to my father and the Bourres. Then we will post it to the *Times*. Then we will stand our ground, here, in London, before this very statue, if needs must be. Lady Howard is not sick, is she?"

"No more than she has been," Esme said.

He smoothed her hair. "Do not spare me anything, my love. It might take me a bit of time to accustom myself, but—"

She put a finger over his lips. "I will never run away from you."

He kissed her, long, and deeply.

"Fitzhugh?"

"Hm?"

"I will be a friend to Miss Bourre. I promise. It has been so long since I had a young, female friend. But she will not have it, not at first. Be patient with her."

"Hurting Dorrie is the only thing about being in love with you that gives me pain. We will try together."

Esme smiled. "We will."

"Flowers, guv'nor, flowers for my lady?" asked a boy in a piping voice behind her.

He held a basket that seemed as large as he was, brimming with flowers of all sorts and colors. He set it down, touched his brown cap with a cunningly deprecating smile. Esme approved of him.

Fitzhugh chose a posy of irises, violets, and carnations, and then would have handed the boy some money.

"A second one, please, Fitzhugh?" Esme asked. "Bigger."

Fitzhugh raised a brow, but said, "A second one, sir, if you please."

"Right you are, guv'nor. Right you are."

Fitzhugh selected a second posy, of pink roses and gladiolas, and paid the boy, who touched his cap, grinned, and hustled off. "He did not want to make change of my guinea."

"For a man who can tell the value of a horse and equipage to the nearest five pounds, you did overpay him."

"I am in charity with the world." He held out the second posy to her.

"No, it is not for me," Esme said. "It is for her." She turned to the angel statue. "Fitzhugh, give her those, and take her gag off. Let us let her talk. It is time for me to build a new reputation."

"I am sorry I believed any of the other."

"I gave you little opportunity to believe otherwise."

"Except our first night here," Fitzhugh said.

"What is one incident against the weight of so much else? Remove her gag." She took the flowers from him and nodded toward the statue.

Fitzhugh climbed the gate and jumped over. "Someone locked it, after our last stunt."

"Of course they did," Esme said. She handed him the flowers through the bars.

Fitzhugh propped them between the crook of the angel's arms and her shoulder, and removed the black mask from her mouth. Then he climbed back over the gate.

Esme took his hand, held it tight. "See, now she does not look like she has secrets to whisper. She looks like she enjoys the sweetness of what is before her. She is happy, as I am. No, I do take that back. I am happier than she."

"I should hope so," he said, amused.

"I will finally grow into my name. A good name. Mine, and yours."

"Whatever your name, you are an amazing woman," Fitzhugh said, "and I love you."

"I love you," she replied. "Take me home?"

"With pleasure."

More Regency Romance
From Zebra